# THE LAKE
## DREAMS
## THE SKY

Also by Swain Wolfe

*The Woman Who Lives in the Earth*

# THE LAKE DREAMS THE SKY

SWAIN WOLFE

Cliff Street Books
*An Imprint of* HarperCollins*Publishers*

HarperCollins books may be purchased for educational, business, or sales promotional use. For information please write: Special Markets Department, HarperCollins Publishers, Inc., 10 East 53rd Street, New York, NY 10022.

FIRST EDITION

*Designed by Christine Weathersbee*

Library of Congress Cataloging-in-Publication Data
Wolfe, Swain.
  The lake dreams the sky / Swain Wolfe. — 1st ed.
    p. cm.
  ISBN 0–06–017412–9
  I. Title.
PS3573.05257L3   1998
813'.54—dc21                                                    97-48898

98 99 00 01 02 ❖/RRD 10 9 8 7 6 5 4 3 2

*For Marley and Zulu*

Thanks to Diane Reverand, editor *extraordinaire*,
Barbara Theroux, friend of writers,
and John Peterson Baker, diver of dreams.

*August 1, 1997*

*Love? What is it? Most natural painkiller.*
*What there is. LOVE.*

William S. Burroughs,
February 5, 1914–August 2, 1997

# THE LAKE
## DREAMS
## THE SKY

## SATURDAY
## AFTERNOON

They said the lake was so deep in places you could never find bottom. When Liz was nine, Jess Beckett and his grandfather tied a three-pound iron bolt to a mile of twine and let it play out into the deepest part of the lake. The bolt never touched bottom. When they pulled up the twine, the bolt was gone. Something a mile down had taken it.

She had known a mysterious, wild, and deadly lake. It left a sensation deep inside that seemed stronger than love. She never imagined this feeling would betray her. She was not prepared for the complexity that shaped her life beyond the boundaries of her youth. Like a selfish lover, the lake had slowly pulled her apart.

Now she was going back, twenty-three years later, her face pressed to the window, searching the ground below for a familiar road or mountain peak. She stretched her neck, giving the short, cowlick of a man next to her a chance to ask where she was going, where she was from, and what she did.

"To visit my grandmother, and get a good rest. I live in Boston. I analyze real estate demographics."

The man perked up on *analyze*. "What do you do with the numbers?" he asked. The way he said *numbers* made them sound precious, like children or peaches.

"We contract to the feds," she said. "But they're used by everybody: city planners, insurance companies, chain stores, housing developers. They all get their fingers in our numbers."

"Interesting work." He nodded and smiled.

She sighed in anticipation of escape as the plane tilted into its descent. Most of the passengers were business-men, stuffed into their pants, mustached and cowboy-booted men with scotch and sirloin bellies who, like the cows they ate, leaned heavily in all directions.

She imagined the plane plunging into the lake, silent and sharp—the bellied men, wide-eyed and gripped in screams. She was happy to trade them to God for the snowy egret or the black-footed ferret or whatever the infinite absorption of scotch and sirloin was putting an end to.

———

Outside the terminal an Indian leaned against an old, blue Ford pickup, his head tilted up toward the sky, read-ing the clouds. Liz studied him through the tinted glass, guessing the facts of his life. Sure that he was her ride, she tapped on the glass and waved.

The Indian failed to notice. He was watching the clouds change from animals to people and back again. She stopped trying to get his attention and went to the door, keeping an eye on her luggage.

"Excuse me," she called. "Are you Ana's man?"

His head came forward as his eyes took in the short skirt and red lips. "I never thought of it that way," he said. He had a pockmarked face, greasy hair pulled back straight in a long braid, and a voice that was flat and soft in a way that sounded thoughtful or menacing.

She wondered if his hair was dirty or if he greased it deliberately.

"Did Ana send you?" she asked. Her tone betrayed her hope that he was not the one.

"I came to give Elizabeth a ride to Ana Hanson's."

"It's Liz," she said. Her voice made a nervous little jump and her eyes darted from the Indian to her luggage. She was only anxious for her possessions, but he assumed she was giving orders. He retrieved the luggage—a weekend case and a larger suitcase—and set them in the back of his pickup. He carefully covered them with a tarp, which he secured with a cinder block at each corner.

She quelled a groan of disbelief. She could imagine the blocks sliding around, letting the tarp sail into the road, causing an accident. And she did not like his wreck of a truck. A van would have made more sense. Her concern showed in her hesitation. She got in, clutching a small computer and a handbag.

A faint smile slid across the Indian's face. She guessed

he was amused by her apprehension. She balanced the computer and the bag on her knees and reached for the seat belt, but the truck was designed before the era of safety consciousness. He glanced down at her searching hands. She could see he thought she was pathetic. She stared at him, seat belt-less and angry.

The Indian ignored her and started the truck. The lack of a muffler glorified their exit from the parking lot.

"You're a magazine woman," he said in his soft tone, barely audible over the gurgle of the engine.

"What makes you think I'm in publishing?" she asked.

"No, not that way. You're like a woman in a magazine."

"How so?" she asked.

"Not too many people dress that fancy. Nobody here."

"Nobody?"

"No."

"Professional women wear blue jeans and cowboy boots, I suppose?"

"I don't know about professional women. My people's women only dress up for church. But, the Father doesn't like those short skirts."

She checked him for humor, found none, and decided to sit out the ride in silence. For a half hour, she stared at the passing landscape as the unmuffled engine rapped at her nerves.

On the higher hills, pale green sage rolled back from the road toward the mountains and their snow-covered peaks. An unusually wet, warm spring had filled the creeks and river, and flooded the lowest pastures. The highway stretched north pulling her toward the lake and old possibilities.

The Indian had soured things for her. His belly hung down over the big silver beacon of a buckle, stretching his shirt taut at the mother-of-pearl snaps. He was a mean, bitter man. She wondered why Ana had sent him.

The truck crested a hill and the Indian shifted down, torquing the engine into a long, loud, irritating rasp. Liz held her hands over her ears and glared at him.

"Stop it!" she shouted. "Stop it!"

The Indian ignored her. He stared straight down the road, hostile and sullen. He meant it to be like this, and that infuriated her.

"Stop this goddamn piece of junk. Now!" she screamed.

The Indian slammed his foot on the brake. For a brief moment, the shrieking of metal on metal came from inside his head. He winced, his first change of expression since the furtive smile that had started it all.

The truck slowed and drifted toward the shoulder, gradually coming to a stop above a deep ravine. As soon as her feet touched the ground, the Indian drove away, leaving her seething at the edge of the road.

She was struck by how suddenly the circumstances of life can change. The word *luggage* jumped into her head. She turned, but too late. The Indian and her possessions were gone.

"You bastard." Her final shout at the Indian triggered a furious, whirling sound in the ravine below. Two pheasants exploded out of the sage and flew down the dry gulch to the boundary between the hill and the green of an alfalfa field. The savage sound stifled her anger. Her eye followed the pheasants' line of flight until she realized she was standing on the hill that overlooked the lake three miles north. She was home.

At that moment she became an alien—the field below marked the perimeter of a fungal growth of condominiums and apartment houses that spread up from the lake and masked the landmarks of her childhood. Nothing remained to match her memory. The lakeshore was encrusted with docks. Fun-seeking powerboats cut wakes across the lake as far north as the haze permitted her to see.

She closed her eyes and inhaled. The image of the mocking Indian drifted up, smiling his strange, elusive smile.

She started down the road toward what she guessed was her grandmother's place, a small, white house with a high pitched roof in the middle of a green field and orchard trees. The property bordered the lake and was surrounded on three sides by a dense maze of flat-faced, obedient, white condos—quick, easy copies of the fashionable penal colony style, what her architect friends referred to as Karl-Marx-with-money. A large section of land farthest from the lake had been invaded by rows of apartment houses treated with Swiss alpine facades.

She had reasonable heels, but they were not made for distance. After the second mile downhill on the thin leather soles, her feet shrieked at her. Deep inside the maze of housing units, she sat down on a curb, took her shoes off, and rubbed her feet. She felt as though she knew the inhabitants because she knew the numbers of their lives.

A large man cruised by in a new cream-colored Ford van with fancy red pinstripes. He stopped about a hundred feet down the street and stared at her in his rearview mirror. She put her shoes on and stood up, checking the quiet condos for signs of life. The van backed up until the driver was directly in front of her. He was a larger, younger version of the Indian who had driven off with her luggage.

"Are you the woman who needs a ride to Ana Hanson's?" It was the same soft voice. There was nothing she could read into his expression, but the sounds of children giggling came from the back of the van. "Hey," he said, "be good back there."

She walked around the van and got in. Three small boys stared at her. They sat on her luggage, holding two golden puppies on their laps. As soon as she turned away, they started giggling again. The small, sure voice of someone in charge said, "Zoom it, Red Crows."

The big Indian put the van in gear. They sailed down through the glass-smooth streets, past the green concrete lawns of the condo maze. He looked at Liz and grinned. "My brother said you don't like his truck too much."

Her lips tightened. "No, I don't like his truck too much."

"My brother doesn't like white people too much. He thinks all his troubles are the fault of white people."

She lowered her voice to sound casual. "What do you think?"

"He's probably right. If it weren't for white people, he wouldn't be here."

"Why? Modern medicine?"

"Beaver hats."

"Beaver hats?"

"Yeah. French fur traders. We're part French. I know some French." He pointed to the last condo before the single strand of barbed wire that marked Ana's property. "That's our place—one on top." He said it as a point of information, so she would know where to find him if she needed anything. Her knee-jerk reaction was that Indians in condos messed with her precious numbers.

Her grandmother's house stood in the middle of twenty acres of field and cherry orchard that sloped to the lake. The size of everything seemed all wrong. She was not even sure it was the same house. It was much too small, and the trees were not right.

"These can't be the same trees," she said.

"The old ones winter-killed. I planted these for Ana and I take care of them for her."

"Expensive property for an orchard."

"Yeah," he said. "We need more of these condominiums. Then all my *peoples* could move here."

She laughed. "When I lived here the Indian kids would come down to pick cherries. In the evening we'd all go swim off the dock."

She looked at the shoreline. It was smooth, uninterrupted by the jutting dock. "There was a dock," she insisted. "It was huge." She sounded alarmed. "What happened?"

"A storm took it out, 'bout eight years ago," he said.

The importance of the dock was a surprise—another piece of the past, gone for good.

"Once I stood on that dock," she said, "and watched a fighter plane come out of the sky and slip into the lake without a sound. Men from the National Guard looked for it for days. The pilot's helmet floated to the surface, but that was all they found. I must have been fourteen. It was my last summer here.

"I was never afraid when I was a girl," she said.

The Indian was silent. She appreciated the fact that he did not say anything. When he stopped at the back gate, she got out without looking at him. She reached into her handbag.

"How much do I owe you?" she asked.

"That's all done, thanks."

The boys juggled their puppies, pushed her luggage to the back of the van, and jumped down.

She took several dollar bills from her wallet and handed them out. "Leave them by the gate," she said. "I'll get them later."

They looked back at the big Indian for approval, said their *thank-yous*, and piled into the van waving their dollars. The smallest, who had short black horsebrush hair, issued the order to zoom it, and they were gone.

Weeds had replaced the lawn. The garden seemed deranged and overgrown. The path to the house bowed around the raspberries that occupied half the yard. Liz pushed the gate back and stepped in.

Several hundred unattended tulip bulbs overran the right side of the garden. Only a few dozen had managed to bloom and those were in various stages of wilt. The long, sharp blades of the threatening irises defended the back of the house and the cellar doors.

The shed, which saved the road from raspberries, reminded her of clay pots and rows of pale green seedlings. The roof was soft with moss. She was drawn into the musty interior, past the thicket of rakes and spades that guarded the door. Inside, a potting bench stood against the low, small paned windows. A faded red car slept in the far corner with a mattress over its hood and strange coils of greenish copper tubing from an old whiskey still balanced above in the rafters.

She stepped around a pile of broken pots, raising the odor of clay. She touched the shards with her toe, then gently pushed at them to hear their dry, earthy echo. The sound and smell of the clay reassured her. She walked to the car and peered in through the passenger window. A cluster of levers sprouted from the floorboard and a mysterious collection of gauges and dials covered the dash. On the back window ledge, several well-chosen stones were arranged so the shape and characteristics of each were revealed by its proximity to the others. Transfixed in the backseat sat a quizzical stuffed bear with a small black bunny on his lap. The car itself had stopped time, marking the end of one innocence and the beginning of another.

Liz had come back to the lake wanting more of the confidence and understanding she possessed as a child—something the dusty shed seemed almost to promise, as though she had stored her deepest secrets with the rakes, the car, and the stones, and returned when she needed them most.

The memory of who she had been only made her feel counterfeit and hollow. Little bristles of anxiety formed under her skin, turning to sharp, glassy slivers. She waited for the sensation to pass. It amazed her, what she had gotten used to.

She heard the soft, distant sounds of digging and left her memories with the car. In the garden, Liz could see a brown-skinned woman with muscular arms crouched in the raspberries, working the ground with a trowel. She moved with unconscious grace—an exotic, blissful animal, deep in a berry patch. Liz walked by on the far side, intent on saving her heels from the soft grass between the flat stones that led to the entropic house of her childhood.

She peered through the back door screen into the kitchen. The odor of oil soap stirred up a vague sensation of regret. She caught sight of her grandmother against a far window in the living room, looking out at the lake. From the doorway, Liz called, "There's a naked girl in your garden, Gramma. What's she doing out there?"

Ana followed the voice to the back door and the bloom of light that silhouetted her granddaughter. "She's gardening." Ana laughed. "She's my sharecropper."

Liz had not seen her grandmother for twenty-three years, though they had sent letters each Christmas. Ana had always been a little distant, and it did not help when Liz became a real estate analyst, a developer in her grandmother's eyes. The natives did not like developers, until they did a little developing themselves. Ana was not likely to do a little developing. She owned the lake in the way lovers own the air.

"Come in, Elizabeth, I'll make coffee."

Liz had discarded "Elizabeth" years ago, but it made little difference. The woman who had saved her from rattlesnakes and a good deal else, including her mother, would call her what she wanted.

They stood in the kitchen, leaned toward one another, and embraced, hands to shoulders, cheek on cheek, but Ana kept a distance between them as though bosoms were sacred.

She stepped back and eyed the black nylon case that hung from Liz's shoulder. "What is that black thing, Elizabeth?"

"It's a computer, Gramma. It's become an appendage."

Ana had always enjoyed irony. She set the tragic and the merely serious against their inherent contradictions.

She smiled. "Well, that's stylish of you."

Ana's way of seeing things made Liz a careful listener. She hesitated.

"I don't think so, Gramma. It's just work."

Liz studied her grandmother in the dim light of the kitchen window and tried to remember what she was like more than two decades ago. They had said good-bye in this spot. Ana seemed shorter now, and her hair was white, but she was very much the same person Liz remembered. Neither of them said anything for several moments. They just stood there in the soft light in the faded kitchen and thought about the past.

Long smoky strands of spiderweb had drifted up and

attached themselves in the dark corners of the high ceiling. Areas of old wallpaper beneath the paint had peeled away, exposing other layers and patches of plaster—an ancient atlas of time and territory.

"So, is it the place you remembered?" Ana asked.

Liz smiled. "The stuffed bear is still in the red car," she said. "And the stones haven't moved."

"Oh, the red car. I haven't looked at it for years. I don't know what you're talking about."

"My bear. I forgot it when I left. I wrote you to send it. Don't you remember?"

"I don't believe I remember a bear in the red car." Ana moved away toward the stove. She reached for the tin angel and took a match from its extended arms. She lit a burner.

"I wrote you," Liz insisted.

"About the bear?"

"Yes, Gramma. And the stones. Right after mother took me back."

"Elizabeth, that was so long ago," Ana said, trying to be herself and Liz's grandmother at the same time. It had been years since she was expected to be someone else. It made her tense. She stared at the strange granddaughter-woman who stood in her kitchen wearing a tight skirt, an expensive, glossy blouse, and perfume that had a sharp, bittersweet odor, like willow bark after a frost.

"Well, it doesn't matter, Gramma," Liz said in retreat.

"No, you're right, Elizabeth. It doesn't matter."

The conflict had a disturbing familiarity to Liz. She could feel herself repeating an old pattern. When she was twelve, Liz decided Ana was intimidating in a way she could never put into words. Her grandmother's silences made her feel transparent. She remembered Ana spitting grape seeds on the ground and saying, "Elizabeth, you have started telling little lies all the time. That's not smart." But Liz thought she had to tell lies. Lies kept her grandmother from seeing into her.

Liz noticed the black felt boot liners on her grandmother's feet and wondered if Ana had the boots that went with the liners. Her eye traveled to the cereal boxes neatly stacked under the old chrome and Formica kitchen table. She estimated, with some alarm, 140 boxes. The table itself was stacked with books, magazines, and plants. Evidently, Ana ate her cereal standing.

Rather than make an issue of the cereal boxes, Liz decided to inspect the rest of the house. She went from the kitchen through the wide doorway into what was once the dining room, now filled with books, boxes, and magazines stacked waist high in narrow rows. Liz navigated the pathway through the stacks that meandered around the room. Ana lived a disheveled, well-informed life.

A miniature minotaur, hidden between stacks of *Science News*, *National Geographic*, and *Natural History*, peered up at her from ankle height. The mythological beast, whatever his appetites, considered his prey too large or too dangerous. Had he been real rather than stone, he would have offered a face-saving snort and slipped back into the stacks between *Esquire* and *Archaeology*. But he was stone, dormant as a doorstop. Liz stubbed her toe on his nose.

The minotaur and the strangeness of the room made her edgy. She stared at the mounting evidence of her grandmother's unstable mind—a labyrinth of words and paper twenty years deep. The labyrinth slithered around the corner and into the living room, consuming a table, a piano, and two windowsills.

In her attempt to retreat, she bumped a stack of magazines that spilled across a Navajo rug. "Good god. This thing's worth . . . at least twenty-five thousand dollars." She marveled at the rug, and its value, and reassembled fifty-seven issues of *The Smithsonian* in their proper place in the wandering wall.

She realized something was familiar in the rooms. Even the labyrinth had a feel she recognized—a kind of shaggy meander that suggested order and logic but led to nothing specific or nameable.

Her grandmother's voice came from the faraway kitchen, "Your coffee's on the table, Elizabeth."

Ana stood at the back door, looking through the screen into the garden. The afternoon light illuminated her long, unkempt hair and accentuated her thin body.

A small amount of very black coffee in a large cup was perched on top of a stack of books on the kitchen table. Liz eyed the stains in the crazed porcelain and smelled the coffee. There was a faint scent of cardboard, but no odor of coffee. The taste was too strong and too sweet. Liz took her cup and went to the back door. She could see out over her grandmother into the yard. "What is this you're drinking, Gramma?"

"That girl got me drinking it like this." Ana nodded toward the garden, though there was no sign of her sharecropper. "She ran away from home. Her people make it this way."

"Where's she from?"

"Alaska. She's a Sea Indian."

"So how does she make coffee?"

"She puts a heaping tablespoon of instant coffee with about a fourth cup of water and two tablespoons of sugar. Makes it sweet, don't you think?"

"It makes my teeth hurt."

"It wakes you up, but you have to take a nap afterward. I thought it would be just your thing, Elizabeth."

"Why, Gramma?"

"Oh, I just thought it was stylish."

Liz looked down through Ana's glow of white hair. She was depending on Ana's firm grasp of reality, but it seemed as though the grandmother who was once so strong was beginning to dissolve.

"Gramma?"

"Yes, Elizabeth."

"You save things?"

Ana had never thought of it like that. "It's not that I save things," she said. "I just don't throw them away."

"Why don't you?"

"It's a bother, just one more thing to do that I don't care about."

"Did you keep my things?"

"Your things should be in the far left corner of the cellar. I think that's where they are. It's mildewy down there. Take a flashlight, and you should put on different clothes. Where is your luggage, Elizabeth?"

"Back by the gate."

"Those boys." Ana snorted. "Which one brought you?"

"Red Crows, I think, but I asked his kids to leave them there."

"There are two Red Crows. The angry one is David. The friendly one is Henry. David's okay, but that Henry's a snake. He gets girls pregnant and leaves them."

"Which is worse, being hated by David or loved by Henry?"

Ana's laugh was followed by a yawn. "I guess I need a nap. There's a flashlight in that drawer next to the sink." Her granddaughter and the Sea Indian's coffee had worn her out. "You can stay in your old room," she called out as Liz crossed the garden to retrieve her luggage. "I fixed it up for you."

---

The room of her childhood was decorated in the house style—books and magazines stacked waist high. Ana's fix-up consisted of clearing the bed of books and putting down fresh sheets. Liz changed into sweatpants, a tee shirt, and denim jacket.

She went back to the garden to challenge the vigilant irises for rights of possession to the cellar doors. The doors lay at a twenty-degree angle to the ground and had to be lifted up and to the side. A rubble of concrete steps descended into the dark cellar, and a fine mist of dirt coated the cobwebs that hung from the joists. Anything that absorbed moisture was caked in gray-white mildew.

Narrow pathways separated the stacks of crates, cardboard boxes, and loose assemblages of ancient bathroom fixtures, stone slabs, and bins of empty bottles.

The cobwebs were drawn to her, clinging to her hair and her face, catching her lips. With each step, clouds of mildew spores floated up into the dank air. Only the fear of inhaling some unknown evil deep into her lungs stifled her reflexive need to gag.

She straightened up and stood in the cellar's dank silence, playing the flashlight over the rusty metal shelves that held her things. Behind the shelves, she could see the rock foundation. Moisture had seeped through the wall and eroded the mortar, turning it to powder, loosening the stones. Several had rolled down and wedged against the shelves. She wondered how the house was standing.

Small piles of mildewed mortar had trickled into the boxes that held her treasures. Delicate, crystal-like feathers of white mold spread across the faces of dolls and sprouted from picture frames. She held her breath and carefully extracted the contents of the first box until she was forced to turn her head to breathe.

There were several manifestations of Barbie, stacks of 45s—the Monkees, Arlo Guthrie, and the Beatles—in paper sleeves, and red and yellow plastic shoes. The 1970s memorabilia seemed sugary. As she went further back in time, the boxes revealed a very different Liz.

She discovered the wood people made from branches and burrs by an old man named Dee. He called them his guys. Some had pieces of mother-of-pearl buttons for eyes, or lips from twigs, and arms made of spoons. One had a hat of tin with an iron sprocket rim. Each doll had a story. One went to the moon and back, one had gone to the center of the earth, and another had wrestled an octopus under the sea, which was why its metal parts were rusty. Dee had lived in a cabin near the lake. Even though he bathed once a week, even in winter, Liz remembered his skin was dark and shiny.

And there were collections of stones, each carefully culled from the billions of stones along the lakeshore. Months of her life had gone to selecting stones. She had been a master of stones. Ana had saved them all.

A thin piece of Masonite board lined the bottom of a box filled with Dee's wood people. She pulled the board out of the box and examined it with the flashlight. It was a painting of a woman floating in the air. A shaft of sunlight illuminated her, perhaps held her in the air above the lake against a dark gray sky. Barely visible beneath her in the black water was a large fish or serpent with scales. In the distance, a storm line moved over the water. In an upper corner flew a small red bird. The picture had a vivid, intense feeling, as though a manic child had painted it. The way the woman leaned forward, floating above the water, drew Liz to the painting. The woman's arms seemed to flow near her sides, the palms open. The painting had been on the wall above Liz's bed for the five years she lived with her grandmother.

She turned it over and discovered the name "Rose" written in dark red paint in a careful, elaborate script. In the bottom right corner the painter had printed his name, "Cody, 1948."

"Cody and Rose," Liz said aloud.

It was a great discovery. She had never taken the painting down from the wall in her room, so she had never realized it belonged to a story she knew as a child. In her mind the story always went with a question: how could love set water on fire?

"Lean forward," he said. "A little more."

"I can't," she said. "I'll lose my balance."

She held her arms down and slightly away from her body like wings at rest, the palms open, toward him, cushioned by the air as though she were landing. Behind her a dark, rolling storm moved down the lake toward them.

Her white dress lifted around her thighs. She was ready. He lay down on the dock, flat on his stomach, looking up at the flying woman against the violent sky, and began to paint. He painted fast, faster than usual because of the storm. The sun angled down, illuminating the woman, holding her in the slant light against the dark sky and the churning lake shadowed in the storm.

He used color to find her shape. Color revealed the fold, defined the edge, and spoke to the light. He dipped the fingers of his left hand into thick red, blue, yellow, white, and black paint from a row of mason jars. With short, swift flicks from a rabbit-hair brush, the paint seemed to fly from his fingers to the white oxide on the board.

"Move your arms out a little, and back," he said.

"Like this?" she asked.

"That's perfect."

"Paint fast," she said. "The rain is coming and the light is leaving."

Miles away, thunder rolled across the water. People and animals around the lake watched and listened. Farther north the scent of the storm started dogs barking. Horses inhaled the charged air and began running full tilt across the pasture. They whinnied and bucked. Horses rejoice.

## SATURDAY
## EVENING

*L*iz had forgotten the dust and the cobwebs, even the mildew that surrounded her in the basement. She moved the flashlight across the primitive painting, searching for the story in its details. Cody and Rose had fixed themselves in her childhood memories. Their story had made love seem possible.

After World War II, a stranger came to town and fell in love with a local waitress. She was an Indian girl who lived in a shack by the lake. Their love was so intense it set the lake on fire and burned the town to the ground.

"Rose." She whispered the name to the dank cellar. He must have loved her very much. She could tell by the wistful way he painted her face, the way her arms floated back, the desire she held in the folds of her dress blown back against her legs. Maybe their love *did* set the lake on fire.

She took one of Dee's wood people, a stone, and Cody's painting of Rose and carefully made her way through the cobwebs to the broken stairs.

The kitchen floor creaked under her step, warning the house of the threat to its established order. Liz worried that she would wake Ana from her nap. She wanted to be alone with her new-found treasures, as though they held the key to a secret door and required the ritual of solitude. She moved through the house to her old bedroom with the care and consideration of a thief.

There on the dirty white surface of her bedroom wall Liz could make out the faded rectangle where the painting had hung for five years or more. The nail was still in the wall. She set the painting back in its rectangle and lay on the bed, contemplating the mysterious Rose. The illuminated woman hovered above, arms and hands supporting her weight against the electrified air of the storm. Or was she waiting to embrace and be embraced? Liz studied her face and the position of her arms. What did he mean to say, she wondered, with the arms like that and the palms open? Was Rose flying?

Liz closed her eyes, arms slightly spread with her palms open, and imagined herself leaning forward into the charged air. Then she reached up with both hands and lightly touched her face. She pressed her fingers against her lips. The kiss had been the key. She had forgotten about it until that moment.

When she was seven, she discovered if things were perfect, if she would lie still for a long time then slowly kiss her fingertips, she would fall into a trance and feel she was flying. The kiss stopped working when she was fourteen.

She lay perfectly still, fingertips to lips, and waited. Nothing happened. I'll never be a kid again, she thought. She drifted into a daydream, pretending she was flying over lush, pale green forests, pink orchards, white condos, and slipping into the deep blue lake.

It was dusk outside and raining when she woke. She could hear Ana in the kitchen, shaking cereal out of a box.

Liz carried the painting into the kitchen and held it up for her grandmother to see. Ana stopped chewing when she saw the painting.

"Where did you find that?"

"It was in a box with Dee's guys and some stones. Do you remember it?"

"Yes," said Ana. "I remember."

"Where did it come from?"

Ana set her bowl on the stove and took the painting from Liz. She held it at an angle to catch the light from the single bulb in the ceiling.

"It was a gift."

"From Rose?" Liz asked, hopefully.

"No. A total stranger. I believe she'd been a nurse."

"Do you like the painting?" Liz asked.

"It seems a little romantic, don't you think?"

"It reminded me of the Virgin Mary."

Ana gave Liz a small smile and rolled her eyes. "What could be more romantic?"

"On the back it says Rose and it's signed by Cody. When I was a kid, there was a story about them. Do you remember it?"

"Yes, I know the story."

"Did you know them?"

Ana paused, searching the patterns on the wall. "Yes," she said. "I think I did."

"Were they lovers?" Liz asked.

Ana reached over and picked up her bowl of cereal. "That's the story," she said. "The legendary romance."

"How do you define romance, Gramma?"

"Shared yearning," said Ana.

He shifted into second for the long, downward slope that stretched north through the night rain toward a town at the edge of the lake. The truck was a covered, 1938, one-ton Dodge. It looked like a stock truck to passersby, but it was his house. He was a saw filer by trade and traveled from lumber mill to lumber mill. Looking like a gypsy was not a good idea. Chinese, Indians, and gypsies were fair game. Being a horse hauler actually had some class attached to it.

Partway down the hill he heard a *pop* in the transmission. A flaw in a steel pin, or a gear tooth—a simple lack of compassion between molecules—gave way and began to reorder the events in his life and the passage of time.

His heart sped up and his hands tightened on the steering wheel. He rode the brakes halfway down the hill, but the truck was heavily loaded. It began to pick up speed until he was shooting through the night on a rain-slick road, held in the grip of surreal time.

The road was relatively straight. He was near the bottom before the truck fishtailed and slid off the shoulder, hurtling sideways into a fence before coming to a hard, jerky halt. The screech of metal against barbed wire absorbed his attention through the crash and clang of tools, dishes, and pans that resounded from the back. The truck stayed upright.

He sat in the dark, counting his lucky stars and listening to the hiss of the radiator. Twenty minutes later his heart had slowed to normal. He climbed through the narrow gap between the seats into the back of the truck, found his bed amid the debris, and fell asleep.

The rain had stopped by morning and the sun was poking holes in the clouds. Several milk cows, mottled white and black, came to investigate. If one milk cow took it to mind that such a truck was filled with sweet rolled oats, then they all did. They pushed and nudged for position until the meanest five nosed up to the side rack and inhaled the scent of the saw filer through the cracks between the boards. After serious consideration and having failed to detect the possibility of rolled oats, they wandered away.

He woke up, surveyed the damage, and walked to town in search of a tow truck. Beside the transmission's problems, the sudden stop had torn the battery loose, put the fan through the radiator, broken two motor mounts, and bent a tie-rod.

A short Norwegian owned the garage and gas pump a half mile down the road.

"No. Haven't got a tow truck, but I got a truck that can tow," he said. He was a no-nonsense man who smiled a lot, unlike most no-nonsense men. He did not have much to say for himself, either. People who came by often wondered what made him smile.

"He's George," said the pretty woman with a curly perm. "And I'm Margaret. We can fix ya up."

Once they got Cody's truck towed, the damage checked over, and part numbers looked up, George said it would be two weeks or more before the parts came in.

"He's a nice young man, George. Why don't we let him park his rig in back of the garage?" said Margaret.

"I can't very well refuse now," he said, but he was still smiling.

They pulled the truck around behind the garage so the tail end looked out on the south edge of the lake and the mountains to the east.

"That way," said Margaret, "you can lie in bed and watch the sun come up—if you get up that late."

There was a cafe about one hundred feet east of the garage. It was one of those cafes that faced the highway, where the action was. The back door of the cafe, where the trash cans were, faced the lake.

The garage and the cafe perched on a rise of land about twenty feet above the shore in a bay at the southernmost point of the lake. At the bottom of the steep, grassy slope, a congregation of charred pilings stood six feet out of the water. They were the foundation for a lumber mill that had burned several years before. To the east, there were some tar paper shacks near the water. Farther east, cherry orchards bloomed to where the mountains rose up, sudden and sharp. To the west, he could see the little town that sloped down and stopped at the water's edge. The lake extended north for thirty-two miles. The south end was about six miles across at its widest. The lake was shaped like a long-necked gourd with clusters of small islands down its middle. The islands were home to heron and osprey. Mountain sheep, deer, and black bear crossed over when it got cold enough to freeze. Grebes, ducks, and snow geese negotiated the feeding grounds in the marshes on the southeast edge of the lake.

---

Early his first morning behind the garage, he sat in the back door of his truck sipping coffee and waiting for the sun to inhale the mist off the lake. He wanted that brief moment just before the mist is vaporized when it comes alive—dancing, rolling, and shooting over the surface, desperate to elude its fate.

At the edge of his vision, from the back door of the cafe, an arm, a strong shoulder, and the graceful curve of a woman's neck flashed out and back. He thought he heard her voice and what she said was still in the air. He could see an afterimage of her dark hair and the curve of her shoulder. She seemed open and free, maybe reckless.

He found himself looking at the cafe, just glancing over in that direction, waiting for her to emerge—for the gesture of her arm throwing an empty bottle at a trash bin. When it happened the second time, she came all the way outside, and he was looking at her, and for a moment she saw him looking.

Already she knew he was waiting for parts from Portland. She had noticed he had nice shoulders and he carried himself well. He was strong, by the way he moved, and that was good. And there was his gaze. It was not the local lake men's stare that asked only, "Can I eat this?" Determined parental guidance or lack of new blood for the last hundred years had given the men and boys around the lake that bovine-against-the-weather look. So from the start, he had a slight edge.

The third time he noticed her that morning, she walked out the back door, sat on a large flat rock, and stared out at the lake. She had dark hair to her shoulders, which were bare, and she wore a white cotton top and a pale yellow skirt. He liked the long muscles of her legs and imagined the shape of her thighs beneath her skirt.

His imagination had been at work on the folds and bulges of the giant cumulus clouds bunched up above the mountains, waiting for the right moment to race across the valley. He had explored the clouds for crevices, shallows, and swells, and those places made hard and soft by the light. His attention easily shifted to the hope and possibility of her body.

She knew he was in his truck, because the door in the back was open. She wondered if he had made breakfast. He had not been in the cafe. Maybe he was broke. After a few minutes she stood up, walked over, pressed her stomach against the high bed of the truck, and peered through the door. She could make him out against the light that came from the cab windows into his little house. He was sitting on a three-legged chair, leaning forward with a short thin brush in one hand and stabbing at a board about sixteen inches high and ten inches wide. The board was propped against some books on a small table.

"Hello?"

"Yes. Hello."

"I came to spy on you. You have a horse in there?"

He appeared in the doorway, looming above her, smelling of turpentine and oil paint. She stared up at him, realizing she had never really looked up at a man from that angle before: knees, crotch, smudges of paint, belt loops, buttons, neck, face, and hair. She smiled up at him. If this were an everyday thing, she thought, shins and knees would take on much greater importance.

"I hear you're our resident saw filer." She grinned and gestured toward the black pilings. "Too bad the mill burned down."

Cody could feel the lyrical warmth of her voice reverberate through his body. He sat down in the doorway and began cleaning the paint off his fingers with an old undershirt soaked in turps.

"I saw you spring out and back a couple times," he said. "My name is Cody."

"After the rodeo guy?"

"Yeah, matter of fact. He died the year before I was born. My grandfather buried him."

"Really? Did he shoot him?"

"No." Cody laughed. "He was a pallbearer."

"Well, I'm Rose," she said and reached up to shake his hand.

"I didn't think it would be this easy," he said.

"What's easy?"

"Learnin' your name."

His hair was light brown and seemed to fly around his large head. The flying hair, in combination with eyes too intense for normal everyday use, made him seem a little dangerous, though his voice was deep and easy. She decided he was in his early thirties.

"Do you paint pictures?" She was puzzled by the globs of paint he had wiped off his fingers.

"It's just something I do. There's no money in it."

"Money's the root of all evil, don't you agree?" She said it straight, to test him.

"Are you one of those religious reformers?"

"Not in the usual ways." She was smiling.

"But you believe in evil?" he asked, not sure if she was joking.

"Just the part with wheels." She looked back over her shoulder toward the cafe. "I better get to work. Can I see what you paint, later?"

"I won't be going anywhere."

She walked away, leaving him to wonder what part of evil had wheels.

———

From inside his truck, he had been painting part of the narrow scene he could see through the doorway—

high rolling clouds above sharp mountains with steep canyons, and the lake below with its burnt pilings waiting in the blue bay. The scene would be framed by the vertical rectangle of the doorway and the cupboards on either side. Enameled tin plates, flour, salt, sugar, and a honeycomb square created one side of the frame. The other side was stocked with mason jars in many colors and levels of paint, brushes in cans, and tins of turpentine. The scene allowed him to paint the border when the light and the clouds were not to his liking.

He had been painting creases on the undersides of clouds before she stepped into his picture and sat on the rock. Only her legs and her yellow skirt showed in the frame. The rock had not been part of the plan, but her legs made it work. It was a perfect accident. Just painting the legs and not the rest of her was a small joke, a way of saying he did not know her yet.

Although he liked her voice, her shape, and the way she moved, he was wary of the way she talked. Her remark about *the part with wheels* sounded a little too smart, like a good exit line. He assumed women who had good exit lines were trouble.

The legs were not working, so he did the skirt and went back to the clouds. When the clouds started their race across the valley and the light changed, he worked on the cupboards.

———◦———

"Hello, the truck," Rose called to him.

"Come see," he said.

She hoisted herself up and through the doorway.

He gave her the three-legged chair and turned the painting so it would catch the light. He sat on a crate just to one side to see her framed in the doorway against the sky. Her hair was a raven black that hid a deep shade of blue. She had it tied back and the light glanced off her cheekbones when she turned her head.

She studied the painting for several minutes. The bright yellow he had used for the skirt jumped out at her. She felt it did not belong with the rest of the painting, which was done in a strange technique, very different from anything she had ever seen—all those dots. And it was a little crude, but not quite childlike.

"You might think about changing the yellow," was her first comment.

"You don't like the rich yellow?"

"It's the first thing you see and it's like a cartoon. If the yellow were pale, then it would be something you would discover, without it saying, look at me."

"Suppose I have my reasons? What if I want a joke?"

"I like to discover things, then they're more mine."

She watched him staring at the painting. She guessed he was angry and she was thinking about leaving. Then he looked up.

"What you're saying is, that I should be painting for other people—not for myself."

"Is it one or the other?"

He leaned toward Rose to get a better look at her eyes, but without the sun they seemed completely black. Her directness made her seem slightly larger to him. "I never had to think about it before. I just paint for myself."

"Do you paint with the idea that other people will see the painting?"

"No. I don't think about it."

"Do you want people to look at a painting when it's finished?"

"Once it's done they can make what they want of it. Take it or leave it."

"But they will change it, make it something else altogether."

"Yes, but I don't think about that."

"Really? How can you not think about it?"

"I just paint. I don't think that much when I paint." He had been watching the sky and realized it would be dark soon. "I should find some wood for a fire."

She turned and looked at the sky. "I need to get home, but come and walk with me. If we go along the lake, we'll find wood."

------

They walked over the bank, down the hillside to the shore. Their long, narrow shadows drew them east, past the burnt pilings that guarded the lake. The air was clear and there was no wind so the water was calm.

He trailed behind her, picking up firewood and watching her walk. He liked her balance and the way her feet barely touched the sand and pushed her forward.

She realized he was watching and became self-conscious. She stopped, waited for him to catch up, and walked beside him.

Several garrulous crows stepped among the stones, examining the shoreline for insects. They gurgled and cawed among themselves, ignoring the human beings.

Rose listened to their garble of sounds, catching phrases and patterns she recognized as crow talk. The crows were busy turning over stones for bugs and were reluctant to fly off. She guided Cody toward the grass, away from the birds.

"When I was three," she said, "the old woman who raised me told me to go outside and talk to the crows. I learned all their sounds and became a good crow talker."

Did she believe she talked to crows, he wondered, or was it a child's game?

His skepticism compressed the air. She stopped and reached out, touching his arm. How could she explain talking crows to a stranger?

"The thoughts of crows," she said, "are as different from ours as their bodies are. They think things we could never understand."

"Did you really talk to crows?"

She watched the crows examining the stones.

"I talked to them and they talked to me. I wanted to believe I understood them."

"And the crows returned the favor?"

"Yes. They wanted to understand too."

He thought about a small, sturdy Rose, squatting among the crows, cawing and gurgling. "It was another time," he said. "The rules were different then. I believed in Santa Claus. He was very real."

"Do you think it's the same thing?" she asked. "The crows and Santa Claus?"

"No, just that what's real keeps changing."

"Changing, how?"

"When I paint pictures I watch the light on the surface of things. The way the world feels changes when the surfaces change, and the way I think about it changes."

"Because of sunlight and shadows?"

"Yes, that, and colors and textures, and the shapes of things—different corners."

"Sharp and smooth?"

"Yeah, and sexy and funny."

She laughed. "Funny corners?"

"Well, the crows think so."

"Yes," she said. "I remember. They think people have funny corners."

"I have funny corners?"

"I'm sure you do."

He paused for a moment. Best to be careful, he thought, and went back to his theory of the world.

"Before the war, the cars were black. The black soaked up the light. Now there're colors everywhere. The shapes and sounds are new. It isn't the forties anymore. What's real isn't what was real ten years ago."

"Were the talking crows real or was it just in my head?"

"How could you ever know? It's all different now, anyway."

"I doubt if the crow world's different. I just can't see into it."

"Did they have names?"

She watched the birds working the stones on the shoreline until she remembered.

"Marley and Zulu." She smiled. "Those were their names."

"You named them?"

"No. They told me. I asked what to call them. One said Marley, the other said Zulu."

"You were three?"

"Yeah. Pretty good, huh?"

He grinned at her and studied the way her eyebrows tapered back like wings, and her dark eyes.

"Marley, Zulu," said the crows. They watched the long legs walk away.

"What did the crows say?" Cody asked.

Rose laughed and made a crow gurgle: "The human bein's are mashin' the stones again."

"That's the way we are," said Cody.

Half a mile down the shore Cody could see two tar paper shacks with smoke rising from them. Past the shacks another half mile was a white house in the middle of an orchard. Beyond the orchard were other orchards with other houses.

"Where do you live?" he asked.

"In the first house."

He was not sure if she was talking about the first shack or the house in the orchard, but the shack had smoke. "Do you live alone?"

She grinned at him. "No. I live with Catherine Red Crows. She raised me before I went away. I came back to take care of her."

"Red Crows sounds like an Indian name." He decided she must have meant the shack. He could see that it was larger than it first appeared. "You were raised by Indians?"

"Yes."

"What was that like?"

"It was good and it was what I knew." She glanced toward the tar-papered structure and smiled. "I came back."

Parts of grilles, headlights, and fenders revealed the hiding places of several old cars among the blackberry bushes behind the shacks. An army jacket and some tee shirts hung from a clothesline that ran from the first shack over a broken boat and back toward the blackberries. About one hundred feet in front, a twelve-foot boat had been pulled up on shore.

Cody's idea of Indians was shaped by poverty. He had seen very little of them. The mills didn't hire Indians. They weren't allowed in the bars and never had money for cafes. He rarely had any dealings with them. When he did, they never looked him in the eye. He liked to see people's eyes.

———◦———

When they came to the boat, she reached down and picked something from the sand and put it in her pocket. She climbed into the boat and sat down facing the lake. He wasn't sure if he should sit next to her or not. He stood in the sand, holding his firewood, and watched the shallow waves wash the shoreline.

For a long time they said nothing, just looked out at the lake and at the clouds reflected in its dark water.

"Could I tell you a story about the lake?" she asked. "It's ancient."

He was lost in the lake. It was a moment before he realized she had asked a question. "Yes," he said. "I'd like that."

She leaned forward slightly, almost as though she were speaking to the lake. The pure sound of her voice seemed to spread through him.

"One day, Catherine Red Crows took four of us kids out in a boat. She said we were going fishin' but mostly she wanted to tell us about the lake and about how the world came to be. So this is what she told:

At first there was only the lake and the sun, nothing else existed. After about a thousand years, Loneliness came to visit and stayed around for another thousand years. So the lake thought about how she might get rid of this uninvited guest.

After a long time, her thoughts turned into fish— many, many colors and sizes of fish. Her fish caught the sun with their scales and flashed their bright colors all through the surface of the lake.

Loneliness hated the fish and their flashing colors. Hate turned Loneliness into a serpent that swam down far below the surface. The lake could not see the serpent, but she could feel it moving around inside her.

The lake was very tired and she fell asleep for another thousand years and dreamed the sky, and the rain, and the mountains to hold the rain. The brightness of the sky made the serpent of Loneliness swim down into the deepest, darkest place it could find. Loneliness never went away. It still comes in the night.

Loneliness made the lake dream the sky and that was the beginning of everything.

He was quiet for a long time, held in the spell of her voice, not knowing what to say. Finally, he asked, "Did Catherine Red Crows believe that story?"

She wondered if he was being dismissive or if he was really curious. "I don't know how to answer that. The lake was the center of her world. She was born here, she grew up here. The lake fed her and it fed her children and her grandchildren. She didn't have to believe it or not believe it. She knew the story in her heart. That is deeper than belief. When your life depends on something wild, it's good to tell its story."

"What did you make of her story?"

"I spent hours staring at the lake, searching for the serpent. It made the lake a magical place."

"You believed her?"

"When I was a child everybody told stories, and their stories told me what was possible. The world was awake, everything could speak: trees, and animals, grass, and stones—they all spoke. Sometimes they would speak to me. And they could see me. They were thinking about me.

"Those stories created a world for me. They let me see things. Some of it was frightening."

"What was frightening?"

"I still look for the serpent, especially when there's a motion in the water."

He heard her, perhaps for the first time. She believed

in something outside his experience. Playing with crows was one thing, believing in a lake monster was different. There was something disturbing about her. She seemed like a cauldron of thoughts.

The story reminded him of a feeling he had when he painted, as though he were on the edge of understanding something important and waiting for the right word or gesture—the invitation that would open a hidden world. These were things he never talked about. People would think he was crazy.

He wanted to go back to his truck, build a fire, make coffee, and paint, but he was anchored in the sand and graceless as a grounded barge.

She sat in the boat watching him, trying to guess what he was thinking, and what had made him tense. She stood and extended her arm slightly with the palm of her hand open.

"Come in with me and meet Catherine."

He set his driftwood by the boat and let her lead him to the house.

No one knew Catherine Red Crows' age, but she had a great-, great-, great-granddaughter. Her grandson, who lived in the other shack with his grandchildren and several other Red Crows, said she was as old as the moon.

The outside of Catherine's shack was covered with several layers of tar paper held in place by thousands of chrome-plated tacks set in diamond patterns. Long thin poles held the tar paper on the roof. Smoke rose from a tin stack with a cone-shaped hat to keep out rain.

Rose led Cody through the door and pointed to the ancient woman asleep under a white spread in a narrow brass bed next to the stove. The walls, ceiling, and floor had a sheen of thin, white paint that seemed to glow in the window light. The white quilt amid the white walls and the white floor freed the brass bed to float upward and suspended the sleeping Catherine in the timeless room.

Cody felt as though he had discovered a secret church. He even wondered if the old Indian woman was dead, until she reached up and pulled a cord attached to a fishline, rattling a cluster of tin cans outside.

"Is that you, Rose?" she asked, squinting against the light.

"I've brought a visitor, Catherine," Rose announced, leading him toward the bed. "This is Cody."

Catherine was the oldest, most shriveled human being he had ever seen. She opened her mouth to speak, but no words came out that he could hear.

"Hello, Catherine," he replied to her silent greeting.

Rose realized she should explain his existence to her old mother. With an edge of enthusiasm in her voice she said, "He's painting a picture of the lake."

Catherine's black eyes shifted back and forth between Rose and Cody. The door opened and her eyes squinted down to slits. The rattling cans had summoned three children with soup, mashed potatoes, and fry bread. When they saw Cody, they sent the youngest back to the other shack for more food. A few minutes later Catherine's room was filled with Red Crows who stood or sat on the floor, shifting their gaze back and forth from Cody to Rose. Other than a soft murmur when Cody was introduced, they said nothing. Although they smiled from time to time, he could not tell what they were thinking. In their midst, he was as alien as a dervish saint.

He and Rose ate their soup and fry bread in the half circle of Indians. One of the children leaned against the bed and spooned Catherine her mashed potatoes. After some difficulty, an old man with long, thin braids managed to light some sage in a tobacco tin nailed to the wall. The odors of sage, smoked leather, and people made the air thick. As the sun set, the light faded until the room was defined by its shadows and brown-skinned people.

Rose explained to the assembled that Cody traveled from mill to mill sharpening the big circular saws, that he was also a painter, and that he was painting a picture of the lake. There were more murmurs. Someone said something in Indian and some of the young people laughed until Rose replied and there was more laughter.

She shook her head. "They're teasing me, because of you."

She pulled her hair down over her face, holding it tight under her chin, then turned and growled at the children standing by the bed. They pretended terror and fled through the door, yelling, "No-face, no-face." The tension in the shack released its hold and allowed five generations of Red Crows to drift away into the evening.

Rose opened the stove door and added a piece of driftwood to the fire, leaving the door open for the light. She sat on the floor by the stove where she could see Cody near the bed, and Catherine, propped up on many pillows, staring into the darkness across the room.

"Catherine?" Rose leaned toward her, but she did not shift her gaze. "Catherine?" Still there was no response. "What do you think she sees?"

Cody watched her for a moment, and replied in a matter-of-fact voice, "She's peering in God's window."

It was something his mother had said of people who were old and distant. Rose's laughter surprised him.

"She's a Peeping Tom? Tell me," Rose insisted, "what does she see?"

"Everything at once."

"How can she see everything?" Rose asked.

He was at a loss for a moment. "In God's house time is compressed into an instant. So Catherine can see everything."

"The past and the future?"

"Yes," he said. "And everything that never happened."

"Catherine has two gods. There's the one whose feet Gerome Red Crows painted on the wall of the church, and there's the one who hides in the deep part of the lake."

He considered the two gods for a moment, then he smiled. "Don't you think they're the same? The one with feet knows everything that happened and the other one knows everything that never happened."

"Loneliness knows everything that never happened?"

"Yes, that one, the serpent."

She grinned that she could draw stories out of him. She watched the curve of his mouth in the stove light. It was a nice mouth, she thought.

Catherine had closed her eyes and her head had fallen back on the pillow. She rattled.

He stood up to go. "I should go back and let you go to bed."

"Yes." She hesitated. "I open the cafe tomorrow."

"How did you know I was a saw filer?" he asked, making time.

"Margaret told me. The one whose backyard you're

camped in. She tells me everything that matters at the garage." They looked at each other in the near dark.

"Well," he said. "Maybe I'll see you tomorrow?"

"Come by the cafe, if you like."

"Sure. I'll be up early."

She held her closed hand out to him. "Here," she said, and dropped something smooth and hard into his hand. "Have a stone."

His palm closed around the stone.

"Thank you," he said. He could feel the heat of her hand.

———————

He collected his firewood and made his way back in the twilight. He stopped to sit on the rock behind the cafe, watching the little church of Catherine, the Peeping Tom. When the truck parts were in, he thought, he could be gone in a day and a half if he worked right through. He had almost run out of money, and for the time being, things were at a dead end. And now—wanting this woman.

There was no way to think about her, because all the problems she created for him could only be resolved by leaving or staying. He had just met her. She was new. There would be no real difficulty in walking away; just avoid her until the truck was running. He thought about hitching a ride to Calgary so he could set up some jobs in Canada. He thought about fishing for salmon in Alaska, or the far end of the lake. No, not the lake. She was the lake now. Or the serpent. He wasn't sure.

Thin streaks of magenta lay between the dark mountains and the blue-black sky. He walked to his truck, hoisted himself in, stretched out on the bed, and fell asleep.

Night Indians swam through the blue lake. They pursued him from the south. They were gaining on him. He knew where they would never go. He dove down and down into the deepest, darkest, blackest place in the world. When it was so black there was nothing, not even despair, his hands felt a tear in the darkness. He entered and discovered the white church. Rose lay on the bed, her yellow skirt pulled up above the thick, muscular trap of her thighs, waiting.

He had little sleep, but the sharp, cool morning air began to draw him back from his dreams. He lay in bed, floating at the edge of the awakening world, watching through the open door as the blackness began to fade from the sky and the birds started their shrill songs of passion and property.

He became aware of something watching him in the dark from the bottom of the doorway. When he looked directly at it, the thing had drifted away. A small panic pricked his heart and brought him fully awake. He sat upright. His mind raced along, recalling the dream and the events of the evening.

She had worked her way into his thoughts. He wondered if that was her intention. She was a curious woman. She saw things, and that made her seem open, not necessarily available. "I'll tell you a story" was not the same as "Come into my life."

Until the parts for the truck came, he could fill his life with other things. He would find a job and he would paint. Perhaps he would see her from time to time. She could help him with the Indians. He wanted to paint Catherine in her white church, and the tar paper shacks with the cars hiding in the blackberries. He would paint Rose's world and take it with him. They would not become lovers, even if she were willing. It was important, he realized, not to touch her.

He started a fire and heated water for coffee. He could not help wanting her, but maybe he could avoid needing her. What was the cafe coffee like? he wondered. Probably not strong enough. He pulled the pot away from the flames, added two handfuls of coffee to the water and waited for the grounds to settle out. He drank his coffee inside the truck and watched the light change on the lake through the frame of the doorway. Wind gusts turned the water blue to black and back again. He painted straight through to midafternoon.

She came out of the cafe twice, and looked his way. She imagined him painting, though she could not see into the dim interior of his house. She was pleased that he was absorbed in his work rather than hanging out at the cafe. By noon, she wondered when he would emerge. By mid-afternoon, she wanted to know what he was thinking.

She took her break and stood on the flat rock look-ing out over the lake. Then she turned toward the truck, shaded her eyes from the sun, and stood there until he came out and waved to her.

"Hello," he called. "Come over and take a look. I've been at it all day."

She walked to the truck and climbed through the

doorway. He gave her his seat so she could see the painting. It was the same scene, but another painting, intense in a way she had never seen. It felt like fire, especially the sky and clouds. The dress was still deep yellow, but the entire painting had been changed to balance the intensity of the dress. The painting was complete except for the legs on the rock.

He looked at her, surprised by how beautiful she was. Desire had transformed the observer.

"I can't get the legs right," he said.

"Why not?" she asked

He stared at the blur of desire left in the paint. Without thinking he said, "They're your legs."

She studied his face, searching for intentions. "I don't understand what you mean."

He didn't know what to say, and for a while he said nothing. His focus wandered through the cab window and settled where the curve of the left front fender made a valley with the rounded hump of the hood. When he looked back, she could tell he was ready to change things between them.

"They're your legs," he said. "They're personal. Your thighs are full of promises. If I painted them the way I think about them, the way I see them, then you'd know how ordinary I am." He could hear himself saying the words and he felt the tension go as he escaped into the truth.

She looked down at her legs, pulling her dress tight against her thighs. She looked at him and smiled. "Whatever you are, Cody, ordinary isn't it."

"No. You think I'm different because I paint pictures and live in a stock truck."

"But you're free."

"I'm as desperate as the next guy."

"Aren't you an artist?"

"No. An artist thinks about being an artist."

"What do you think about?"

His expression turned boyish. "Today I thought about the woman in my painting."

She smiled. "I've thought about you too."

Her eyes were made bright by the lake and the sky. The afternoon heat had penetrated the little house, making her cheekbones glisten. An accident of lighting and a belief in beauty began to pull him into her. At the same moment he felt the slow excitement of curiosity driven by fear.

She got up to go back to the cafe. "You tell me your story and I'll tell you mine." At the doorway she looked over her shoulder, smiled, then turned, plunging into the afternoon sun.

He saw her image recede into the hungry light. He wanted to say what he felt. No restraints, no prohibitions, no rules. And he wanted to know her story.

## SATURDAY NIGHT

"After my grandfather died, did you ever love anyone enough that you wanted to marry him?" Liz asked. That her grandmother might have led an interesting life had never occurred to Liz. She suddenly realized how little she knew about Ana's past.

Ana smiled at the memory of Liz's grandfather and the ancient phrase, out of wedlock.

"What?" asked Liz, embarrassed that her ignorance might have inspired her grandmother's amusement.

Ana was stopped from answering by a small, electronic sound that came from Liz's room. "Something's chirping," said Ana.

"It's my phone."

"You travel with your own phone?"

"I'll be right back, Gramma."

Ana washed her cereal bowl and balanced it on top of

the dishes in the drain rack. She pulled a chair from the table, sat in the middle of the kitchen under the bare, hundred-watt bulb, and waited for her granddaughter to return. She stretched her hands out under the light, flexing her fingers for circulation, and watched their shadows play against the floor.

She wondered if Elizabeth's interest was in romance or family history. To Ana they were the same. Being deeply in love had charged the air around her—transformed how she saw the world, what she remembered, and the way her body moved. Although the intensity of that union was far in the past, as if another person had lived in her body and thought her thoughts, her memory of it still lived in an emotional landscape. Nothing could alter the reality of what she had experienced.

A half hour later Liz walked back from her room through the shadowy fortress of magazines. She could see Ana asleep in the kitchen, her head slumped forward on her chest. An erratic moth batted at the solitary light above her.

Liz patted her grandmother's shoulder. "Wake up, Gramma. Your neck'll get stuck like that and you'll have to look at feet for the rest of your life."

Ana opened her eyes. She twitched her toes inside the boot liners. "Felt feet," she said and smiled at her granddaughter. Liz's mood had changed, her lips were tight. "Are you all right?" asked Ana.

Liz turned away and watched the maze of magazines dissolve into the darkness of the living room. "I'm just fine, Gramma."

"You're obviously upset about something, Elizabeth."

"Just a phone squabble. It's a man I've been seeing. He's at a meeting in Tokyo. He wants us to have more time together. He's too . . . desperate, I guess."

"Is that why you've been so tense since you arrived?"

"That's part of it. Tom really needs a wife. It's the right move for him."

"But not for you?"

"There's no smoke, you know?" Liz laughed. "He'll make a good husband—for somebody. Oh, God, marriage. Did the monkish life ever appeal to you?"

"No. I lived a life of extremes. In the old days I liked men too much, now I own property—the general pattern for the decline and fall of civilizations. What's really bothering you?"

Liz gazed at the moth's demented dance. She drew in a deep breath and exhaled.

"I guess I feel lost. I wanted to come back here and find it the way it was. When I was a kid, I felt solid. Now everything feels fake." Her mouth made a quick, little twitch. "I'm an emotional spastic. I'm like that moth."

"What feels fake?"

"I did everything I set out to do—I got the degrees, I'm a major success in my career, I make a lot of money, the nice condo, nice car, nice nice. It's all nice. Then one day the bottom dropped out."

"Are you doing what you wanted, or what was expected?"

"I don't know. I just want to know how to fix it. How do I make a life that feels real again?"

"You want me to tell you?"

Liz pressed her fingers against her temples and began rubbing them. "God, Gramma. I can't figure anything out anymore. I wanted to come back and be quiet and for it all to go away."

"Well, I'll be the grandmother if that's what you want." She gave Liz a small, ironic smile. "When was the last time you ate anything?"

"Lunch, yesterday."

"It wouldn't hurt you to eat."

Liz eyed Ana's cereal boxes.

"You don't have to eat cereal, Elizabeth. I've put in some things for you. Look in the fridge."

"That was thoughtful," said Liz. "Thank you." She found a banquet of steaks, chicken, and vegetables stuffed into the small refrigerator. She made space on the edge of the drainboard and started chopping vegetables for a salad.

"So, can you give me a little advice?"

"I doubt what I did in my life would work for you."

"Why not?"

"Because we're different people and it was different then."

"What's so different?"

"I was stubborn and took risks in a particularly unforgiving time."

"Did that get you in trouble?"

"Of course, but being careful comes with its own troubles."

"I know," said Liz. She found a bowl for her salad, shook some bottled dressing on it, and stood by the sink chomping through her greens. "Most of the people I know gave up their dreams for the promise that they'd be taken care of. What they do and who they do it for doesn't matter. They just need to feel safe, but they're swallowed up by their meaningless jobs."

"The problem with being a drone is you never get to learn anything that counts for much—nothing you can carry with you."

"How did you avoid it?"

Ana laughed. "It wasn't always deliberate. Sometimes I just did something dumb and got lucky."

"Dumb, how?"

"Finding myself in situations I should have avoided, but making a discovery in the process. It was a way of seeing."

"What did you discover?"

The first thing that came to Ana's memory was a warm, long-ago night in Mexico. Something slightly wicked found its way into her expression. "One night I went out drinking," she said. "It was in a bad section of Guadalajara. I drank too much and got lost, which is easy to do, and ended up in an alley behind a garage. There was a woman there, fighting with her drunken husband in the moonlight. I saw her hand yank at his neck, like this." She put a clenched fist to her throat and made a quick, little jerk. "He slumped down like a sack of sand. She'd slit his throat. I was mesmerized. When she saw me she threatened to put her *blado minito* in the *gringa*'s throat. It was the kind of thing that broadens your horizons."

Liz almost choked on her salad. "Not if you're the husband. How did it broaden your horizons?"

"I realized how much of an outlaw I was. It never occurred to me to report her."

"But she murdered him. You never reported it, even later?"

"She had her reasons. I saw my own passion in her. Every day in business and government, people's lives are destroyed. It's just as deadly. Where do you report that?"

Liz flashed a quick smile. "Very revealing. Now maybe you'll answer my first question."

"What question?"

"About the love of your life."

"I had someone. I wasn't always a hermit."

"Was it my grandfather? The one who was killed in the war?"

"No. It was a man I met several years later."

"What happened to him?"

"He died fairly young."

"Oh, Gramma. I'm sorry."

"Life went on. It does that if you let it."

"What was he like?"

"He was a bit of an outlaw himself."

"Was it shared yearning?"

Ana laughed. "Definitely shared. That doesn't go now, does it? The authorities prefer the controlled burn to the wildfire."

"When I first heard the story of Cody and Rose, I wondered how love could set water on fire."

"In my experience, gasoline and fuel oil heighten the intensity."

Liz laughed. "Were you a terrorist, Gramma?"

"Some would have said as much."

BILLY OGEEN OWNED THE BEGINNINGS OF A MARINA AND
a fiberglass boat business. He also owned the Roadside
Cafe, where Rose worked. Every morning he stopped
by, had coffee with some friends, and caught the gossip.
He had built the cafe after he came back from the war.
His wife had wanted it to face the lake, but Ogeen was
not naive. He knew the action was on the highway.

"That lake"—Ogeen pointed toward the kitchen—
"is just one damn big hole full of water. When we were
growin' up it wasn't such a big deal. All you could do was
paddle around on it—the fishin' was nonexistent. Now
we're makin' a livin' off the clowns who come here to
drink an' chase pussy."

"Jesus, you're a cynical son of a bitch, Ogeen," said Willis, the Chevy dealer.

Ogeen laughed. "Just practical. I'm a realist."

"I could use some of that," hooted Larry Morgan as he sat down. Larry was an insurance broker. "You got that on the menu, Ogeen?"

"What's that, Larry?"

"Real ass," Larry said in a deep voice, and looked around.

"So what followed you through the door, Larry?"

"Yeah, cow butt."

"Hey. Keep it down, guys," said Ogeen. "What the hell's wrong with you?"

Beside Larry and Willis, there was Earl, in farm implements and real estate, and Lloyd, who managed his father's lumberyard. Their jokey remarks and guy-swagger reminded Rose of high school boys, but she never thought of them as mean or dangerous. They were business regulars and they wore suits. They were fascinated with the workings of the town—who had built what and when, who had plans, where the action would be in six months, in a year, or five.

When Cody came in, they all noticed. He walked to the counter, sat down, and waited for Rose.

"Hi," she said. "Glad you could make it."

"Thought I'd try your coffee, Miss."

She poured him a cup and watched. "So?"

"It's about what I expected."

She laughed. "Oh, we're not good enough for you, huh?"

Earl leaned over to Ogeen. "Who the hell is that?" he asked.

"I'd guess he's the drifter camped in that truck behind George's place."

"How so?"

"Did you hear a car pull up? Not many people walk out here."

"What's his story?"

"His transmission went out on the hill. Lost his brakes. Nelson's fence saved him."

"Too bad."

"You never know," said Ogeen. "Well, I need to order supplies for the cook. See you later, fellows." He got up and walked past Cody into the kitchen.

Three women came in and sat down in the booth next to the window. They all waved to Ogeen's friends and said hi. Earl, Willis, Lloyd, and Larry waved and nodded. Rose set water out for the women and waited to take their orders.

The short blond with a tight perm shouted their good fortune to the boys across the cafe. "We came over to celebrate—Esther's husband just bought her a beautiful new washer-dryer. It's General Electric—real nice."

Esther was jubilant and radiant, she bounced. Her husband's expression of love filled her to the brim, spilling over to her friends. Appliance frenzy filled the cafe. Even the customers at two other tables caught a little of Esther's bouncy enthusiasm. The linoleum and chrome seemed brighter. For a moment the place was aglow. The man at the counter was looking in their direction. He looked lean and strong, he was easy on the eyes, and he was new. Esther thought he was damn near perfect.

"Would you like to order?" asked Rose. She had been waiting for the women to settle in, but they kept fussing with themselves and enthusing over one thing and then another. They had taken over the cafe, changing its shape and colors. Rose felt as if she had left her body and was watching them from high above. She called down to them, "Would you like to order?"

They looked up, surprised to see her standing there. All three registered Rose's clothes and hair, noticed the lack of makeup, and remembered she was the Indian girl who looked almost white.

Gail, the tight blond, said, "Coffees for me and the girls, and I'll have a piece of cherry pie with ice cream."

"Me too," said Shirley.

"I'll have the same," said Esther.

"Did you want your pie heated?" asked Rose.

"Uh-huh." "Sure." "That would be fine." They watched her walk away. She did not seem to care about the washer-dryer. They saw her turn her head and smile as she went by the man at the counter. The entire time she was cutting pie, the man had a smile on his face. She said something over her shoulder and he laughed.

When Ogeen's buddies got ready to leave, Rose was busy serving pies and pouring coffee for the three women. The men filed up to the cash register, took toothpicks from the dispenser, and stood around waiting for Rose. They made a slow, surreptitious scan of the new guy. At first they just glanced down at his boots—loggers, no corks—and the Levi's. After a little small talk they made their way up to his forearms and shoulders.

"Ready, boys?" asked Rose. "That's Cody there. Cody, these are the boss's friends, Larry, Willis, Lloyd, and Earl."

Cody nodded to each of them. "Good morning, fellows."

"His truck broke down," said Rose. "Like that pie, Lloyd? Your change. Thanks, Larry. He's waiting for parts."

"Yeah," said Earl. "We heard."

"Good luck," said Willis, and they all nodded and left.

Cody turned and watched them go. "Why is it," he asked Rose, "that women's dresses can look like the magazine ads, but men's suits never fit quite right?"

"Maybe they only design suits for nervous little men who live in cities. Do you get magazines?"

"No. In the winter I spend a lot of time in libraries."

"Do you read a lot?"

"Mostly machinery manuals and biographies."

"About pirates?"

"Some of them were definitely pirates, but they were written up to be inventors and explorers." He smiled, leaned forward slightly, and lowered his voice. "Did you know there was an Englishman in the seventeen hundreds who sailed around the world and collected over thirty thousand plants and animals?"

Rose started laughing. "No. I didn't know that," she said. "How did he get them all home?"

"Well, he pressed the plants in books. You can get hundreds of plants in a book. And there were a lot of little things. Bugs and such."

"Bugs and such? We should put that on the menu."

They were both laughing when Ogeen shouted from the back. "You've got other customers, Rose."

She turned and looked over the order counter into the kitchen. "Everybody's fine, Ogeen. Are you okay?"

Sue Ellen, the cook, set a plate of cakes on the counter and called out, louder than necessary, "Order up."

Rose took the cakes off the counter. "Thanks, Sue. Could you put up an order of bugs and such?"

Cody was digging in his pocket for nickels. "I should be going."

"The coffee's on me," she said.

---

That afternoon Cody walked down the road toward town to buy some supplies and to look for a way to make a little money. He was irritated by Rose's boss—another jerk who needed to humiliate the people who worked for him. Cody felt protective of Rose, yet it was obvious she was fearless around Ogeen. Some women could handle obnoxious bullies by treating them like boys. It took the right woman, and perhaps the right bully. Well, he decided, it's not any of mine.

On the lakeside of the road he came upon Tidyman & Son, an oil distribution company that consisted of a small office building attached to a warehouse. A gravel-covered yard and several large fuel tanks overlooked the lake. West of the yard was a shed for trucks and machinery.

A staunch, roundish man with a black wool cap and a chewed cigar stood at the yard's edge looking over the bank at the water below. He began waving his arms, bringing them up and letting them fall in a gesture of futility. He did this several times then turned away from the lake and walked toward the office. He saw Cody on the road, watching. They stood and stared at each other.

"What in the name of hell are you gawkin' at?" the man shouted.

"You look like you're conducting fish—wavin' your arms at an inert body of water."

"*Inert*'s a damn fancy word for a drifter," the man retorted. He waved an arm at the lake. "There's nothing inert about it." He walked back to the site of his agitation. "Look at this," he demanded, pointing down at the deep undercut eroded by the sleepless lake.

Cody walked down from the road and looked over the edge. The entire yard had been made by dumping rock and dirt into the lake, and the lake was gradually eating its way back.

"You need a break wall to stop that," Cody said.

"Yeah, found that out," the man said. "Goddamn lake." He looked Cody over, as if he were inspecting for lice. "The problem is, anybody who isn't retarded or Indian is workin' on the dam. You need a job?"

"The name is Cody."

"All right, Cody," the man wheezed. "Mine's Tidyman. Do you need a job?"

"Yeah, I do."

"You have any experience at this sort a thing?"

"I'm a saw filer, but I've built a couple of tepee burners and I put in a steam shed and a green chain for the mill in Whitehall." He walked around on the bank and surveyed the shoreline on either side of the yard. "I can do the job, but I'll need some equipment."

Tidyman smiled. If prayer doesn't work, he thought, dumb luck will do. "When can you start?"

"I can start now if you can provide the equipment, material, and two strong boys, and pay me eighteen dollars a day. It should take about twelve days if we do it with stone and the stone's close, less if you can get a pile driver and timbers."

Tidyman thought about the offer long enough so it looked like he was a reasonable businessman. "Well, the pile driver's doin' a dock on the west side. So it'll have to be stone. The boys may be a problem. They're all on the dam. You might have to find some Indians." He pointed to a dock that was about a half mile to the west. "I have a barge down there. I have a winch, and I have trucks."

"What's wrong with the Indians?" Cody asked.

"Nothin'. You just have to give them a good enough reason to work. It's not something they do on a regular basis."

"What do they do on a regular basis?"

"They hunt and they play poker real good. Nobody can catch more fish in a day than one of their women. Those women know the lake better than the men."

"Why don't Indians ever look you in the eye?" Cody asked.

"Yeah, they don't, do they?" Tidyman said. "I don't

really know." He laughed like an evil gnome. "Maybe they just don't like what they see." He took the cigar out of his mouth and looked up at Cody. He grinned until his fat cheeks made his eyes squint.

Cody smiled down at him. "Where do we find the stone?" he asked.

He walked back along the highway in the noon heat, carrying his box of groceries. He passed a Dairy Boy Shakes ice-cream place, a new motel with its six small cabins covered in green shingles, and the old Harmmon Boat Works building. The boat works was the only building that faced the lake. The pavement soaked up the heat, until the road began to shimmer. He was sweating by the time he got back to the truck and discovered Rose, sitting in his doorway, drinking a cold beer.

"That looks good," he said.

"Would you like a beer?"

"Sure, a beer'd be fine."

She opened a bottle and handed it to him. "One fine beer. What do you think of Mr. Tidyman?" she asked.

Cody took a pull off the bottle. He was not surprised that she knew already. "Different. Strange sense of humor. What's the burr under his blanket?"

"He inherited the business. I don't think he likes it, but the times have been good to him, with the war and the dam."

"He's unhappy because he's a success?"

"I told you, money's the root of all evil. Maybe he has a secret, unfulfilled passion."

"A deviant pleasure?"

"Of course. Maybe he's the kind that fixates on body parts—toes, elbows, knees?" She paused. "Thighs?"

"Did I offend you by what I said about your thighs?"

"No. You should say what's on your mind." She had kicked her shoes off and was twisting her feet around and banging her toes together.

"It could be risky—saying what's on your mind," he said.

"Just any run-of-the-mill mind," she asked, "or yours in particular?"

"Depends on what's on my mind. What's on yours?"

She laughed and set her bottle inside the door. "Bad day at the Roadside Cafe."

"Ogeen?"

"He's just a modern bastard. Nothing special." She shrugged. "Would you go for a swim with me? I think it's too damn hot for my brain."

He climbed into the truck and stripped down to his shorts. Her back was to him but she could hear the rustle of clothing. She stared at the lake and the cafe and thought about him naked.

He stood next to her in the doorway. "You're wearing your dress in the water?" he asked.

"Yes, why not?"

He jumped down and held out his hand to her. "Why not."

They walked down the steep bank to the lakeshore and into the water toward the burnt pilings. Her dress billowed up around her thighs until it soaked through and spilled out behind her like a thin blue cloud. He trailed along, watching her move through the water. She turned her head and smiled, then dropped below the surface and pushed away.

Sunlight swam down through the water and dappled the thighs full of promises. She swam with her legs apart, slowly fanning the water, undulating in the swimming light.

He moved under and around her, never touching. Flickers of light played with her curves and crevices, sending coded messages to the ancient parts of his brain. She reached the floating dock and pulled herself up. Her dress stuck to her breasts and belly. He stayed in, treading water and smiling.

"That was nice," he said.

"What?"

"Do you always go bare?"

"Not always." Her expression turned serious. "You're not going to talk about this to anybody, I hope."

"No, I wouldn't."

"I'm in enough trouble around here without the lakers talking about my bare bottom."

"What trouble?"

"I'm different. And I was raised by the Red Crows, which makes me part Indian—to the whites, but I'm still a white woman to the Indians. Behind my back they call me white meat."

He was cold and his erection had receded, so he climbed up onto the float and sat next to her. "When you went away, where did you go, and why did you come back?"

"When I was about three, a man, who was maybe my father, asked Catherine Red Crows to watch me for the afternoon. He never came back, so I became an Indian. When I was about twelve, I got sent to Indian school in Oklahoma City, where they taught me to be a white person. We had to wear those itchy, black wool jumpers.

"A young man got me pregnant. I was fifteen, my baby was put in a foster home, and I was sent to a school in Wichita. After that, I went to teachers' college in San Bernardino till the war broke out. Then I got a job at Grumman Aviation. When the war ended, I came back home to be with Catherine."

"A hard life."

"I liked living with the Indians when I was a kid, and I liked working with the women making fighter planes. Those were pretty good years. I don't regret anything."

"Nothing?"

She was quiet for a while. "I want my daughter back."

"Did you love her father?"

She smiled. "Yes. He was wonderful to me. He went to the war. I got a letter from him once, all the way from Rome, Italy."

"He didn't come back?"

"No. Just the letter."

"Were there others?"

She laughed. "Others? Other lovers?"

"Uh-huh, those others."

"You want everything? All my stories?"

"Sure."

"There was a war, remember. Those were fast times."

He looked embarrassed. "I meant, were you ever in love again?"

"When I worked in Los Angeles, I met a man who came out from the east to translate Japanese for the army." She laughed and shook her head. "I guess, at first, I fell in love with his ideas, all his talk."

"What happened?"

"Most of what I understand came from Catherine and the Indians, and living on the lake. My linguist was like salad—all that leafy stuff, and I was really hungry. I wanted a good, bloody piece of meat."

"Was he in love with you?"

"We loved each other, but he wanted the world made into words. What I knew never fit into words."

"What do you mean? You're very good with words and you're full of ideas nobody ever heard of. Did you tell him about the lake and Loneliness?"

"I think that's different. I can tell stories, but I can't explain them. He had to know the meaning of everything."

"Do you tell everyone your stories?" The possessive edge in his voice surprised him.

Rose smiled. "Only the ones I think can hear them," she said. "I was wrong about him."

He realized he did not want her to be wrong this time.

"What will you do when Catherine dies?" he asked. "Will you stay?"

"No." She looked out across the water. "The lake is a big part of my life, though." She looked up at him and smiled. "If I could change who I am, I would."

"How would you be different?"

"No one would know who I'd been. I'd be invisible. I could be myself. I wouldn't be Indian or white or poor or rich."

"Would you be alone?"

She laughed. "I'd be a bear to live with."

"Yes," he smiled. "That wouldn't surprise me."

She reached over and gently poked his shoulder. His eyes closed and her touch spread through his body like ink in a pool. When the touch had saturated him, he heard a sound, like a stone dropped in water. He opened his eyes and she was gone.

He slid into the water and swam deep, along the outer edge of the pilings, searching for her. She appeared, swimming above him against the light. She drew him farther out into the lake. One hundred feet beyond the pilings she pointed toward the bottom. Gradually he began to see what appeared to be giant logs partially buried in silt, thirty feet beneath the surface. There were hundreds of them scattered along the bottom like giant matchsticks. She swam down into the green-gray light, turning from time to time to see if he was following.

As they made their way back toward the truck, picking their way through the rocks, Rose explained the logs. "Before the mill burned, they'd corral a thousand logs at a time in a floating boom and bring them down the lake from the rivers up north. The booms would sit out there for days waiting to be pulled into the mill. Some of the sap-heavy ones would take on enough water to sink them."

He heard some of what she said, but not all of it. He was caught up in how she moved, how the dress clung to her bottom and thighs, and how desperately he wanted her. Finally he laughed to break the tension.

"What's funny?" she asked.

"Desire. Desire is funny, and lust. Common, ordinary, everyday lust."

She gave him a long, deliberate look and smiled.

It was too direct for him. He looked away and changed the subject. "How long did the mill operate?"

"Forty, maybe fifty years," she said. "I was away when it burned."

"Then there's a lot of timber down there."

She looked up at him and smiled. "Lots of some-body's money."

He laughed. "Evil money."

"Well, whoever tries to salvage that mess would have to work pretty hard to get it off the bottom. And then they might only have a bunch of rotten logs."

"Maybe. I've been around logging camps and mills most of my life. I've never heard of anybody loggin' a lake."

They walked up the slope behind the garage to the truck and Cody climbed inside. When he reappeared in the doorway, he had his clothes on. He jumped down.

"I put a shirt and my other pants on the bed if you want them. I can dry your dress on the hood."

Rose wondered why there were no stairs for the back of his truck, but in an odd way she liked having to hoist herself in every time.

Her dress stuck to her skin. She had to work it up from side to side to get it off. She put his shirt on and rolled the sleeves back. It was long enough to cover her bottom, which was fortunate because the pants were impossible. She peered out and handed him her dress. He walked around to the front of the truck and spread the dress on the hood, carefully smoothing it with his hands.

She watched him through the cab window. His hands stroked her dress. The hot metal surface against the wet material made steam rise through his fingers. Cody looked up suddenly, but the glare off the window kept her secret. He smiled that she might be watching and find him out, stroking the recollection of her body.

"Where were you raised?" she asked when he came back.

"In the woods, mostly. Canada, the Idaho panhandle, and outside Coreen."

"Where're your folks?"

"My father died in a logging accident just before the war. Mama married some fellow in Coreen. I have three sisters. They scattered."

"Older, younger, married, single?"

"All younger, all married."

"Nobody to tie you down?" It was a joke, said with a slight leer.

He laughed. "There was a schoolteacher I liked a lot, but she found a pharmacist. We wanted different things."

"What do you want?"

"I decide as I go along."

"You don't have plans? I thought everybody had plans these days."

"I like projects. One thing, then another. Sometimes I like to make a little evil money. I read for days. I paint."

"How do you make money? The file business?"

"Usually. Sometimes I'll contract a project, like the one for Tidyman, or install machinery. I do a little trading. The usual pirate stuff." He grinned at her. "I know of some military surplus Vicker's wobble-plate drives if you'd be in need."

She laughed. "Wobble-plates?" Pirate, she thought, was not far off.

"Did you go to college?"

"For a year, after the war. I realized I couldn't learn what I wanted in college."

"What did you want?"

"Adventures, discovery, hidden treasure." He laughed. "The usual."

"Now what?"

"I've got a job for a couple of weeks, a truck to fix, and some paintings to do. That's for now."

They looked at each other without saying a word, and then, as though their mouths were connected to the same mental mechanism, they began to smile.

She leaned toward him and gave him a gentle kiss at the arch of his eye.

"For now," she said. "I've got to get home."

"Wait here. I'll be right back." He leapt through the doorway, all legs and arms flying in an air dance. He returned in an instant with her dress, still smiling.

"It's wet," he said, and handed the dress up to her. "You can keep the shirt."

"I'll bet you have two shirts, and this is the best one."

"I can buy another. I'll make a good piece of change in the next two weeks."

"You'll need some help, won't you?"

"Need a job?"

She laughed. "Not yet. But Gerome and Joseph Red Crows need to make some money."

"Are these Indians of yours any good?"

"Bad Indians, good work."

"We'll start early."

"Thanks, I'll tell them. Can I just borrow your shirt, for now?"

"Sure."

She jumped down, holding the shirt from flying up, revealing her everything.

"They'd be surprised to learn they're my Indians. It's me that belongs to them." She laughed and disappeared over the hill.

———————

He lay on his bed and looked out on the evening sky. The hands of her laughter curved around his shoulders, drawing him in, holding him against her skin. She pressed in, her breath on his neck, her mouth on his mouth. He could feel her soaking into his body.

His dreams were filled with logs and Indians crossing and diving into the darkness of the lake. They reemerged, floating toward the surface in shafts of soft green light. He saw her, through the crisscross of logs and Indians, swimming down into the black water, wearing his good white shirt. He swam after her. She became a speck, then disappeared. He was lost.

Indian eyes watched him from the darkness. He could hear their soft, faraway voices speaking the words of a strange and difficult language.

The voices of his dream became the shadows of men in the doorway of the truck. He woke and discovered the door open. It was still dark and he could see several people standing in the moonlight waiting for him. He tried to ask what they wanted but was too tired and fell back asleep.

———◦———

Two Indian men sat on the ground and watched the lake change its shape as light came into the sky. Cody had eased himself down from the truck and was starting a fire for coffee before he realized the men were there. All he could see at first were dark shapes. They sat motionless and said nothing.

"Good morning. Would you like some coffee?" he asked. It seemed to Cody that a lot of time went by before one of them turned to him and answered.

In a slow, quiet voice, the bigger of the two men replied, "Good morning." It was a thoughtful voice. "Coffee would be good. Thank you." Then he turned back to his lake.

Cody took cups and coffee over to the Indians. They nodded. He sat on his haunches and poured the coffee.

"This is good coffee," said the big man. "Thank you." He extended his hand. "My name is Gerome Red Crows. This is Joseph. He is also a Red Crows. We came to help you build a break wall for Mr. Tidyman."

Gerome was over six feet, a bit taller than Cody, and several years older. As the light improved, Cody could see the transactions of a rough life carved in the Indian's face: old scars on a cheek and the chin, a slight realignment of the nose. He wondered if Indians or whites had done this to him. Male or female?

The other Indian, Joseph, was in his late forties. He had a thin, tough look. He seemed a little nasty, but someone liked him well enough to weave bright pieces of cloth into his braids. He wore an old red cowboy shirt with silver snaps. The heels of his army boots were worn down on the outside. He stood bowlegged and drank his coffee.

Joseph had a wife named Sally, a much younger woman whom he had purchased several years before from her intoxicated mother. He believed women, like farm animals, had no souls—a notion that often enough brought him grief. He fought the world in secret ways. His goal was to become a shaman. Such skills, he believed, would allow him to control the unbound spirits that could occupy the bodies of wild animals or women.

Gerome did not believe in this shifting spirit world. Animals had souls. They could give a person a little luck in life, or *oomph*, as his great-grandmother called it. So his attitude toward the world was shaped more as a request.

Cody had not expected the men to come at all. Their early arrival made him wonder what magic Rose was able to work on them.

There was a gentleness in Gerome's voice that belied the fierce, murderous design of his face. This worked to his benefit in poker games or whenever bluffing became an important factor in his survival. The full effect on the listener was a sense of relief and an unconscious tendency to trust the Indian.

"Would you like some breakfast?" Cody asked.

"Thank you, we have eaten this morning," Gerome replied.

Cody liked Gerome's formality. He wondered if the

Indian was aware of what he was doing, of how he sounded and looked.

Cody made himself some biscuits and heated a slab of salt pork on a flat piece of iron he used as a frying pan. He ate sitting on the front fender of his truck and thought about stones: how heavy? how many? how far? how long?

Before they left, Cody took three blankets from the truck, giving one each to Gerome and Joseph. The Indians took the blankets without saying anything or looking surprised, but it was their first hint that they would not be sleeping at home. In a small grocery down the highway from Tidyman & Son, Cody purchased a block of ice and enough food for three days' worth of hard work.

Gerome went through the boxes, looking at each label. "It is a good thing white man's food has pictures on it," he said. "Otherwise we wouldn't know what we were eating."

Cody smiled.

The Indian held up a can. "You have a lot of this one, but there is no picture."

"That's Spam. Nobody knows what's in it."

"Yes," said Gerome. "I know Spam."

Two hours later they were making a wake through the glass-smooth water toward a rock slide, five miles north on the west side of the lake. Gerome lay on the deck and stared over the side as the sky slid endlessly beneath the bow. Cody stood midbarge, captivated by the water and the wispy clouds that funneled downward, opening into feathery plumes. Joseph guided them north and west, hands on the wheel, taking in the deep vibrations of the diesel engine.

The barge was thirty feet wide by fifty-five feet long. Its deck and the hull were made of thick oak planks. The hull was sealed with lead and oakum and several years of paint. It leaked badly and had to be pumped at least once a week for several hours to keep it afloat. If it were loaded down to the gunnels, two pumps, running day and night, were required. In case of a pump failure, several balsa-wood life jackets hung from the pilothouse. The effectiveness of the jackets had, fortunately, never been called into question. Years of sun bleaching and mildew had rotted the cotton strapping.

Cody calculated that the barge could haul enough rock in three trips to build Tidyman's break wall. They would have to pick the rock off a slide and move it two hundred feet to a stone outcropping at the water's edge. The drop-off at this point was deep enough to allow the barge to pull in close, where it could be loaded from a gangplank.

They loaded rock into wheelbarrows and brought them to the barge, up the gangplank, unloaded, and returned to the slide. This went on all afternoon. The rock was piled around the edge of the deck until it began to resemble a walled fortress. Late in the afternoon, on the lake side of the barge, Gerome began building three extensions at right angles to the outer wall. Cody said nothing. The rocks could be placed in any configuration, as long as the barge was in relative balance. By evening three separate rooms with doorways had appeared. Still nothing was said, but that night each man spread his blanket in one of the rooms, lay down, and fell into a deep, exhausted sleep.

ROSE HAD COME BACK TO THE TRUCK AFTER CATHERINE had fallen asleep, and waited for Cody to return. There was no note and he had said nothing about being gone overnight. The door was open, so she climbed in and stretched out on his bed.

It was dark when she woke. She lay perfectly still and imagined the weight of his body pressing her into the thin mattress. She could feel him on her belly, against her breasts, his breath against her neck, and waited for the press of his mouth against her mouth. She reached up and touched her lips with her fingertips. Her imagination lifted her off the mattress. She drifted through the doorway and floated above the blue truck, out over the lake, searching the shoreline until she found the sinking barge weighed down with its wants and its riches.

Late in the night, a young woman came to the doorway and listened for sounds of breathing.

"Hello," she said to the dark interior of the truck.

"Hello?" said Rose. She had forgotten she was in the truck.

"It is you, Rose?" the woman asked.

"Sally?"

"Yes. Do you know where Joseph is?"

"I don't know, Sally. They haven't come back."

"Are they drowned?"

Rose came to the doorway and sat down. "I dreamed they were drowned, but my dreams are never true."

"It's good your dreams are bad," said Sally.

"Let's go wake Tidyman up and find out."

They set off in the cool night air down the warm highway. The sky was clear and black and filled with stars, but the road through the trees was dark. They could barely see each other, so they held hands and walked on the soft asphalt for two miles through the racket of a million crickets.

Sally was short and thin. She worried about many things, probably things that did not need worrying, which made her nervous and kept her thin. Her high cheekbones and her sharp black eyes could make her look angry when she was only daydreaming. She worried more than she daydreamed.

Sally squeezed Rose's hand a little to let her know something was going to be said. "Rose, did you ever wonder why the Red Crows never have anything?"

"You mean why are we always so poor?"

"Yes, that."

"I think it's because we're lazy. The men would rather hunt and gamble than go to work."

"Yes," said Sally. "That is true. But what is the reason they have no desire to work?"

"I don't know, Sally."

"I will tell you then. It is because when the black robes came, long ago, none of the Red Crows would follow them. They're being punished because of their stupid ancestors."

"But most of the Red Crows go to church now."

"They just pretend. None of them use their eyes to see God. I'm being punished because I married a Red Crows."

"Joseph was never one for God."

"If Joseph believed in God, he would try to trick him to get more power."

"Yes," said Rose. "Everyone tries to trick God."

Sally's mind raced down the dark road. She would never try to trick God. Sally was quiet for too long.

Rose guessed her thoughts and gave Sally's hand a gentle squeeze. "We're all part of God's mind," said Rose.

⸺✦⸻

The oil distributor's house sat on a steep hill across the road from the oil yard. They climbed the wood stairs to the house, caught their breath for a moment, and turned to look down across the bay. It was light enough to see the barge was not moored anywhere nearby. Rose knocked on the door. She waited then knocked again, harder.

"Coming, damn it. Coming," someone yelled from inside the house.

The door jerked open and there stood Tidyman peering into the night. He had not planned on callers and women were never expected. He could tell they were women because of their hair, and he guessed they were

Indians because of the scent of woodsmoke and tanned leather. His hands immediately covered his private parts. His concern was not so much that the women might see his pecker, but that his pecker might see them. His hands fanned out to cover his pecker eyes.

"What? What?" he asked in distress.

"Do you know where the guys are?" Rose asked.

"They camped up where they're loading rocks on the west side. It'll take them a day or two." He paused for a moment. "They didn't let you know? What a bunch of bastards. I'm sure they're all right. You should go home and get some sleep."

"Sorry we woke you," said Rose.

"It's okay. Well, good night ladies," he said, and closed the door.

"Those bastards," said Sally.

"Maybe," said Rose. "And maybe they just don't think anyone cares about them."

"It's true. I don't care. To hell with him. Anyway, it's that damn Sho-shon who calls himself a shaman. Some day God will teach them a lesson."

"Sally, maybe you shouldn't talk about God so much. He might give you a swift kick in your behind."

"God would never kick me there."

They walked on through the din of crickets, guided only by the pathway of stars above the trees. Near the top of the hill the sky opened up and they could see the distant outline of the garage and the cafe. Sally giggled at the sign by the road: "It's big. It's thick. Enjoy it now. Dairy Boy Shakes."

Sally released her hold on Rose's hand and drifted away slightly, now that they could see the edge of the road.

"I hear the animals call his name," said Sally out of the blackness.

"Whose name?" Rose asked.

"God's name. If the animals do it, it must be all right. Don't you think?"

"The animals call God's name?"

"At night. I've heard them." Sally was quiet for a few steps, thinking hard. "When I say his name, I'm afraid sometimes."

"Why are you afraid?"

"When I say God's name, it comes out of my mouth."

"Yes."

"Well, sometimes I put Joseph's thing in my mouth."

"Oh," said Rose.

"You see?" asked Sally.

"Yes," Rose said in her serious voice. "That is a problem."

"Do you do that, Rose? Put the man's thing in your mouth."

"It's all right to put the man's thing in your mouth." Rose sounded very sure of herself, which was a comfort to Sally, but then Rose went too far. "You can put it wherever it fits."

"Rose!"

"Just be happy you've got holes in your body, Sally."

There was a long silence from Sally. Images and implications and God's wrath played through her thoughts. "Rose," she said, "does Cody have a big . . . ?"

"Yeah."

"Then you've done it with him?"

"No."

"How do you know it's big?"

"We went swimming. It got hard in the water."

"Are you goin' to do it?"

"If I see him again, and if I don't kill him first."

Sally walked along, touching Rose's shoulder for guidance and comfort. "Maybe I should go swimming with Joseph," she said and laughed.

Rose stopped and reached her arm around Sally. They stood in the middle of the asphalt road.

"Sally, you are beautiful and desirable. Joseph will learn to love you. And if he doesn't, you'll find someone who does."

Sally's tears rolled down her cheeks in the dark. If she made a sound, it was lost among the droning crickets.

## SUNDAY
## MORNING

$A$na and Liz walked east along the shore toward the condominiums until they came to the block wall that defined the property line. It was as far as they could go without wading out past the wall or climbing over it. Neither of them said anything. Liz studied the row of docks that jutted out into the lake from each cluster of condos. Struck by the real-world display of her statistics, she turned and started back.

"Slow down," Ana called. "I can't keep up."

Liz turned and waved at the condos. "We could be anywhere. It looks like a thousand other places."

"There's a spot I sit in my living room where I can't see these things. It's like having blinders on that let me look into the past."

"What was it like when you were a child?"

"I was raised by an old Red Crows woman whose family lived here for generations."

"I never knew you were raised by Indians."

"I never held on to it, but that life made me curious about the way people had lived long ago. What caught my interest went clear back to the primitive hunters in Europe and here. So that was what I studied and that is where I dream."

"I had no idea you were interested in anything like that."

"It taught me a lot about how people operate."

"Would I have made a good primitive, Gramma?"

Ana laughed. "Probably. You're always figuring out what things are worth."

Liz flinched. "What do you mean by that?"

"I mean we're all made the same. Those people weren't fools. They thought about the worth of things as well as their own worthiness. They invented middle-class values. Their stories are full of pride and spite. Lots of courage and vindictiveness too."

"That's what would have made me a good primitive? Thanks a lot."

"Those are survival skills, Elizabeth. They have a purpose or they wouldn't exist."

"It never occurred to me that being middle class was in our blood. It's not the kind of thing I think about."

"We all have little mysteries we need to solve."

"Is that what the maze of magazines is all about?"

"Oh, those. I've meant to get rid of most of them—

have a big housecleaning someday." Ana waved at some imaginary future and laughed. "But there's always something better to do, like take a nap."

"I'd be glad to help get rid of them."

"That's very nice, but why would you want to spend your visit hauling trash?"

"To feel useful. I need a project."

"Well, thank you. It'll make a nice fire. I'd have asked those Red Crows boys to do it—they're the ones that sold me the subscriptions in the first place—but I don't want them in my stuff."

As they walked back through the cherry trees to the house, Ana began to have doubts. Her paper fortress provided an odd comfort. The uneven edges of the stacks absorbed sound and softened the light.

"There're some papers I should save," she hedged, "out of respect, if nothing else—monographs and some articles by people I knew."

When she walked through the kitchen and examined the maze with the thought of it gone, she remembered long ago, how open and inviting the house had been.

"We used to push the rugs back and dance. We thought we were pretty good." She looked at Liz and smiled and hummed a tune.

"What's the tune?"

"'Doin' What Comes Natur'lly.'"

"Gramma and the outlaw?"

"Yep, him."

They sorted and carried for several hours, creating a large pile of magazines on the lake side of the house at the edge of the grass. Ana was stiff and her bones hurt. She moved slowly, dividing letters, articles, monographs, drawings, and photographs into smaller stacks along the living room wall. Occasionally, she would collect an armload of magazines and carry them outside. It was well into afternoon before they took a break and sat down in the newly exposed living room chairs. Heat and dust had tired them as much as the work. They sipped Ana's industrial-strength coffee from crazed, white cups and surveyed their attack on the maze.

Among the magazines, Liz had discovered reprints from professional journals, photocopies of unpublished articles, and correspondence from several anthropologists and archaeologists. She was surprised by the extent of Ana's interest.

The collection held other surprises as well—copies of *Vogue, Esquire, Playboy, Playgirl, American Trucker, The Whole Earth Catalog, Good Housekeeping,* and dozens of comic books.

She was startled to find a porn magazine and wanted to ask her grandmother about it. Instead, she dropped the magazine at the edge of the pile outside and waited until Ana was in the house to flip through it. A series of pictures of a thin, strung-out–looking blond having sex with a lithe, muscular man aroused her. She felt surreptitious and fourteen again. Her sneaky horniness invited in sensations she would remember and take with her—the placid lake, the intensity of the cherry trees in bloom, and Ana's surprising passions.

The rooms were clear except for the considerable pile of journals and correspondence Ana had stacked against the living room wall. Dust drifted through the stream of sunlight. Liz followed a faded path—the last evidence of Ana's maze—across the newly revealed rug, through the pool of sun to the spot where Ana had sat for years, reading her magazines and journals and watching the lake. Liz took a wicker chair they had reclaimed from the stacks and pulled it next to her grandmother. She pointed a toe at the remaining evidence of her grandmother's past obsession.

"That was a major project."

"Many years. I've forgotten the theories already. The stories were interesting. They'll stay with me."

"Stories about what?"

"Animals, mostly."

"I didn't know you were an animal person."

"It wasn't simply the animals. When we were hunters, our relationship with animals was sacramental. They allowed us to negotiate with the forces that were hidden in nature."

"What was there to negotiate for?"

"Food and good health, luck in finding the right mate, strong babies, the usual."

Liz's brow crinkled. "Were we killing the same animals we were asking for help?"

Ana leaned forward slightly, regaining her energy. "You have to understand that life was seen as cyclical. If you thought about an animal in the proper ways—respected it, and performed the right rituals—its spirit would eventually return in another animal and allow you to kill it again."

"And if you didn't think the right thoughts?"

"The animals went away and you starved."

Liz felt a slight twitch. "This entire relationship was based on fear?"

"There were other emotions." Her hands began to accentuate her words. "Rapture and awe sharpened our senses as well as fear. They let the animals speak to us."

Her grandmother's exuberance surprised Liz. "How did they speak to us? They didn't just come out of the woods and start talking, did they?"

"The stories inspired people, particularly the teenagers, to have visions. The spirit of an animal would appear in a vision and offer to be a youngster's helper."

"Like angels?"

"Yes, in ways—we must have felt animals were always watching us, that the slightest thing we did could draw their attention. Before horses or farming, we were totally dependent on wild animals. That had to have an enormous effect on us. In fact, we believed nature had a mind that could see into our minds."

"That sounds very intense. Even paranoid."

"We were certainly compelled to speak to nature and to negotiate for more control."

"It seems strange to me that anyone could believe those things."

"It was more than belief. We experienced it. To a great extent our livelihood shapes our reality. What we see is what we learn to see."

"If this was supposed to be a negotiation, what did the animals get out of it, besides getting to terrorize us?"

"We sang songs to them, and danced, said prayers and performed rituals. We told stories and painted images to honor animals."

"But did we tell love stories?"

Ana laughed. "You have a one-track mind, Elizabeth. We told erotic stories. We told about deep attachments and jealousy, about territory, murder, and treachery. Mostly the stories were about animals, even about people marrying animals or being transformed into animals, but there seems to be a shortage of stories about people becoming immersed in each other."

"No romantic love?"

"Maybe not. Perhaps romantic love is a modern invention."

"What do you mean? We just copulated like a bunch of animals?"

"We fell in love, of course. But how far did we need to fall? Perhaps rapture and awe became unnecessary in our negotiations with animals and found another expression. Maybe the vision of the animal spirit was transformed to a vision of the beloved."

"Have you had visions, Gramma?"

"I did. But instead of an animal, my vision was that I was the lake and I was dreaming."

"What did that feel like?"

"Deep and full of fishes."

"Like love?"

"Like making love."

THE SUN WAS HOT ON THEIR HEADS BEFORE THEY WOKE the next morning. Cody felt ill at ease—a sense of great luck undercut by a lurking threat. They went ashore, made a fire, and cooked breakfast. As they ate, Cody studied Gerome.

Gerome looked up from time to time. He nodded his approval of the scrambled eggs and pork more than once, then looked away, wondering what the white man had up his sleeve. For his part, Gerome wanted to get Cody in a stick game. Maybe after the job was done.

One moment they were all languishing in the morning sun with full bellies, feeling their aching muscles from the day before, and then, as though they were appendages of a single being, they all felt the need to get to work. For hours, they loaded and pushed and unloaded their wheelbarrows.

Cody discovered slide rocks with lichen in many colors, intense yellow, orange, green, and black. He would see the lichen, reach for the rock, lift it into the wheelbarrow, set it down, and reach for another. The pattern of color and shape on each rock opened a separate room in his mind, a kind of atmospheric chamber, which held a memory from his childhood. He saw his mother's arm reach down for a stretching cat. Three horses rolled in the dust, then stood, legs apart, shaking themselves. He watched his father jump from log to log across a mill pond. All day he was immersed in the colors and patterns on stones.

There was no talk because Cody was lost in the thousand things the stones brought back.

There was no talk because Joseph hated white men.

And there was no talk because Gerome was reluctant to speak because Joseph hated white men. To speak to Cody would upset the delicate balance in Gerome's relationship to Joseph's mentor, Sho-shon, who thought of himself as a shaman. Sho-shon possessed a chickadee medicine bundle that had belonged to an old chief who lived before the buffalo were all killed off. The chickadee had been the chief's helper and had made his luck strong. Gerome wanted to purchase this bundle and the sixteen songs that went with it. How much luck, if any, was left in the bundle was a question that could not be settled until Gerome bought it and learned the songs. It was like buying a horse he had never ridden, or a used car—there was no way to know what you had until your life depended on it.

The three men worked well into the afternoon, lost in memories, hatreds, and dreams. About two o'clock, Joseph mentioned to Gerome that he was ready to eat. When Gerome told Cody, they looked at the sun for verification, unable to believe the day had gone so fast. Memories and dreams were more sustaining than hatred.

The barge was sitting low in the water. The rock wall was two layers deep around the edge of the deck. They would be ready to head back well before dark.

———◆———

"Damn it," Cody shouted and jumped up.

The three men had finished eating and were lying in the shade of a rock outcropping, resting before going back to work.

"What is the matter?" Gerome asked.

"I forgot to tell Rose we'd be gone overnight."

Gerome thought it through, then said, "Rose and Sally would've gone down to Mr. Tidyman's last night and asked him what happened. Then they got mad. Sally cried some. Rose stayed mad. Maybe you won't see her again. I don't know."

Joseph stared at Gerome for talking so much. Joseph's bucket was full—his hatred was spilling over in all directions now. Gerome was tired of Joseph's hatred.

"Who is Sally?" Cody asked.

"Joseph's wife."

Cody felt a surge of guilt. He looked at Joseph, who looked away.

"The women will understand," said Gerome. "Sally will forgive."

Gerome realized Joseph would not have told Sally he was going, anyway. Thinking about this hardened his feelings against the tough, angry Indian.

The men went back to work, loading, pushing, and unloading stones, building their fortress over water, forcing the barge deeper and deeper into the lake. The difference was that each man's concentration had changed.

Cody thought only of Rose and her anger. His memories no longer flowed from the stones.

Joseph realized he had lost his hold over Gerome and thought about how to regain his advantage.

And Gerome knew Cody was in love with Rose, which meant they were brothers, because Rose was Gerome's little sister. How quick things change, Gerome thought.

———

They could have worked for two more hours, but a bearing on one of the pumps froze. Cody and Gerome jumped down into the hull and inspected their prospects. After ten minutes, they realized the remaining pump was barely keeping up with the leaks, and both of its bearings were hot. They climbed back on deck and Gerome called to Joseph to get on board.

Cody moved the barge into the lake, tied the wheel off, and set to bailing with Joseph and Gerome. Each man bailed from a separate hatch—fore, center, and aft. For the next two hours, the bailed water gushed across the deck and spilled over the sides while the barge powered its way toward town. As the men weakened, the waterline inside the hull began to rise. It became obvious that they had to dump part of their cargo of stone to avoid sinking the barge.

Cody went on deck and began heaving stones over the side. Gerome and Joseph bailed with a steady ferocity. In half an hour, half a day's work loading and hauling stone was pitched into the water.

The barge quivered. It faltered and slowed. Then the water in the hull began to create a wave, moving back and forth on its own.

Cody was bent double, furiously throwing stones, when a long shadow slid across the deck. He turned and looked up at Gerome's dark face.

"I'm getting that sinkin' feeling," said Gerome.

Cody sat down against the stones. "We're going to sink Tidyman's barge along with our jobs, and you're making a joke?"

Gerome handed Cody one of the last three beers and sat down. "Yes. Pretty good joke."

"I don't think so."

"You have to think about these things in the right way," Gerome said. "Mr. Tidyman sank his own barge. He did not take care of the bearing. The barge is very old. It is okay for it to sink. Its time is come."

Cody looked back at the fury of water shooting from Joseph's hatch.

"Why are you so calm about this, Gerome? Joseph's still in a froth back there."

"I don't think Joseph knows how to swim."

"You do? I heard Indians can't swim."

"I am a very good swimmer. You probably should not believe the things you have heard about Indians."

Cody thought Gerome was smiling. He did not know what it meant when Gerome smiled.

They sipped their beers and let Tidyman's barge sink deeper into the water. They eyed the balsa life jackets and the rising water. Soon they would be bobbing in the lake waiting to be rescued.

"Do you think we will be rescued?" asked Gerome.

"Have you seen a flare gun on board?"

"I haven't seen a flare gun."

Cody pointed toward town. "We're getting close."

In the distance they could hear a fire bell. "Someone is coming," said Gerome.

They stood up to watch as the fireboat approached, its brass bell clanging and a water plume rising behind. It was a race. Either the miracle of military surplus would save the day or the barge would wallow and sink. The fireboat made a loop so it could come in, moving with the barge, and tie up alongside. Two lines were dragged on deck by the Lake Volunteer Fire Department and plunged into the center hatch. The pumps were engaged to prime the lines, then reversed to draw water from the barge.

Deafened by the barge's roaring engine, Joseph was oblivious to the fireboat. He was in the rear hatch, bailing for his life. Cody took the last beer and went back to save him from exhaustion. He handed Joseph the beer and pointed him toward the plumes shooting up from the fireboat. When it dawned on Joseph what had happened, his expression told the white man the Indian intended to kill him.

The fireboat's twin diesel pumps screamed, shooting water plumes eighty feet in the air. The barge and the fireboat moved along arm in arm toward town. An hour later the barge was visibly higher.

A new aluminum outboard speedboat, two small sailboats, a ChrisCraft inboard Speedster, and six kids in two rowboats joined them. All took turns challenging the heavy plumes that jettisoned from the fireboat. The men in the outboard seemed to enjoy an affinity between faster and drunker. Three boys in a rowboat capsized in the spray and had to be rescued by the wealthy Philadelphian in the ChrisCraft Speedster. To the delight of everyone, the ChrisCraft nearly swamped, but Mr. Philadelphia pulled the boys in, saved their boat, and finished as hero of the day.

Cody felt distant from the carnival that encircled him. He sat on the stones near the prow, watching the antic swirl of boats, voices, and engines. He was tired and fragile. He wondered if Rose was angry.

Joseph felt he had been tricked. His terror of drowning had driven him to exhaust himself bailing water. Gerome and the white man had let him suffer. Joseph sat on the deck with his legs crossed and stared north, away from the frivolity of the slap-happy rescue.

As the heroic flotilla approached the south shore near Tidyman's oil yard, the fireboat pulled its pumplines and cast off. Cody grounded the barge close to the dissolving embankment near where they would begin building the wall. He looked up at Tidyman, who was watching from the edge of the yard, hands in pockets, cigar in teeth.

"We lost the bearings on both pumps," Cody called to him.

"Get me the model numbers," Tidyman shouted back. "I'll go in and get your bearings. You can break the pumps down while I'm gone."

While Cody was below looking for numbers, the outboard made a pass near the barge. The boat slowed and one of three men inside waved and shouted up at Tidyman.

"Hey, Tidy, I hear your stupid Indians tried to sink your stupid barge." They began laughing and whooping.

The oil man picked up a fist-size rock and hurled it at the boat. The stone whacked the motor housing and ricocheted into the water. The men looked up at Tidyman.

"Ya stupid Jew bastard," one of them shouted.

"Yeah," said another. "Stupid kike bastard."

Tidyman reached down for another stone and hurled it toward the speedboat. The boat gunned away, made a half circle, and cut a wake before roaring off toward the town docks.

Gerome watched them go. "What is a stupid kite, Joseph?"

Joseph had nothing to say.

---

She saw Cody walking up the road toward the cafe. Gerome and Joseph had walked by two hours before, so she was expecting him. He stopped at the edge of the road and looked at the cafe. He was wearing the same old blue work shirt with the sleeves rolled back. His hands were on his hips. He studied the windows, trying to see through the reflections of sky and mountains.

He was thinking about going in, when a hand appeared in the cafe window, flat against the upper pane, fingers spread, then another lower down. Her nose flattened on the center pane, then her lips pressed full and hard and kissed the glass.

Yes. Thank God. He jumped high like a boy, spun a full circle, and landed facing her. He smiled and bowed slightly. Cody in ecstasy.

She opened the door and looked straight into him. She knew what he was thinking. She led him through the cafe to the back door past Ogeen, who had seen it all. The cook looked up from her soup.

"I'm takin' my break," said Rose.

And they were out the door.

———————

They stood face-to-face in the truck. Nothing was said. In their gaze the expectations of their lives were revealed, and forgotten. Only the memory of strong shoulders, a full mouth, or a sensuous curve remained as surfaces to absorb their needs and wants.

He wanted to press his lips in the hollow made by her collarbone and her neck. She reached up, as though reading his mind, and touched the hollow place his lips wanted. She turned her head to give him access. Her skin resisted as much as it yielded to his touch. Hungry lips pressed to hungry skin.

She held his head against her neck and pressed her belly into his thigh. It felt vulgar, needy, and demanding all at once. They came out of their clothes in a slow frenzy, and she pulled him down onto the bed.

His hand held her sleek belly then slid down through her black thicket of fur. The fingers, made hard and dry from rough stones, discovered the slit of wet flesh, small clusters and knots of nerves, and the pulse of her beating heart.

Her breathing stopped and all the little fishes in her body shivered between his lips on her neck to the tips of his fingers. She reached down and took him in her hands.

"Oh, God."

"I'll go slow. It'll be okay."

He did and it was.

She was floating, dazed and smiling. A strange sensation began in her hand. At first it felt as though a small calf or a lamb was sucking gently on her thumb. Its slow, tingling began moving up her arm, over her shoulder, and gradually settled in her breasts. It felt like stardust.

"What do you want?" he asked.

"Everything," she said.

And he did.

THE BIRDS WERE SINGING THEIR WAR SONGS. STILL asleep, he barely opened his eyes—only small slits into his dreaming mind. He did not look directly at the dark shape in the doorway, but it was there, waiting and watching.

"Go on sleeping, I am telling you a story," said the doorway smudge. It was quiet and said nothing, waiting to see if Cody was asleep. After a long time the voice began to tell him a story:

On the edge of the lake a boy lived with his old grandmother. What he knew came from her. She taught him to catch fish, kill deer, and make fire. He knew nothing about being a man. The old grandmother said, "Be careful or the serpent'll get you and I'll be alone." She never said anything about women.

He met a woman walking along the shore. Shadows from tall cedars hid her face. She came close and spoke. Her voice was in his mind. She led him underwater. She took him down and down, into the dim blue light. She kissed him, and felt his penis. He had a strong desire. She parted her legs and in slid his penis. It grew longer and longer.

Then something was changing inside his body. He began to dissolve. He felt all mushy inside, soft—like ice cream. She smiled. Her eyes twinkled. "Welcome home, Dairy Boy," she said, drinking him up. The last thing he saw were his toes.

"Haw, haw, haw," said the doorway smudge, and slipped away. Cody woke up. He was sweating, but he was laughing too. He got up and went out to pee. He was piss proud and had to wait in the dawn light for the flow to start. A chickadee sang "chick-a-dee, chick-a-dee, chick-a-dee-dee-dee." Some birds sing for love, others for terra-toree. Cody stood on the edge of the hill holding the wand of his passion, making impressions in the sand. He knew the world was alive and aware and laughing.

---

Rose mixed, Sally rolled and cut. They took turns searing the fry bread. There were fourteen Red Crows to feed, plus potatoes to mash for Catherine next door, so they started early. At first they worked fast, not talking. Rose pumped and squeezed the dough. She was thinking. She decided he would be gone in a week.

"That would be best," she said.

"What would be best?" asked Sally.

"He'll leave when he gets his truck running."

"How do you know?"

"I don't. Maybe I want him to go away and let me be. I don't know how to be two people. I want to be Rose. I want to live Rose's life. How can I do that if I'm some guy's woman?"

Sally gave her a dirty look. "Rose, you have weird ideas flyin' through your head from makin' areoplanes. What if you never find a man? Who's goin' to take care of you?"

"Sweet Sally, who takes care of you? Not that pompous, self-righteous shaman's apprentice. You and I do more work than any man in this family. Most of the cash money that comes in is from my pay and tips. Why can't I take care of myself?"

Sally mushed the fry bread around in the pan, then she gently patted some flour on the soft dough.

"I didn't mean it like that, Rose. I meant, who's goin' to take care of your heart?"

Rose was quiet. The dough slowly squeezed through her fingers and she looked Sally in the eye.

"Well, honey," she said softly, "who do you think should get that job?"

"Please don't look at me like that, Rose."

"Well, I'm not going to be a nun or a whore, and I'm not going to be alone. So I guess I better figure on something else."

"You could be partners, like Annie Big Horn and John Cameron."

"Who?"

"That white man who logged on Little Deer Creek. He lived alone in his dugout till he got goin' on Annie

Big Horn. She'd come up from the South somewhere pullin' a little tin house on wheels behind an old pickup. She parked that tin house on blocks next to Cameron's dugout."

"They're called trailer houses," said Rose, "and they're made of aluminum, not tin."

"Alu-mun-im?" Sally asked.

"Yes."

Sally smiled. "They made a little windbreak between them so he could go back and forth, but she never took the wheels off her trailer house. She said that way she could leave any time she damn well pleased." Sally smiled. "She used to make pretty lamps out of sagebrush wood. She polished them up shiny."

"So?" said Rose, squeezing her dough.

"So?"

"So, what happened? Were they happy? What happened to them?"

"She shot him."

Rose looked up at her.

"But she got away," Sally said and flipped her bread.

"This happened when I was in California?" Rose asked.

Sally nodded.

"She didn't shoot him," said Rose.

Sally laughed. "How do you know?"

"Gerome would have told me about a shooting."

Sally gave her a big smile. "Okay, she didn't shoot him. She hitched up her house and drove off. She got loose."

"So she left him."

"You and Cody could be partners if you have an aluminum house. When you don't get your way you can hitch up and drive away. No fuss."

Rose looked at her straight-faced. "You think this is about having my way?"

"I'm just having fun. I can be serious."

"Okay, be serious."

Sally turned away and watched the bread sizzle. "You were raised by Red Crows but you're not ever goin' to be Indian. Some women are jealous and some young men have a bad name they call you."

"I know that, Sally. They call me white meat."

Sally flinched. She stared at Rose, trying to see the hurt in her eyes. "You'll leave here when Catherine dies, won't you?"

"Yes."

"You're full of strong feelings, Rose. You'll get a man, even if it isn't Cody."

"I know I'll get a man. I just don't want to be swallowed up by him."

"That's how I'm different from you, Rose Red Crows. I want swallowed up."

Rose looked at her, thinking things better left unsaid. "I know."

A thin wisp of smoke began curling up from the fry bread.

"Your bread's burning," said Rose.

Sally smiled. "No, that's Joseph's bread. He was mean this morning."

———◆———

The sky was bright and clear. At any moment the sun would come up over the mountains. Cody sat on a rock, holding his coffee and watched the large, solitary Indian walking along the shore toward him, seeking out the invisible pathway of solid footing between wet sand and dry.

In a perfect moment, the light off the lake embraced Gerome, lifting him into the air, and set him on the rim of the hill before Cody. The Indian's ascension was a simple trick of light and water, though to Cody it felt like a kind of sorcery, an antic magic that came from the lake itself. The ascended Indian smiled.

"Good morning, Cody. It is a fine day."

The vision put Cody in a mind fog. He stood and extended his hand to Gerome. "G'morning," he mumbled.

They sat on a log and watched the light. Cody wanted to tell the Indian how the light made him seem to rise up and float through the air, but there was no way to say it without sounding strange.

"Is Joseph coming?" he asked.

"No. Joseph will not come. He would like me to bring his pay to him."

Cody's head cleared at the thought of Joseph's hatred. "Am I the evil white man?"

"Joseph is an angry person. He hates the white man, but he is part white. I wonder if he hates the part of himself that is white."

"What about you? Are you angry?"

Gerome looked at Cody's smooth white skin. He pointed to his own scarred face. "Sometimes I forget these."

"Do you think things were better before the whites came?"

"I don't know. An old man told Catherine's father about a real bad winter, before the whites came. People survived by eating ptarmigan droppings. We live longer now and there're more babies. We have many things. It all depends."

"Why is Joseph so angry?"

"The days before the horse we call 'dog days.' People used dogs to pull the travois." The Indian paused and thought about how his words would sound to the white man who sat beside him, sipping black coffee.

"We've gone back to dog days," he said, "but now we are white man's dogs."

His laughter sounded soft and deadly. Then he shook his head.

Cody felt embarrassed. He squinted into the rising sun, searching for a place in his mind where Gerome's words would not take hold. He flung the words out with his coffee and watched them splatter the ground.

"We should be going," he said. "Let's see if we can sink Tidyman's barge today."

A yellow freight truck pulled up as they walked by the garage. When the driver opened the back gate, Cody caught sight of two boxes and a tie-rod. He assumed they were his truck parts. He kept walking and said nothing.

Gerome saw the parts, and he saw Cody look at them.

They walked along the blacktop through the mottled light of the cottonwoods, thinking about the importance of truck parts.

Cody knew that the day after the retaining wall was finished he would have a working truck and some extra money. He could go up to Canada on the road over Glacier Park, work the rest of the summer in the mills around Calgary, then cut back across the mountains to British Columbia. He wanted to see the Adams River in the fall when it was thick with salmon.

"Do salmon come up this far?" he asked Gerome.

"When I was a boy, salmon came to the lake. Before they dammed the big river. Every other year it turned red with salmon."

"The whole lake?"

"Along the edge of the bay. We'd get them with spears. The women would cut the bones out, and skin them. Then they'd lay the meat on aspen poles to dry it. All our people would come to spear the salmon and dry them. Those salmon racks were lined out in a big curve along the bay. At sundown they would glow, like a necklace of little fires."

"Did the whites spear salmon too?" Cody asked.

"No. It was just something Indians did."

"Why didn't the whites do it?"

Gerome shook his head. "Don't know. Probably 'cause it was something Indians did. . . . Why do you want to know about salmon?" he asked, searching for the connection between salmon and truck parts.

"I thought I might work my way over to the Adams

River by fall," said Cody. "There's a run this year. I could spear some salmon for you."

Gerome's voice seemed a little tight. "All the way up to British Columbia?" he asked.

"Yeah."

Cody looked up at the Indian, then his eye drifted back to the blacktop. There was going to be a problem about truck parts. If he had a working truck and he stayed, it would be because she made him feel solid and real. He wanted to find that on his own. He felt lost most of the time, wandering around the country. If he depended on her to make his life work, nothing would change. He would still feel lost. And there was always the matter of trust.

When they went past the shake parlor with its big goofy sign, he remembered the dream of the lake woman sucking him up through his dick. He had made a joke of his fear. That made him smile.

They walked down the highway through the splotches and dots of sunlight. They were silent and full of questions.

After they had started the Daimler and cast off, Gerome stayed in the pilothouse, keeping their course, north and west toward the rock quarry. Cody stood on the edge of the rear deck and looked back at his stranded stock truck and the little cafe on the hill above the bay. Rose was already at work by now. He concentrated on the back door, waiting for her to come out and wave to him.

If he stayed, would she want him to stay? He needed to find something to do until she knew. And there was the larger problem of being stranded. Nothing people considered exciting or important filled him up. He had to change his life or drift forever. That was the trouble with truck parts. He had to decide everything by the time Tidyman's wall was done.

Rose was the only person he could talk to, and she mystified him. He was drawn to her because she was different from other women. She did not need what they were desperate for. He knew men who liked desperate women. It made them feel reasonable and in control. He had seen enough to know that never proved to be the case. The desperation had a way of taking over.

He had chosen wrong before. Or he had been chosen. He was never sure who did the choosing. His father had told him the most important part of being in love was respect. You had it or you didn't. If you didn't, things fell apart. You needed to treat a woman as if she were something wild, otherwise she would hurt you. Finally, after she hurt you real bad, she'd kill something in you. You'd be glad to get away, but you'd have somethin' floatin' around dead inside you.

He realized his father had not been in his mind for a long time. The old man had spent his life in the woods, cutting down trees, until one of them cut him down. Now Cody wanted to ask him about this woman.

Half an hour later his eyes were still fixed on the door of the cafe. Nothing seemed to have moved. He felt frozen in place as the shore-bound buildings grew smaller and smaller.

They were a mile out when he saw a tiny yellow patch of color emerge from the cafe door and move toward the rock that overlooked the lake. Without thinking, he had his shirt off, waving it back and forth like a boy with a flag.

Then he stopped and stared closely at the yellow patch. It had moved higher above the rock and was waving back.

In all that expanse of open water, sky, and soft green hills, a flash of bright color had fused his thoughts.

At that moment he knew she would be the one to decide whether he was going or staying. He trusted her to know.

"How are the boys this morning?" Rose asked. She poured coffee for Ogeen and his buddies.

Their eyes swarmed over her, searching her body for an answer to their riddles of need and desire. She smiled at the men-children, spoiled, boisterous boys. She could have put them in her pocket.

Their suits and ties and just-pressed shirts said wives and stability. Their eyes flirted or telegraphed sincerity, but their mouths gave them away. The million little muscles that shaped lips and cheeks into smiles were attached to their deepest fears.

Rose had learned to keep the customers at a distance, out of her mind, and in their place.

Several months before, in the late winter when she had started the job, their belligerence had swamped her senses. One day, she had retreated from the raucous men to the kitchen, embarrassed, wondering what was happening to her. The cook set her straight. Sue, who considered herself a tough old gal, oscillated between self-righteousness and episodes of moody anger. She looked at Rose as if she were eyeing a young mare with potential.

"Sweetie pie," she blared, "ya need 'em to respect ya. How ya gonna tuit?"

———◦———

It had been a cold winter. The wind had blown in from the east, made drifts of fine snow in places, and left the frozen ground bare and lonely in others.

Rose walked back to Catherine's shack at night. She punched through the fragile crust in her open galoshes, letting snow spill in over the tops.

She stopped outside the shack and inhaled the icy air. She was afraid she had lost her grip.

She kicked the snow off her boots and went in. The house was dark. She sat on the floor and cried.

Catherine called, "Come to me, daughter. Let me see you close." Rose found her way to Catherine in the dark and lit the lamp by the bed. The old woman peered up at her.

As Catherine grew older, she believed it was easier for her to see into people—that their voices and the way they moved made little eyeholes into their souls. Catherine knew what Rose had learned from the Red Crows was lost when she went into the white world.

Catherine was quiet, listening to the air and concocting a cure for her daughter's affliction.

"Have you forgotten everything?" she asked.

"I didn't forget, Mother. Everything changed. I came back expecting to fit in. It's not that way, is it? I'm not a Red Crows."

"I'm afraid that's true."

"I don't belong here anymore. I'm not even a white woman."

Catherine reached over and touched Rose on the arm. "I've known you a long time. I can make a cure for you. I want you strong on the inside so you can be brave when you're alone."

Rose had grown leery of Indian cures. Such things only seemed to work for the true believers and even they had the same problems over and over again. "What can you do?" she asked.

"This is not a good time to find what we need."

"No? When?"

"In the spring. When things start comin' up from the ground we'll find what we're lookin' for. In the meantime you should try talkin' to the crows, like you used to."

"I talked to crows?"

"When you were little. You'll remember. It'll come back."

For the next month Rose talked to the crows whenever they came near. She listened intently, sometimes repeating their sounds with great care. The crows ignored her until she came too close, then they heaved into the air and flapped away. In time they let her come closer and closer. Eventually, they would land nearby and comb the beach for insects. A dialogue of sorts developed between Rose and the crows as they mimicked her attempts to mimic them.

When the snow began to melt, Catherine sent Gerome to the cafe to say Rose was sick. It was time to fix Rose. Her secret intention was to remove the nuns from her daughter's soul.

"I'm a pretty good medicine person," Catherine said to her dubious daughter. "I can tell you don't believe me. You'll see. I'll fix you up good."

For two days and nights, at Catherine's direction, Rose washed all their clothing in cold lake water and scrubbed the walls of the little house with ashes, lye, and whiting. The floor she polished with white soapstone. If nothing else, Rose thought, Indian magic was good for getting the house clean. Had she known what Catherine was planning, she would have fled.

When the house was done, Rose colored her face with beet dye, dressed them both for the cold, and carried Catherine on her back toward the trees to the east. Waitressing had given Rose strong legs and Catherine was light, but the old woman's weight pressed Rose into the soft ground as they moved deeper into the woods.

"Mother, my bones ache," Rose complained. "I have to stop soon."

"No. No. There's no time. We have to find bear leaf fungus and a skunkbush before it gets dark."

Catherine seemed glued to her. Rose was sick of the whole Indian act. She wanted to lie on her back and roll around like a tired mare ridding itself of mosquitoes.

By late afternoon, they had reached the foothills. Rose was in agony and still the old woman insisted they keep moving toward the mountains.

Just before nightfall, they found a skunkbush by a spring in a meadow. Catherine dug the root out with her digger stick and instructed Rose to collect the bear leaf fungus from the nearby cedars.

"I am tired now and hungry," said Catherine. "You can't have anything to eat, though. You can't sleep either."

She ate her pemmican and drank from the spring while Rose cut boughs from a small cedar and made a bed for them. Catherine curled up inside the curve of Rose's body and fell asleep.

———◦———

Two crows sat on the lowest branch of an ancient cedar and watched the two sleeping humans. It was barely light.

"Caw, Caw," they shouted. Catherine opened her eyes and listened. "Wake up, wake up, Grandmother bein'," Marley screeched. "You'll freeze in your sleep."

Zulu cocked her head to the side, then rotated it back and forth. Snowflakes began to settle on her glossy feathers.

"These two are the Grandmother bein' and her lost girl," Marley gurgled.

"They're not movin', Marley. They'll freeze in their sleep. That'll be the end of bacon fat and tripes."

"We'd disappear if the humanbein's and the spirit bein's didn't use us to do their talkin'."

"Keep your eye on the bacon fat," said Zulu.

They dropped from the branch, cawing, and flapped their wings above the sleeping humans.

"Thank you, crow person," said Catherine. Her voice was weak. She was stiff and could not turn her head. She felt dead, all shriveled—her legs and feet drawn up against her body.

The birds flapped away into the gray, cawing their cry through the giant cedars and the falling snow.

"Wake up, daughter, you're not suppose to sleep," Catherine croaked. "Daughter? Wake up. If we freeze, who'll feed the crows? Who will they talk to, daughter? Wake up, wake up."

———◦———

Rose woke from her dream. Catherine was poking her in the ribs and mumbling about the crows.

The trip home made Rose wish for death. She stopped several times, weak and shaky, and leaned against a tree to rest. When they reached home the house was cold. Rose put her mother on the bed and covered her with blankets.

"Take the root and fungus and make tea," said Catherine.

Rose put the bear leaf to her nose. It smelled like pee. Maybe a fox or a wolf. She cut the root in thin strips. The strips were dried on a tin plate on the stove, then pounded and ground in a bowl with a stone. She broke the bear leaf apart and ground it into the root.

Rose was past talking. Her dark eyes, shining in the half-light, and her long tapered eyebrows gave her the look of a crazed bird. She sat on the bed and leaned forward, holding the bowl out to her mother. Catherine reached in and took a pinch of the powder, rubbing it between her thumb and forefinger. She squinted and smelled her fingers.

Catherine touched the powder to her tongue. A soft, dry laugh rattled from her throat.

"Boil this," said Catherine. "Drink it all. You'll be pretty sick, so go outside."

Rose made a tea of the powder and poured it in a thick, white cup that said PROPERTY OF UNITED STATES NAVY on one side. She went out into an overcast afternoon, wrapped in a blanket, and sat by the shore.

The weary haze of a thought floated through her mind: this is the easy part. She put her awareness in the cup and drank from its thick whiteness. The hot tea made little beads of sweat on her forehead.

Her breathing quickened. Fear reached down from her brain, through her neck, into her chest. She fell through the dark sky until she was only a speck. She knew she was dying. She began to retch.

It was dusk when Catherine woke and realized Rose had not returned. She managed to reach the cord and rattle the cans, calling the young Red Crows. When they were told to find Rose, the children raced off calling her name. Amy, who was four years old and who came last, stood quietly on the steps and listened. When the others had gone and their shouts were far away, she heard the crows talking, down by the water. They were watching a dark thing on the ground.

The hand-me-down wool coat that Amy wore made her look unbalanced. She walked slowly toward the crows, across the rocky beach. She was afraid the dark thing was Rose. As Amy approached, the crows moved back from the still form lying on the rocks. Rose was quiet and pale. Amy knew she was dead.

Amy's screams brought Gerome and several other

Red Crows out of their shack and down to the beach. They carried Rose back to Catherine's, where four young Red Crows women stripped off her clothes and massaged the blood back into her arms and legs. They washed her body and matted hair, and rubbed her skin with sagebrush leaves. The women chattered and cooed and talked about boyfriends and food. When Rose could sit upright, they wrapped her in blankets, gave her hot water to drink, and dried her hair.

She slept for two nights and a day. On the morning of the second day she could hear the rain on the tar paper roof. She lay in her bed and listened. Something was different in her face and arms. At first she thought she had lost weight. The sensation flowed through her spine into her legs. When she stood she could feel down into the ground. Tree feet, she thought. Her ordeal had let the past loose in her body. Instead of feeling more white or more Indian, she was simply relieved to be alive. The world had opened up.

Billy Ogeen felt like a shell of thin glass. He flinched, then looked up, and smiled at Rose.

"We were out last night," he said. "Drank too much."

Ogeen sipped his coffee. He laughed, but it hurt. His hangover made the world sharp. The cafe was too bright and his buddies too loud.

He watched Rose pour coffee, watched her arms and shoulders and the curve of her collarbone. Had Rose changed, he wondered, or was it his hangover that made her so different?

When she leaned in to pour his coffee, he caught the scent of leather and woodsmoke and remembered she was Indian. In high school before the war, he had an Indian girlfriend who was several years older. He broke it off before anyone found out—anyone white. His parents would not have stood for it. The girls at school would have beat her up and ignored him forever. He just stopped coming around. When she saw him in town, he crossed the street to avoid her. Ogeen never spoke to her again and he never forgot. His betrayal haunted him. It was one of life's lessons and the secret of his success. It made him trustworthy.

Rose stretched across the table to reach the insurance man's cup. The shiny cotton slid against the bulge of her thigh and made soft static crackle in Ogeen's brain. He wanted to pull her thighs against his chest and press his crackling head into her stomach. He felt a shock of regret. More than anything he wanted her to hold him, to forgive him.

In the weeks that followed, Ogeen forced himself to deny his affections for Rose because he knew she would not have him. It became the worm that quietly ate at his confidence.

Then spring came with its changes and possibilities, and everything began to green up. One morning the stranger in the stock truck appeared out the back door of the cafe, and Rose fell in love. Ogeen was hearing about Cody from his coffee buddies and anyone else he talked to in town. The new man was cute, handsome, striking, tough, could handle himself in a fight, was from a wealthy eastern family, a Communist, an ex-con with a bad temper, and a heavy drinker. Cody had become everyman's fear.

Ogeen's craving for Rose deepened with every mention of the saw filer. Even though she was out-of-bounds, his sense of territory expanded. He became a moralist.

———◦———

Cody and Gerome spent ten days loading rock onto the barge, hauling it down the lake to Tidyman's oil depot, and constructing the break wall. They finished the wall late in the afternoon. Cody had gone across the highway to the little store and returned with two quarts of beer. They sat on the wall with their feet dangling in the water.

Gerome ran his hands over the stones. "We build a pretty good wall," he said. "I like stone. It's good to touch."

Cody looked up at him and grinned. "Nothing smells as good as wet stone," he said and raised his beer. "Here's to stone."

"I'm getting too old to work this hard. I'll have to go out in the woods and sleep for two, three days."

———◦———

Rose leaned against the back of the truck and peered in at Cody. He lay in bed, watching the colors fade from the sky. He had heard her coming.

"Hi," he said from the dark interior of the truck.

"How did it go?" she asked. She wondered if he knew his truck parts had come in.

"Did a good job. We made good money. Tidyman's happy. I'm on speaking terms with every muscle in my body, and you're here. Life is good."

She could make out his shape, rising slowly, turning, and standing. His legs were stiff. When he moved into the light she could see his hands were scraped and bruised.

"Oh, ouch."

"What?"

"Your hands."

"Oh, those. Yeah. Lots of oh, ouches." He sat down in the doorway and pulled her close, wrapping his legs around her. He nestled his head in her thick hair and whispered, "The parts came in."

She knew he was saying, give me a reason to stay. He wanted to stay, it was obvious. What she wanted was elusive, but she was not afraid to make it easy for him, at least to give him a chance to see what it might be like.

"Remember the logs in the lake?" she asked.

"Uh-huh."

She put her arms around his waist and held him. It seemed as if he had been away for weeks. She reached up and kissed him, a long kiss, and ran her hands over the muscles in his back and thighs until she could feel his penis enlarge against her chest.

"I can't stay," she whispered. "I promised Catherine a bath."

He laughed and pushed her away. "Then you can't make me crazy."

"Sure I can," she said. "It's easy."

"Tell me about logs in the lake, or did you forget?"

"A guy came in this morning who manages the mill at Pardee. His name's Dumas. He says the logs should still be good. They just have to be cut wet so they won't crack when they dry. He said they'd be good for studs and he'd pay ten dollars a thousand board feet."

Cody smiled at her and wondered where she was going. He had thought about getting the logs out, that was the kind of thing his mind did on its own, but he never guessed it could be practical. He assumed the logs were rotten. Now she was opening another door.

"Did you get fired?" he asked.

"No, but that's a possibility."

"What happened?"

"Ogeen said my moral character is weak, and I said, self-righteousness was a nice dress-up for jealousy."

"What's he jealous of?"

"You, of course."

"Me? But he's married."

"Yes?"

"Has he been watchin' us?"

"He's seen enough, and Sue fills him in."

Cody did not want to think about Billy Ogeen's warped jealousy or the gossiping cook, or that he could be the reason for Rose to lose her job.

"You want to go into the loggin' business?" he asked.

"You and me and Gerome. You take half. Gerome and I'll split the other half."

"You're generous. Why not thirds?"

"You'd know how to rig everything and keep it running. You'd make it work. I don't know that stuff, and Gerome won't think about anything unless it's something he loves doing."

"What are his loves?"

"Women, deer, cars, and gambling."

"A pretty good life. The deer and cars even out with the women and gambling. Is that how it works?"

"Careful."

"Uh-huh. As far as the split goes, you and Gerome should get thirds. He's real good. He took up Joseph's slack. And he can swim."

"Of course he can swim. Indians can swim from birth."

"I've been told not to believe anything I've heard about Indians," he said.

"Gerome said that?"

"Uh-huh."

"So how do you see me earning my keep in this deal?"

"You could handle the pumps and the air lines and take care of business with the mill."

"You've been thinking about this all along, haven't you?"

He smiled at being found out. "Maybe Tidyman will let us use his barge," he said.

"Christ no. We'll all drown."

"Speak nice about the barge. It's got new bearings in its pumps and we couldn't afford anything else. We named her in your honor."

She smiled. "It's a her?"

"Ships at sea, barges at bay, ladies, every one."

"I'm honored. Cursed, but honored."

He gestured toward the interior of the truck. "Do you want to come in?" he asked.

"I need to get back home. I'll see you tomorrow."

"Tomorrow."

She ran away in his line of sight, over the rock in the painting, down the hill, and disappeared between the land and the lake a step at a time.

---

The next afternoon, they walked the shoreline past the little church of Catherine toward a small marsh with cattails that divided the Indian shacks from the orchards that surrounded the nice white house.

"When I was a little girl, I would follow the big kids to the mountains. We'd cut through those orchards. When we came back in the evening, sometimes we heard strange sounds floating through the air. We thought they were hungry ghosts looking for small children."

He followed her along a path that led to a walkway made of mushy old logs. They went deep into the reeds until Rose stopped and pointed to the hulk of a rusted car. Its tires were gone and its wooden spoked wheels were sunk to the hubs. The logs led directly to the driver's door.

"What's that doing here?" he asked.

"It belonged to a remittance man who got drunk and drove into the lake one night."

"Remittance man?"

"They used to come here all the time. They're rich kids who were so irresponsible their parents couldn't stand them and sent them out west. Every month they got a remittance to live on. They all had boats and big cars and drank like fish."

"That's a Stutz. They were beautiful."

"It was Gerome's first car. After everybody had given up looking for it, Gerome found the car and dragged it out with a team. He spent six months fixing it up. The Stutz was like new. He loved that car so much he slept in it. Then one day the remittance man and the sheriff came to get the car."

"They had no right."

"He was just an Indian kid. What could he do?"

"What did he do?"

"They chased him up the old east side road. He hid the car in a Red Crows lodge. Later, when they caught him and asked where the car was, he showed them tire tracks to a cliff above the lake.

"What happened?"

"They beat him up bad. He couldn't see for a while and he limped for nearly a year. Later he hid the car down here in the cattails. Sometimes, when the sheriff was looking for him, he lived here. I'd bring him his supper."

"You grew up with him?"

"Yes. Gerome is my brother."

"From the looks of him he's had a mean life."

"He always acted crazy. He was angry. He killed two white guys in fights. He was in Leavenworth for five years. But he changed. I think he's normal. For an Indian, normal."

"What changed him?"

"He found God and a chickadee."

"God and a chickadee?"

"They bring him luck and luck makes him sweet. I love my brother very much. I want him to be a sweet man."

"That's why he helped me with the break wall, because he's your brother?"

"Maybe. But, if he gets you in a stick game, he'll try to take you for everything."

"What's a stick game?"

"It's an old game. It takes some practice and you have to be smart in certain ways—you need luck."

"What's it like?"

"It's fast. I'll teach it to you. But I don't know if you have luck."

He pushed the car's hood back and leaned in to look at the engine. His words rattled around under the hood. "I was raised Lutheran," he said, "but I can still get lucky."

She smiled. "No, it's not getting lucky. Something or someone gives you luck for certain things."

He was stretched over the car's fender, divining its mysteries, distracted by the pleasures of pistons and cast iron.

"Maybe I should stick to poker. What do you mean by *certain things*?" he asked.

"If you're a hunter and the deer gave you luck, you could ask the deer to come to you, if you asked the right way and at the right time."

He emerged from the reassuring womb of ancient metal. "It's some kind of power?"

"Power is just shaman tricks—heavy and ugly, like rape."

"What is luck, then?"

"Luck is sweet, like dancing."

Cody smiled and looked up from under the hood of the Stutz. "Like dancing?"

"Yes."

"Gerome gets luck from the chickadee and he's a church Indian?"

"It's that kind of church," she said.

"Why does the chickadee give Gerome luck?"

"Gerome gives him respect."

"What is the chickadee's luck?"

"The chickadee sees and hears everything."

"When you say the chickadee gives him luck, you don't really mean the chickadee, do you?"

"No," she said. "Not chickadee, but chickadee."

"What do you mean?"

She looked at him, thinking of how to say it. "I can't say what I mean unless you already understand," she said.

"So how do I learn anything from you?"

"Maybe you can't. I lived in a world that was magical when I was little. I could talk to crows. I thought I could, anyway. Like you said, what's real changes. I live in two different worlds now, and don't fit in either of them. That makes me a little crazy."

"Do you have luck?"

"No."

"What kind of luck would you want?"

"The luck to cure illness"—she paused for a moment—"or love."

He realized she had the same doubts about him that he had about her. He started to laugh.

"What's funny?" she asked.

"You said *luck to cure love?*"

"Yes. That's funny?"

"What brought it to mind?" he asked. He was gleeful and merciless. "Why would you want to cure love? Do you have a love that needs curing?"

Her eyes brightened and a grin spread across her face. "You know, don't you? You know, because you've been thinking the same thing, haven't you?" She started laughing. "Haven't you?"

"No. I wouldn't think such a thing," he said, and opened his palms to her. "My heart is pure. I am a simple man."

"A man, pure and simple, yes." The light danced in her eyes. Their laughter aroused her.

He reached for her, pulled her against his body, and ran his hand down her spine into her bottom cleavage. "What you need," he said, "is luck to cure lust."

"We'll see who needs a cure," she said, sliding one hand into his pants and opening the car door with the other. She pulled him down with her onto the seat, legs spread to receive.

"You Red Crows are strange people," he said. "What if someone comes?"

"They'll have a laugh watching the mosquitoes bite your bare ass."

---

"May I?"

"Yes."

"Yes?"

"Yes."

"Like this?"

"Yes. I want you inside me. I'll suck you dry as a wasps' nest."

"Welcome home, Dairy Boy," he whispered.

"What?"

"Never mind," he muttered to the dark nipple on the white breast.

---

They had fallen asleep. Far away the silky purr of a motorcycle reached through the cattails into his consciousness. He realized he was on top of her and she had her arms around his waist. The purr of the motorcycle was coming closer. He felt her fingers move along his spine.

"It's a Vincent," he said. "Who the hell has a Vincent around here?"

"The motorcycle's a Vincent? How can you tell?"

The purr shifted down into a long, throaty rasp, reverberating through the reeds.

"They had a thick manifold and a long stroke." He climbed onto the back deck of the car and looked out over the cattails. "It's pulling a small trailer and it's headed to Gerome's."

She jumped up on the deck and stood next to him. "I'll bet it's Dee LeClair. Want to meet a madman?"

"What brand of mad?"

"He was a machinist in the aircraft plant where I worked. On his own time, he invented beautiful machines that were useless. He made a machine powered by water-wheels that ran off a garden hose. It had chromed gears and the frame and axles were painted red, yellow, and blue."

They stood on the back deck of the Stutz, nestled into their corresponding curves, and watched the approaching motorcyclist. The glow of sex and sleep held them together, while the intrigue of the mad inventor drew them apart. They broke loose like fresh horses and ran through the cattails and back along the shore toward the shacks. He held back at the end to give her time, and to watch how she was with the goggled machinist.

The goggles and the leather flyer's helmet came off and revealed a white man in his forties with a kind, open face. He had an average build and beautiful hands. No energy was wasted being manly. She embraced him, and the beautiful hands were easy and knowing.

Cody felt his heart quicken and he turned his gaze to the bike. Painted in fine gold script on the gas tank were the words EVIL ON WHEELS. Life seemed terribly complicated.

Rose drew back, a little embarrassed. She reached out for Cody and pulled him toward her. She held him close and looked Dee in the eye.

"This is Cody." She smiled at Cody and squeezed until he relaxed. "And this is Dee."

The mad machinist was not crazy. He was quick to redefine his relationship with Rose. There was a flicker of disappointment and the small silly smile of a man who was easy with failure. It was a quick retreat.

"Is Gerome around?" he asked.

Rose pointed at a shack behind the white house in the orchard to the east. "He's playing poker with Louie Desoto."

"I should let him know I'm here," he said. "See you guys later."

He left the bike between the shacks and started down the path a quarter mile to the poker game. The Vincent was loaded with Dee's life and the little trailer with more of his life, including a small machine lathe. He had come for the winter.

Rose pointed to the red torpedo-back Pontiac hiding in the blackberries.

"That used to be Dee's. When Gerome came down to get me after the war, he and Dee sat up for two days and played poker. Gerome won."

"Chickadee's good at poker?"

"Maybe the white man had bad gambling luck."

"What kind of luck do white men have?" he asked.

"The Indians think the white man's luck is business—being in the right place at the right time."

"Indians don't have that kind of luck?"

"Not much anymore," she said.

# SUNDAY
# AFTERNOON

The house had begun to absorb the afternoon heat. Liz suggested they move to the front porch and switch from Sea Indian coffee to red wine. They eased into the least decrepit of Ana's bent-willow recliners and waited for the clouds to drift across the lake.

"I like the heat," said Ana. "I think my thermostat's broke."

Liz eyed the pile of magazines beyond the yard. "Are you ready for a fire?"

"Let's wait until evening," said Ana. "The Red Crows used to make fires at night along the beach." Thinking about the fires made her chuckle. "When I was little, the old women told me they could see the fire thinking my thoughts."

"Did you believe them?"

"Yes, and I always tried to think good thoughts around the fires."

"The Indians seem to have been very caught up with the idea that something was always watching them. What became of their spirits and the rest of it when they converted to Christianity?"

Ana laughed. "Catherine Red Crows said when the black robes first came here the head priest gave a sermon by the lake. He said the gods of the Indian had been lording it over the valley for years and that their time had come to an end. These lesser gods, he claimed, had run into the mountains to hide, quaking in fear of the great Christian God. Catherine said he may have been right, but what the priest didn't know was that the Indian gods were up there peeing in the creeks, and when the white man drank the water, it made him crazy."

Liz laughed. "I think they were upstream of Boston."

"Well, we have good reason to feel crazy. We have the nervous system of an animal that came from a slow-moving world where all its energy came from the food it ate. Now look at us. Evolution never prepared you for this."

Liz wondered if Ana's little lecture was getting personal. "Prepared me for what?" she asked.

Ana laughed. "Among other things, the consequences of love after horses."

"You keep putting these crazy things together."

"Horses were one way we escaped the wilderness. They probably caused more mischief than automobiles, and certainly changed the way we lived. They let the Plains Indians kill a lot more buffalo, which changed how women and men thought about each other.

"People became dependent on horses and buffalo, which gave a lot of power to some families and ruined others. It increased the demand for slaves and for women and children to work the hides so the men could trade for goods.

"Young men on horses were always going on raids or starting wars to gain glory and enhance their pride because it made them desirable in the eyes of the girls. Teenagers became more powerful and rude. And they could buy stuff. The wisdom of the grandmothers fell on numb skulls. Over all, horses made people stupid."

"What would have happened without horses?"

"It wouldn't have mattered. We were desperate to escape nature's power over us. The really desperate became farmers. Shamanism, astronomy, and pesticides were all attempts to control nature. Romantic love and the Chevy Suburban were the result. But it all started with trying to invent an advantage, to find a sharper blade."

"And rapture and awe became romantic love?"

"And several other things, I'm sure. What else makes our hearts beat faster and our minds cloud over?"

Liz laughed. "Singing national anthems."

Ana raised her arm in a grand gesture. "And the adoration of kings and commissars."

TIDYMAN STOOD BY THE WINDOW OF HIS OFFICE. CODY watched him lean his face against the window in order to spy on a piece of the lake. During a storm and often at sunset, he would have his face pressed to the glass, cigar sogged in his mouth, enraptured.

Cody stood in the middle of the room about to pitch his plans for salvaging logs from the lake. He was trying to imagine what Tidyman's face must have looked like from outside.

Even though he thought of himself as bad at business, Tidyman knew he was about to be asked for something. Business required manners and some empathy for the middle class. His empathy only reached so far and it was mostly for the underdog. However, often enough he managed to be in the right place at the right time, which kept him going, kept him rolling high, in fact. Someday, of course, it would fall apart. And he knew that.

Without turning around, he asked, "What's on your mind, Cody?"

"I think there's a good piece of money lying on the bottom of the lake."

Tidyman's shoulders sagged a little. He turned away from the window. "Tell me about it," he said.

Cody explained that the logs in the lake were still useable. "The logs pretty much cover the bottom, three hundred feet north of the pilings and about five hundred across. They're mostly two to two and a half feet at the butt."

When Tidyman gave him an encouraging nod, he continued. "We'll need to get a contract on the logs and we have to do some rigging on the barge. I think we can be working the bay in two weeks. We'll stop at the end of September. That gives you time to make all your deliveries before the middle of November.

"They'll give us ten dollars a thousand board feet at the Pardee mill and they'll load and haul. The logs won't check if they cut 'em while they're still wet. We'll only be able to work the smaller logs, but there're plenty of them. We can probably deck twenty thousand board feet a day. Maybe more.

"Rose, Gerome, and myself will split the profits three ways. We should be able to give you sixty dollars a day for the barge, fuel, and a truck with a heavy winch."

Tidyman was distracted. The logic that was designed

to carry Cody's plan into reality evaded him. What he heard was the enthusiasm in Cody's voice.

"You'll never guess what I wanted to do before I had to take over this business," he said. "I wanted to be a poet, Cody. That's right. My father sent me to Juilliard to study the cello, but I discovered poetry. I went to France and Algiers to write. Then Father died, just before the war. I had to come back to take care of Mamma and run this goddamn business."

Cody waited for Tidyman to come to the point, but he was without a point, floating between his impassioned past and his pointless present.

"The business really took off during the war," Tidyman continued. "Forty-four and forty-five were real good. And I'll do even better with the dam. Christ, I'm a poet and I'm netting over fifty Gs a year. Since I came back to this hole in the mountains, I haven't written a word." He turned an eye toward Cody. "Am I boring you?"

"I don't know about poetry," he said. "I'm just tryin' to make some money before winter sets in." The fuel oil poet was not making sense. Why, Cody wondered, couldn't he make his *fifty Gs* and write poetry in the off-season? Did he have to go to Algiers to write poetry? It would have all changed by now, anyway.

Tidyman scratched his stubble and studied the man with a plan. Cody had the energy. He moved and thought in ways that could make him a wealthy man. Tidyman did not expect Cody to understand. This drifter had his own strange dreams, perhaps every bit as exotic and improbable.

"I can let you use that one-ton Dodge in the shed. We call her Gretchen. There's no key for her, just a switch. Sign for your gas. Oh, yeah, one other thing. You'll have to get new life jackets for the barge." His voice trailed away. "The straps on the old ones are rotten."

Cody started for the door. "I'll replace the jackets," he said. "And thanks." He stopped and looked back at Tidyman. "Why can't you write poetry here?"

Tidyman reached up slowly and removed the cigar stub from his mouth. "There's only two things white people do here," he said. "They kill things and they make money. That's what's allowed. Kill and sell. They pave it over, cut it down, dig it up, then they crap in it. If you care about anything, they'll drive you nuts. That's the key to livin' here—don't give a damn, and you'll get by."

Cody knew Tidyman was right. It was hard to live in these places if you cared about anything, especially if the locals figured you out. It kept him in motion. He lived in a stock truck, painted his pictures, and stayed on the move.

"Why are the Indians so different?" Cody asked.

"Give 'em time," the fuel oil poet said. His hand fluttered like a bird's wing, then he smiled and walked across the room toward his desk.

Cody shook his head, unable to believe the Red Crows would ever want to be like white men. He pulled the door shut. Gerome was standing in the yard, waiting. They went to look for a truck named Gretchen.

She was parked in a long shed west of Tidyman's office. The shed held four or five other 1930s vintage vehicles. Another one-ton Dodge, missing its tires, sat on blocks next to Gretchen—an old lover and sharer of parts.

Gerome placed his huge hands on the dashboard and looked over the interior of the truck. "I know a Gretchen. Gretchen's a good name for this truck." He smiled at his secret.

Cody waited, expecting more, but Gerome's eyes continued to explore the truck. Evidently there was nothing more. The truck turned over several times before it would start, then lurched out of the shed and rumbled down the highway. Gerome had nothing to say the rest of the way home.

They turned off the highway onto the dirt tracks that slithered through the high grass to the shacks. The grass brushed against Gretchen's faded blue fenders, making a sound like rain. Gerome closed his eyes and smiled. His hands were spread out on the dashboard, taking Gretchen's pulse.

"Do you think Indians will ever think like white people?" Cody asked.

Gerome opened his eyes. "I don't know about that. I like this truck okay. Lot of things from the white man are okay."

"What things?" Cody asked.

Gerome watched the grass slide by. "I won that Pontiac car off Dee LeClair when he worked in the airplane factory. It had an Indian-head hood ornament. I thought it was made out of glass, but it was plastic. I like plastic. The sun burns it and makes it cloudy, like snake's eyes."

"Why don't most Indians look white people in the eye?" Cody asked.

Gerome was silent until Cody brought the truck to a halt behind Catherine's place, then he got out and closed the door.

"We are afraid of what we might not see," Gerome said.

He turned and walked to his house. He did not mean to be rude. Because of Rose, Cody was a brother to him. And for a white man, he liked him. So he had to tell him the truth.

Amy sat on the front step looking out at the lake. Although Gerome had looked normal enough to Cody, he looked sad to Amy.

"What is wrong, grandfather?" she asked. "Are you some sad?"

"Yes, granddaughter, I am some sad." He sat down and held out his giant hand. She spread her fingers wide in his palm. She saw the little hand inside the big hand and giggled.

She leaned over, looking Gerome in the eye, and asked, "What time is it?"

OGEEN'S FRIENDS HAD BEEN PASSING GOSSIP BACK AND forth for an hour and a half. Their excuse was that business was slow. The real reason was the new man, the drifter, Cody. At first they kept their voices down so Rose could not hear, or they changed the subject when she came around with refills.

Their anger was fueled in part by the fact that a stranger had stolen what was rightfully theirs. Rose had abandoned them. She was, they came to realize, but never said, the woman of their dreams.

It was Ogeen, whose brain was infested with little black worms of jealousy, who violated the gentlemanly code of discretion and loosened the swarming instincts of his buddies. "Any woman," Ogeen muttered, "who gets it from a worthless drifter's no better than an Indian whore." It was unlike him. He had crossed the line and there was no going back. She was such a deep source of pain. He wanted her gone forever.

He got up and walked into the kitchen. "Sue, you're going to have to take tables for a couple of hours. Rose isn't working here anymore."

Rose stared at him as if he had lost his mind. "You're firing me?"

"I don't want this place getting a sleazy reputation. As of now, you no longer work here."

———◆———

She came out the back of the cafe, walking flat-footed and stiff, and sat in the weeds next to Cody, who was smoothing the inside of Gretchen's brake cylinder with his thumb and a piece of emery paper. She watched for a while, then put her lips just under his ear, and closed her eyes. She stayed there for several seconds, breathing slowly, feeling his neck on her mouth.

"Bad day at the Roadside Cafe?" he asked.

She looked back at the cafe.

"He's a jack-ass hypocrite," she said. "I didn't want to finish up like this." She watched Cody's hands work the cylinder. "It was a good job. I would've gone back after we got the logs out." She reached up, putting one hand on his chest and another on his shoulder. "Being a waitress isn't a grand deal, but I was good at it."

She undid one of his shirt buttons and slid her hand inside. Her fingers played across his skin, searching out ridges, bones, and nipples of flesh.

She glanced back toward the cafe. "Sue's watching. Let's make love under the truck. It'll make her nuts."

"Rose, we can't do that."

"Yes we can. She's the only one who'll see us." Rose slid under the running board and pulled her skirt up above her thighs.

The bright sun made their shadows black. The rhythmic motion beneath the truck could as well have been neon at night.

The flicker of Rose's supple thigh short-circuited the cook's brain. She pressed her pelvis against the cutting board and squeezed the thighs and breast of the cold chicken in her hot hands.

———

They lay stretched out in the grass under the truck.

"Not a lot of room to maneuver under here," he said, staring up into the array of cables, tubes, shaft, and pipe that cluttered the undercarriage.

"No," she said, thoughtfully. "Not for two."

"They call it workin' on your truck, even if you're underneath it," he said. "It's as though the truck were a planet. Wherever you are, you're on it."

"Anytime you need help on your truck, let me know."

"Thanks."

"I have a request, sexiest and bravest man among men."

"Most anything."

"Catherine wants to go out on the lake once more before she dies. I'd like to take her out on the barge early in the morning, when it's still dark and it's cool. The whole family could come."

He squeezed her ass. "You have good heft. Do you know that?"

"I am a partner in this operation, right?"

"Yes. A full one-third of the debt."

"And Gerome has a third, which gives me two-thirds of the vote in this matter. So at four o'clock tomorrow morning we will take Catherine Red Crows out on the barge? Yes?"

"Okay, partner."

———◦———

That evening, Cody and Rose walked down past Tidyman's to where the barge was moored. Cody fired up the engine and steered east along the shore toward Catherine's, past his broken stock truck and the cafe on the hill. Rose watched everything he did and checked out the machinery.

"How fast will it sink with a full load of logs if both pumps quit on us?"

"Several days. Logs are a lot lighter than stone."

"Do you plan to deck the logs lengthwise or cross-wise?"

"Crosswise. It's not as stable, but we'll be faster unloading. We'll use our first logs to build catch frames just offshore. We can butt the barge against a frame and roll half a dozen logs off at a time. When the frames are full, we'll use Gretchen's winch to skid the logs out of the water."

She liked the sounds the barge made—the Daimler's purr, the water singing against the hull, and the deep constant vibrations that came off the deck through her feet and into her body. She could hear the muffled whine of the pumps below.

"This thing is always sinking, isn't it?"

"If it's dead in the water with no load it takes about a week to sink. Every five days you have to run the pumps for five or six hours to get it clear."

Rose smiled at him. "Yeah, I know the feeling."

"We can do this, Rose. I've thought it through. There isn't a problem we can't solve."

"The check is in the mail, the rent will cover the mortgage, and I won't get you pregnant. How did it happen that fate held this barge together for fifty years until we were blessed with it? Just think of the odds against that happening."

"You like this old box, don't you?" asked Cody.

"Yes. I could live here, floating around the lake in the morning mists. I could dock at a different tourist dive every day and sell genuine Indian artifacts. The Red Crows could dress up in idiotic costumes and make up Indian dances for the whites. What do you think?"

"You'll need a partner."

Rose stood between Cody and the wheel with her bottom arched against him, swaying back and forth.

"You wouldn't ever do that tourist stuff," she said. "You're too holy. I know the type."

He steered with one hand and stroked her belly with the other.

"You think that's it? I thought I just needed a better sense of humor."

She turned around and pulled her skirt up.

"Don't get mean with me. I'll use you for fuel." She slipped a hand into his trousers and caressed his erection. She laughed. "It's big an' it's thick," she whispered. "Stoke me, now, Cody. Right now." She unbuttoned him and pulled him out.

He lifted her up onto the instrument panel next to

the wheel. She spread her legs and raised them up, setting her feet on his shoulders.

"Are you a gymnast?" he asked.

She smiled and watched his eyes as he slid into her.

"Not gymnast, frog," she whispered.

He kept one hand underneath her where he could
feel himself inside, sliding back and forth. She came fast
and hard, all arms and legs clenching his body, like a
crab with a fish.

They lay down inside the pilot's cabin, out of sight
of shore-bound eyes, bellies touching, hands exploring
for every nerve, protrusion, and crevice. With eyes,
touch, teeth, and cock they re-created the image and
form of the other and set them to memory. Memory
bound to passion. Passion bound to love. Love magni-
fied the secret in desire.

⸺◆⸺

The meadowlarks had already divided the visible
world when the Red Crows carefully folded a thin mattress around their matriarch, placed her on a narrow
door, and carried her from the white church to a rowboat. They set her crosswise on the boat so her head and
her feet floated over the water. Several sleeping babies
wrapped in JCPenney blankets were nestled in among
bundles of clothing on either side of their ancient ances-
tor. The Red Crows swam through the reflected sky,
propelling the boat of their old and their new.

When all were aboard the barge, Cody started the
engine and lifted the anchor free. The Daimler worked the
water, pushing them north as the sun pulled the moun-

tains' shadow off the lake. By eight o'clock, the sun came over the mountains and caught the Red Crows staring at it.

Catherine had been dreaming of the lake, of water moving through water. The light filtered down warming her body. She woke and discovered she was floating on the lake. She could hear the voices of her family behind the bright light of the sun. She squinted to see. Why am I dreaming this dream? she wondered. She turned and saw Rose, who was holding her hand.

Catherine was quiet for several minutes, listening to the murmurings of her family, and looking for clues or signs in the lake. Was she alive or dead? She studied Rose, squeezed her hand, and looked for a spark in her eyes.

Catherine's soft voice was direct and clear. "Are we in a dream?"

"No. This is not a dream, Mother Red Crows."

"I was dreamin' an' woke up, but it still feels like a dream." She grinned at Rose. "Maybe I'm dead, finally."

"Not yet," said Rose. "You wanted to go on the lake and asked if we'd take you. When you were sleeping we carried you out to the rowboat and brought you here. It was almost dawn when we left the house."

Catherine looked up into her white daughter's eyes. The ancient woman knew she had imagined so many things she was no longer sure of what was real and what was a dream. Maybe death was a dream without a body. She looked at the shrinking body she was attached to, at the arms and the outline of fragile legs curled up against the thin ribs. The breasts that had swayed men and suckled babies were thin leathery sacks. Each breast was marked by a small black indentation. She even remembered losing her nipples in a dream. They had turned to raspberries. In the late evening the deer came. They kissed her and nuzzled her, and reached up with sweet deer lips and plucked away her raspberries. Catherine no longer needed breasts.

Rose stroked the wispy white hair floating up from her mother's bony skull.

"You have a man," Catherine said in her flat, old-Indian-woman-knows-all voice.

"How do you know about that?"

"Your hands tell me. They've been holding a man. Your voice tells me he makes you burn under the blanket."

"I brought him to the house once to meet you," said Rose. "His name is Cody. He's steering the barge. I'll show him to you."

Amy held Gerome's hand and leaned far over the edge of the barge.

"What are you doing, Amy?" Rose called to the small girl working the water.

Amy hung from Gerome's large hand. She twisted around to look at Rose. "Making the boat go fast."

"Would you go tell Cody to come say hello to Catherine, please?"

"Who'll steer the boat?"

"I hadn't thought of that. Maybe you could."

"Okay, Rose," she said, and led Gerome toward the pilothouse.

"Is your new man good in fights?" asked Catherine.

Rose frowned. "Why does that matter?"

"In the old times," said Catherine, "the eyes of the young women couldn't see a young man who didn't care about fighting. That's why the men went away in the evening. They would travel all night and the next, sleeping in the daytime, to raid another tribe for horses and slaves."

"But why did the young women want men who fought?" she asked.

At Amy's instruction, Cody had come over and sat down next to Rose. He felt strange and awkward when she introduced him to Catherine. The old woman paid no attention to him and went on talking about a life in the distant past.

"If your man was good in the fight," said Catherine, "you could have a better life and more babies."

"Why would life be better if your husband was good at fighting?" she asked.

"The best fighters took the most horses," said Catherine, "and they killed the most buffalo. We traded buffalo hides for things we wanted, and the horses let us carry our things from camp to camp. We could have big lodges made with many skins."

"Do you mean that before horses, people had to start over every time they moved?"

"They could only carry their things or drag them. Some people used dogs. Some people had slaves to help. Then horses came. They were strong and ate grass. They were better than dogs or slaves for carrying things and we didn't have to hunt to feed them."

Behind her passive, dark eyes, Catherine could see the young boys playing *coup*, moving slowly and gently from horse to horse, dancing and gliding under their bellies, hiding among legs. The patient girls stood for hours picking burrs and mud from the long tails. All day, old men examined hooves, going from horse to horse, singing softly and telling them how beautiful they were. The horses listened to the sweet voices of the old men and knew that what they said was true because the young girls pressed against their long, thick necks, caressed their silky muzzles, and told them they loved them.

Cody had only seen Catherine as mute. Her voice had come alive. A younger woman lived inside her withered body.

He was surprised the tribes once lived without horses. That the Indians had kept slaves seemed incredible.

"Did people let the slaves go when they got horses?" he asked.

"No. With a good horse, a good man could kill more buffalo and feed more slaves and more wives, and the slaves and the wives could work more hides for tradin'. The more buffalo a man killed, the more horses he needed for all his wives and the things they had traded for hides. A rich man was busy all the time."

The idea of a busy, rich Indian was a strange notion to Cody. "Beside killing buffalo and trading hides, what did rich men do?" he asked.

"They traded horses and slaves. They combed their luck. They held council and led the young men on raids.

They had to make plans with the chiefs, and keep their younger wives happy. Some men had hundreds of horses to be looked after."

Cody looked at the Red Crows sunning themselves on the barge like tourists on a holiday. Some had feathers in their long braids. It was hard to imagine Gerome with a herd of horses and no fences.

"How did they manage hundreds of horses?" he asked.

"Children and old people made themselves useful watching the animals. It was a way for poor people to get a horse."

"Didn't slaves watch the horses?"

"Of course not. They'd steal a horse and get away. The old wives kept slaves busy workin' on hides and makin' clothes from skins."

Cody wondered if he would have been a good hunter, if he would have been rich. Would he have had slaves? What kind of luck would he have had?

"Did the animals give you luck?"

"When I was a young woman," she said, "I had the luck to cure children of bear fever, but then I lost that luck. It went away because I did something I wasn't 'sposed to do. That kinda luck never came back to me."

"What did you do that you weren't suppose to?"

"I had strong feelings for a young man. I think that's why the bears took away my luck."

"What became of the young man?"

"He killed a man in a fight and the man's wife killed him, so after a while I killed her."

"How did you kill her?"

Catherine thrust out her bony hand. "I stuck a knife in her."

"What happened?"

"I went to stay with another tribe. My husband's father had many horses. After a while it was forgotten, and I came back."

"You were married then? What did your husband think about you and the young man?"

"He never knew. He thought I killed the woman because he was sticking his thing in her."

---

Amy and Gerome guided them north toward the islands of the great blue heron. The birds lived in huge nests made of moss and branches at the tops of the trees. As they approached the island, there was a commotion in the sky. Directly above them a screeching osprey attacked a giant heron. The osprey sank its talons into the heron's long neck, and the two of them spiraled down into the lake. The osprey released its grip as they hit the water and flew away. The heron floated on the surface, motionless except for the crimson stain that grew along its neck, announcing its death to the osprey.

Gerome and Amy turned the barge toward the dying bird. A young Red Crows boy, nine or ten years old, darted forward to grab the heron as the barge brushed by.

The barge moved toward the waiting bird. Cody could feel himself reach for the bird as the boy reached out, his hand ready to close around the lifeless neck. At the last moment, the boy saw into the eyes of the bird. He extended his fingers, barely touching the feathers, and stroked its long white neck. The boy laughed with delight. Ignited by the laughing boy, the heron lunged into the air, flapping its huge wings against the water until it rose up parallel to the moving barge. For a moment, the bird seemed held in the air by the boy's elation. The many braids of the Red Crows turned as the heron flew past and sailed low across the water toward its island home.

———————

Amy steered the barge around the east shore of the island, while the Red Crows stared up into the trees at the great nests. Baby heron, waiting for their mothers to return from the marshes with fish, peered down at the small floating island and the pointing Indians.

As the barge approached the west shore of the second island, Cody searched the trees for nests, but the Red Crows showed no interest.

"Where're the nests?" he asked.

"Snakes," said Catherine. "They eat eggs."

"Why are snakes on one island and not the other?"

"Long ago a tribe that ate snakes lived with the heron."

"Those must have been big snakes to eat heron eggs," he said.

"Do you doubt an old woman who talks to crows?" she asked in her soft voice. "The snake is wise and good because it dies and comes back to life. It sees everything."

Looking into Catherine's eyes made him feel strange. He studied her eyes for her thoughts until she mirrored his own. In this wrinkled, old woman-mirror he saw something that had haunted him since childhood—the memory that the world knew every move and thought he made. Now he was staring into its dark eyes.

"There's a man," she said, "who lives alone on the island of the snakes. Even though he's an Indian, his skin and his eyes are white. He's a snake eater."

Catherine's raspy, ancient voice seemed to put the albino snake eater deep in his mind. He felt slightly drunk and his breathing quickened. Then Rose's hand was on the back of his neck, as though to direct him so he could not look away. The island receded into the distance.

"I love you," Rose whispered.

The Red Crows turned their gaze on Cody. The Daimler's pounding beat grew louder. He felt his craziness lift away. He could see Gerome in the pilot's cabin and Amy beside him, standing on the chair, steering north, past the island of the snakes. A small chill of realization caught hold of Cody. This outing was meant as much for him as for Catherine.

---

He became euphoric and happy, smiling like a boy. They were past the last of the islands, churning toward the northernmost bay. Beyond the bay the land rose up to a steep, vivid green hillside. Stone retaining walls supported a road that zigzagged up to a three-story mansion near the top of the hill. Several other buildings were scattered across the hillside, connected by wide walkways. As they came closer, Cody could see several people in white pants supervising other people who were working the landscape—digging, planting, trimming, and mowing. The place was a hive.

"It's called the Springhill Dairy," said Rose.

"What?" asked Cody.

"It's an insane asylum," she said. "A place for crazy people."

For an instant Cody thought the Red Crows meant to bring him to the asylum, to lock him up—put him in white pants in a green pasture milking brown cows. Cody laughed. The Red Crows turned and looked at him.

He could see several cows in long pastures separated by stone fences. There was a barn for milking and for storing hay. There were other buildings on the grounds, some grand, some small, all white and trim.

The narrow, stone-fenced patches of lush green pasture, and the little men in their bright, white pants, were perfect, clean, and proper.

"It's all in order, isn't it?" he said.

"I've always thought it was a little evil." Rose stood and stretched. "The buildings are too big. It's too tidy and too official."

"I didn't think you believed in evil."

"I think officials are evil."

"Why?"

"That place is like Indian school. They make slaves out of everybody."

"Maybe it's the job," he said, watching the little men in their white, tubular pants. He looked at her with a small, wicked grin. "Maybe evil's official."

"So what made them take their evil jobs?"

"Were the Indians who used slaves to work buffalo hides evil?" he asked.

She glanced over at Catherine to see her reaction.

The old woman grimaced. Her face seemed ready to break apart. When the laughter came—several short, throaty giggles—they realized she was smiling.

"Sometimes we took slaves. We were stronger than our enemies." She sounded wistful and happy. "Sometimes we wiped them out. The others are gone. Nothing left."

She dismissed the others, slicing the air with her hand, cutting them off from the living.

Her voice was very matter-of-fact. "We are the ones who have life," she said, and opened her gnarled hand to Cody. She was including him in her circle of the living. He knew she could be his enemy, but she chose to accept him.

Cody and Catherine looked at each other for a long time, until Rose touched his shoulder. She had seen something happen, she was sure. She had seen his face catch its youth and saw the smile flash in his eyes. He was riding on a sea of new things.

She drew herself against him, kissing the arch of his eye. Catherine watched the kiss seep in. She remembered when the meaning of life could be felt in a kiss. An old woman knows everything.

When they approached the dock below the Springhill Dairy, one of the attendants ran down the hill toward the lake waving his arms. He puffed along the dock and pointed to a fancy hand-lettered sign just above the

waterline. The letters were small and made with flourishes. Gerome maneuvered the barge close to the dock so
he could read the message. Except for Catherine, everyone on board went up to the bow to read the sign and get
a good look at the attendant, who would be remembered
as Mr. White Pants. He began waving his arms again,
fearful they meant to disembark *en masse.*

Rose read the sign aloud for the youngest and oldest
Red Crows.

"This dock is personal property to be used by our-
selves and our special guests. Any and all persons treading
without permission will be reported to the sheriff. Respect
others' privacy. Thank you, The Superintendent."

Cody motioned to Gerome to reverse the barge. As
they came closer to the dock, Cody held his hands apart to
indicate the remaining distance. He realized Gerome had
shifted into reverse too late, and began waving him back.
Gerome revved the engine, but too quickly. The whirling
prop created an air pocket and lost its bite against the
water. The unstoppable barge continued toward the dock.

Cody stood on the bow, hands held high, showing
Gerome the ever diminishing distance between barge and
dock. He was wide-eyed and grinning, like a magician,
commanding the dock to disappear beneath the bow of
the barge.

At the last moment, White Pants jumped to the bow.
Cody grabbed him and saved him from falling as the
dock crumpled beneath the barge.

"Welcome aboard," said the happy magician.

"Charges will be filed," White Pants said and pushed

away from Cody's embrace. He balanced on the bow beam, confused, staring at the Red Crows. The barge sighed and stopped. White Pants fell backward into the water. Several Red Crows laughed.

Cody jumped into the water and helped the attendant onto the broken dock. The man glared at him.

Cody stifled his laughter, but not his wicked grin.

"You okay?" he asked. "If you didn't wear those funny pants, this sort of thing wouldn't happen."

The glaring man lost control. He swung, and missed, losing his balance. Cody grabbed his arms and held him upright.

"I'm sorry about this," said Cody. He felt embarrassed by the attendant's humiliation. "We'll fix your dock. We'll make it like new."

The attendant was turning colors. He was an angry rattlesnake in Cody's grip.

More white pants, followed by a dozen inmates, came running down from the stone walls and the perfect green lawn.

"Let go of him," one of the attendants shouted.

"Okay," said Cody, calm and deliberate. "I'm going to let go, and you won't try to hit me again, all right?"

Cody relaxed his grip. The man lunged away and into the arms of the waiting attendants.

"You've done it now, mister," he yelled at Cody. "The sheriff will deal with you and your savages."

The words "your savages" saturated the air. Even the white pants crowd felt awkward. They turned and retreated up the hill, herding the inmates before them.

They watched over their shoulders for a possible attack.

For a brief moment Cody felt lost. Hilarity, embarrassment, and anger overwhelmed him. Amy was standing in the very front of the Red Crows who were lined up along the bow. She seemed confused.

"Are we your savages?" she asked. She said it slow. It was a new word and she liked its sound.

The warm rain of the Red Crows' laughter pulled Cody back onto the barge.

"Savages, savages, savages, savages," they began to chant, making soft, small waves with the words.

Cody turned toward the green hillside where the men in white pants stood, staring down. He felt the blood pumping through his chest and shoulders, through his neck, into his head. He found himself smiling at the men on the hillside.

"Savvv . . . ages," he sang out to the white pants and the inmates on the hill.

For a brief moment, the inmates were part of the stunned silence. Then one of them let out a loud, shrill laugh. Others followed. Their raucous laughter ricocheted off the hillside and across the still water.

Cody and the Indians stared up at the men in white pants and their laughing charges. Cody waved at the figures on the hillside. The attendants stood firm. An inmate hesitantly raised his hand and waved to the assembled Red Crows. Then, one by one, all the patients began to wave. The uprising agitated the white pants into action, herding their charges toward the main building.

Gerome revved the Daimler and the barge screeched

and groaned its way off the dock. Rose was not among the assembled Red Crows. Cody found her sitting beside Catherine, avoiding the scene on the bow.

Rose saw him coming. "It isn't good to make men in white pants feel ridiculous," she said in an even voice.

Her old mother was thinking about trouble.

"You've seen some things that belong to us Indians," said Catherine, "but you're not an Indian. White men can get away with things. It's different for Indians."

"It might be hard for you to be around the Red Crows," Rose said to him. "They won't be your savages. You'll be their white man and the whites won't like that."

"How do the whites think of you?"

"They think I'm a half-breed woman. It makes me interesting to the men and dangerous to the women."

"Because the men are interested?"

"That, and some women think I have powerful magic."

He laughed. "I knew to be cautious."

"Yes?"

"I dreamed you swallowed me."

"Really?"

"I was a milk shake."

"Dairy Boy?"

"Just the way you like it."

He saw her blush and realized it was not a subject she wanted to pursue in front of Catherine.

Amy climbed down from the pilot's chair and went to find her mother to help steer the barge, because Gerome wanted to talk Cody into a poker game. She returned with her mother, a tall woman with high cheekbones and dark slits for eyes. Amy's mother and her two sisters crowded into the pilothouse with Amy. Gerome gave them a few brief instructions and they assumed the duty of guiding the barge back home.

---

The poker game took place at Gerome's house. The Red Crows, normally a talkative family, stood silently for three hours and watched Gerome lose forty-two dollars to Cody. Gerome was determined to stay in the game and win back his money, but he lacked funds.

"Would it be all right if I put up the red automobile," he offered, gesturing in the direction of the blackberry patch. "It still runs. Louie Desoto's usin' the tires. He's s'posed to bring 'em back."

Cody thought about the lovely shapes of the car's fenders and hood. "Instead of the Pontiac," he said, "I would like you to stand in front of the car while I make a painting."

---

Gerome Red Crows stood in waist-high grass beside the chrome grille of his red, torpedo-backed Pontiac. He assumed a traditional noble-savage profile, arms crossed on chest, head held high, eyes on the horizon, disdain in the face.

Cody stood twenty feet back, sizing up the Pontiac, the blackberries, and the Indian. "Gerome, just relax," he said, frustrated.

The Indian was immobile. Cody was not going to paint him ridiculous. Cody glared at Gerome and his irritation rose.

"Could you drop your arms to your sides?" he demanded.

"I would like it this way." Gerome maintained his stiff, eyes-on-the-horizon, chin-to-the-mountains pose.

"I'm not goin' to paint you standing there like a stone Indian."

Gerome did not move. Cody stared at the obstinate Indian.

"Well, to hell with it then. Who needs a picture of an ugly Indian, anyway?"

He picked up his box of paints and the easel and was turning to leave when he realized Gerome was standing rigidly in position. Gerome's conviction held them both in place, fixed in the history of the meadow.

The air was still. A chickadee sat on Catherine's clothesline, waiting for the moment to fly into the picture. Everything was ready.

Cody realized the Indian was right. Gerome was making a joke about painters and all the Indians who ever posed for them. Cody set the easel sticks in the ground. He studied the shape and slope of red fenders, the thick gleaming grille, Gerome's slanted forehead, heavy nose, and thick flat lips. The green leaves vibrated against their shadows. Cody opened the jars of colors, set a board on the easel, and began.

A MY STOOD ON THE FRONT SEAT OF THE RED CAR. SHE
had the side window rolled down and was moving
the steering wheel back and forth. She was flying. The
sound of the tall grass against a car fender brought her
back to the real world. She froze and waited for the mystery car to appear.

A blue Mercury with a white star on the door
cruised down through the grass and stopped almost in
front of Amy. A huge man opened the door with the star
on it and unfolded himself from the car. He straightened
out, stood very still, and listened for signs of life. After a
moment he reached into the car and pulled out a cowboy
hat. He leveled the hat on his head and looked at Amy.
He walked over and bent down. He had a big hat and a
giant face.

"Hi, sweetheart," he said.

Amy knew if she did not know what to say, to say
nothing. She stared straight ahead, both hands on the
thick plastic wheel.

"Are your folks around?" asked the face. She said
nothing and finally it went away.

The sheriff checked the shacks then drove back to

the highway and cruised west, looking for the barge. He found it tied up at Tidyman's dock where Cody, Rose, and Gerome were loading some iron rings for timber collars, bolts, cable, and planking. Gerome saw him first.

"Sheriff Joe's coming our way," he said.

Cody and Rose peered up at the dock. The sheriff was standing at the top of the gangplank looking particularly large. He was smiling.

"Hi, Rose," he said.

"Hi, Joe," she responded.

The sheriff nodded toward Cody. "You'd be Cody?"

"Uh-huh," said Cody.

"I'm Sheriff Black. Sorry we're meetin' like this, but I've got some bad news here." He held up a large brown envelope. "The funny farm says you broke up their dock with Tidyman's barge. In addition, you're charged with the further aggravations of restrainin' one of the attendants and agitatin' the inmates."

"I was steering, Sheriff," Gerome said. "The barge had its own mind about that dock."

"That's well and fine, but it's your friend here's responsible."

"We're all partners," said Rose.

"Doesn't matter, far as the court's concerned."

Rose shook her head. "That's not the law, Joe. You know that."

"I didn't say the law. Said the court."

Cody understood small towns were mostly indifferent to the idea of justice. Lumber camps had a similar outlook. There were ways of maintaining an orderly world without resorting to written codes. He knew he was on dangerous ground.

"I intend to fix the dock," he said. "That's what this lumber's for. I wrapped the attendant up to keep him from takin' a swing at me, and the inmates were just laughing with the rest of us."

Sheriff Joe smiled. "Just laughin' along with the rest of you?"

To Cody, the sheriff's tone seemed slightly dangerous. Anything Cody said was liable to get him in deeper.

Rose knew he was not prepared to deal with Joe. She stepped in. "It was the attendant who started all that. He referred to the Indians as savages. The Red Crows picked it up and made a little song out of it. Then the inmates started laughing. We weren't agitating anybody."

"So, other than running this barge into their dock, none of you did anything, or said anything, to get this attendant riled?"

There was a noticeable pause before Cody spoke up.

"Well, I said something about his white pants. That probably didn't help matters."

Sheriff Joe's face lost its ironic twist. It turned heavy, almost sad. He walked down the gangplank and handed him the envelope. "Bad things come from bad manners," he said. The sheriff gave a small nod and walked back to his car.

Cody read the charges against him and handed the papers to Rose. Gerome peered over her shoulder.

"Looks like trouble," he said.

Cody studied the bluish haze to the north that veiled the Springhill Dairy.

"Let's go up there," he said, "fix their dock, and be nice, and see what happens. Maybe they'll cool down."

Rose shook her head. "What do you think, Gerome?"

"We should go to the funny farm and build them a dock," said Gerome.

"All right. Why not?" she agreed.

"Why not?" said Cody. "We'll build them the best damn dock on the lake."

When they finished loading materials, Rose called Erickson, the pile driver, from the phone in the little store across the highway and arranged to have four pilings set for the new dock.

"Middle of next week's the soonest," she told her partners.

Cody decided to fix his truck in the meantime so he could move it onto the Red Crows' place. Gerome took off. He wanted to find DeSoto and LeClair and play poker for a couple of days. Rose stayed around to help Cody with the truck.

Working together was easy. It made them feel sane. He liked watching the way she moved. She would gaze at him and smile, just because he was there. Sometimes they would brush against each other, stop to embrace, to kiss, and sometimes to make love in the truck. He would let his hand fall across her bottom almost by accident, only the motion would be too slow, too deliberate for a chanced touch. Everything about these two days together felt like the caress of skin.

After the truck was running and Gerome came back, smiling, they spent the next five days on the barge preparing for the logging operation—connecting air pumps, building slide runners and a catch frame for decking the logs, and installing pulleys and winch cables. The underwater gear was primitive and direct. A hookah pump provided breathing air through three-quarter-inch rubber hoses that were draped over the side of the barge. Rose rigged weighted diving belts from bicycle inner tubes, filling them with lead sinkers and iron bolts. They experimented with air pressure and weight, walking on the lake bottom wearing wool long johns, with air tubes in their mouths.

In the floating light of their underworld, the three of them made up hand signals, danced a jitterbug in slow motion, and somersaulted in weightlessness.

Their days assumed an unconscious pattern. In the early evening, they would call it quits and drive Gretchen over to Catherine's for supper, where they would talk about the day's work and plan the next. Before it was dark, Gerome went home to the Red Crows' shack. Cody and Rose walked back along the narrow highway through the cottonwoods and droning crickets to sleep on the deck of the barge.

The time on the lake preparing the barge was without margins. The physical sensations that invaded Cody's dreams drew him into the waking world. The feel of his bare feet on the wooden deck, morning air on his naked skin, cold water shrinking his testicles up into his body, and transitory images of muscles, eyes, and hands were his guardians in the world of iron motors, winches, and steel cables. Breathing and thinking took on the motion of the lake and the sky.

---

Rose woke before first light, watched the stars fade, and waited for Cody to open his eyes. Finally, she got up and made coffee. She sat cross-legged, watching him sleep, and sipped her coffee. His breathing aroused her. She began stroking his body. His first sensation was of teeth and lips on tender flesh, then her legs spread, moving against his thigh.

"Bunny Conners," she whispered.

"Who is Bunny Conners?" he asked.

She leaned forward and put her lips to his ear. "Funny corners," she whispered. "You have funny corners."

"The crows think so," he said.

Gerome arrived when the sun came over the mountain. Rose fixed breakfast for the three of them before they began work on the rigging. The first decking rig they tried to construct was based on a hay-stacking boom. It was too awkward and dangerous. They took it apart and built an extremely simple set of ramps that angled down into the water. Even then they knew it would be difficult to operate.

The logs were as long as thirty-three feet and could weigh three tons out of the water. They lay side to side in rows on the bottom, settled by the motion of the water into positions of least resistance. Every log had to be pulled up parallel to the back edge of the deck. Then the barge would be moved forward so the log would trail far enough behind to clear the underside of the ramps. Once the log cleared, it would be winched up the ramps onto the deck.

Cody found a smaller log that tilted up and was easy to grab. They used it for a test run. Gerome climbed onto the deck after fifteen minutes of trying to maneuver the log parallel to the back deck so Rose could winch it up. Cody followed him up the ladder. They stood facing the sun. Their feet soaked in heat from the oak deck.

Gerome smiled as the warmth seeped back into his body. Slow dancing in cold water at the end of an air hose was new to him. "We'll finish this job 'bout the time we figure it out," he said.

When Cody closed his eyes, he saw the afterimage of the Indian, distorted through forty feet of water, swimming in the mottled light.

Rose killed the air pumps, walked to the back edge of the barge, and looked at the log she had winched beneath the ramp timbers. She came back and sat between Cody and Gerome.

"This won't work," she said. "It would be good if I could see what I'm doin' with that winch, so I'd like us to run control lines for both the winch and the barge back near the ramp. And if you spaced the tongs a little farther apart it would help center the log a lot easier."

Cody smiled at her. "I didn't know this about you."

"I built airplanes, remember?"

Gerome kept his eyes closed. "We will do what you say, Rose Red Crows." The cold water gave his skin a strange gray cast. It made him look like stone.

———◦———

Before they started logging the lake, they took the barge north to the Springhill asylum and worked on the dock they had wrecked the week before. Erickson had driven the required pilings and cleared away the debris. They spent three days putting in timbers and a three-inch plank deck. At first the white pants kept their distance. After the first day, they stopped trying to herd stray inmates back up the slope. Eventually attendants and inmates would come down and watch the progress until they got bored. Late in the afternoon of the third day, the dock builders stood on the barge and admired their solid and handsome piece of work. The inmates cheered and the attendants waved.

"It'll be here after we're long gone," said Rose. And they clinked cold beers together.

"Hear! Hear!" said Cody, waving to the small crowd gathered on the dock.

She set the Daimler's throttle on the half notch and headed the barge south, taking them past the island of the snakes. Cody studied the trees for the albino snake eater. He stared into the foliage until his eyes hurt, hoping for some sign of the white Indian. For a brief moment, a spiral of smoke curled up through the trees, then it was gone. Neither Rose nor Gerome seemed to notice.

When they were past the islands, into open lake again,

Rose spotted a heron streaming across the magenta vein in the evening sky.

They brought the barge into Tidyman's dock with just enough light to find the mooring posts. Cody and Rose slid into their bedrolls before Gerome made it past the end of the dock to where Gretchen was parked.

They lay on their backs and watched the stars come into the sky.

"Do you know about the stars?" she asked.

"Only that they're other suns, far away."

"Suppose we'd never heard about galaxies or solar systems, and there were just these pinpoints of light in the sky. What would they be?"

"The eyes of many small gods who run this operation."

"They run things?"

"With big levers, lots of little Bakelite gears, and too much coffee."

"Is there one god in charge or is it just chaotic?"

"Strictly an every-god-for-himself deal."

"And Cody against them all?"

He laughed and reached over, drawing a finger down her neck and along the clavicle to her shoulder. "Maybe so." He let her question spin through his thoughts for a while. "Not when I'm painting, and not when I'm around you."

"Where did you get the idea to paint pictures?"

"My father and the latch on Charlie Joseph's water house." He had drawn himself up in a sitting position, one arm wrapped around his legs. His free hand floated over her shoulder while his fingers spoke with her skin.

"Tell me," she whispered.

"Charlie had a thick, bull neck. He squatted down when he walked and twisted his body from side to side. He was old and he lived by himself in the woods. One day, when I was a kid, my father took me to visit him, but Charlie wasn't in his shack. We went down a path through the trees to the creek to see if he was in his water house. There was an iron latch on the door—a very beautiful latch. It was just something Charlie had hammered out on his forge. He was a strange old bull who lived alone in a dirty shack—I never would've thought he could make anything beautiful. My father saw me staring at the latch and said, 'You could do somethin' like that someday.'"

"Your father was unusual."

"Yeah, he was. He was okay."

"How did you get from Charlie's latch to painting?"

"I started to see shapes and surfaces more. The way a surface absorbs the light made me think about what's real and what we think is real. Sometimes it feels like there's another place hidden behind this one."

"The Red Crows used to believe in a hidden world."

"They don't now?"

"They say it quit talkin' to them. It disappeared."

He studied the shape of her mouth in the moonlight. "Don't disappear," he whispered, and kissed the moonlit mouth.

---

In the morning Rose made coffee, bacon, and hot-cakes on the tin stove as the sun moved across the water toward the barge. She could see Gerome in the pale blue truck, gliding along the highway between buildings and through the trees, then turn and coast down the dirt road in a haze of luminous dust to the dock. She knew he was tracking the sun's progress, that he was aware of his timing. Whether he felt it was significant, joyful, or humorous, she did not know. He had arrived, as before, with the sun.

They sat on the edge of the barge, looking out across the water, and ate their breakfasts on enameled tin plates borrowed from Catherine.

"This is good coffee," said Gerome. "The cakes are good too."

"Thanks," said Rose.

"And the bacon. Very good."

She looked over at him and smiled. "Yes, it is."

"This is a good way to live," he said.

Cody had been calculating prices, weights, and possibilities. He looked over at the big Indian. "What are you two talking about?" he asked.

"Hunting," Gerome replied.

They heard a car door close and looked back toward the shore. The big sheriff got out of his car, adjusted his hat, and walked down the dock to the barge. The sheriff held up a paper.

"The court forbids you to rebuild the asylum dock," he announced and handed the paper to Cody.

Cody, Rose, and Gerome stood together, reading the restraining order. Cody looked at the sheriff, trying to tell if the man knew the dock had already been rebuilt.

Rose pointed at the date and looked at Cody. "That's today." She said it with a soft whisper that managed to reveal disbelief, disgust, and an undercurrent of caution at the same time.

The sheriff had an official face that revealed nothing.

Cody carefully folded the paper. He shook his head and walked away. The sheriff nodded to Rose and Gerome. He went back to his car, removed his hat, and got in. He watched the trio through the rearview mirror as he drove away.

"What do you make of that?" asked Rose.

"Let's forget about it," said Cody. "What were we talking about before?"

"Hunting," said the Indian.

"Hunting?" said Rose. "I thought we were talking about bacon and pancakes."

"I was thinking about hunting," said Gerome. "It feels strange to go to the store. Do you feel that way too?"

"What if the store stops?" she asked. "Is that what you mean?"

Gerome smiled and in his soft, sweet Indian voice he said, "Could I have some more of those flapjacks?"

"Flapjacks?" said Cody. "Flapjacks?" He giggled and looked at Rose. "Gerome said flapjacks."

"You've never heard them called flapjacks?" she asked.

He was laughing. "I thought flapjacks were foreskins." He was gasping for air. "More flapjacks," he gasped, "before the store stops."

Too late he realized Gerome had him under the

arms. Rose had his feet. He was flying up over the edge and falling down, into the water. He resurfaced sputtering and grabbed for the barge.

Rose peered over the edge. "Hi," she said and handed down a pancake. "Have a flapjack."

"Thanks. They're very good."

"So's the bacon," said Rose.

He ate his pancake, treading water.

# SUNDAY
# NIGHT

"This is going to make an immense fire, Gramma. Are you happy to be rid of all this, or not?"

Ana watched the matches flare in the darkness, then fly into the mound of magazines and papers. "I know it must have seemed creepy—those piles all through the house," said Ana. "But I'd gotten so I liked it. They muted the sound."

The fire flared up in several places, illuminating Liz as she moved along the edge, flinging matches into the mound.

"Do you want me to stop?"

Ana laughed. "No. I'll start on something else. Come back in a couple of years and I'll have the place filled again."

"What got you started on all this?"

"The more distance you get from your own culture,

the better you can see through it. The less it terrorizes you. The irony is that the more you can see your culture for what it is, the less able you are to live in it. A culture requires you to suspend disbelief."

"When the whites came, what happened to Indian culture?"

"Some of the Indians said that when the tribes stopped listening to the spirits, the animals went away. Many believed if they returned to the old ways the whites would disappear. Instead, the Indians got wiped out. They felt betrayed. Their own culture failed them. They were not prepared to harden their hearts to live with the whites.

"David Red Crows' grandfather, Gerome, said Indians could never be themselves in the white world. They couldn't be Indians either because they didn't depend on animals anymore. A man could still see the shape of a woman waiting in the trees on a moonless night, but he didn't know when the gnats were telling him a storm was coming. Gerome thought it would take another fifty years before the Indians thought of nature as a dead piece of junk. Then they would understand the white man."

"When did he say that?"

"About fifty years ago."

"He had a sense of humor, anyway. What did he do?"

"Lots of things. He was in the fuel oil business for quite a while. Made a lot of money, too. He's retired now and lives in the condominiums over by the supermarket."

The flames had settled down into small hot spots, flaring from time to time to illuminate the smoldering mass of unburnt paper. Liz waved a magazine at the futile flames.

"Haven't we been betrayed by our culture, as much as the Indians were by theirs?" she asked.

"Culture always betrays individuals. That's its job."

"Another day, another humiliation?"

"That's one way to look at it. But when all the humiliations and betrayals are totaled up at the end of the day, it's supposed to add up to cooperation and survival."

"You are an optimist, Gramma." Liz laughed. "I think it's ironic that the Indians felt betrayed because their hearts were not hardened and we feel betrayed because ours are."

GEROME SWAM DOWN INTO THE WORLD OF SLOW, MURKY light and sleeping logs. The cable trailed back with the black air hose—his tentacle to the overworld. He found a smallish log to experiment with and set the hooks on either side of its midpoint. Slowly, Rose winched the cable in, pulling the barge to a center point over the log.

Gerome signaled for Rose to take up the line. The winch was geared down, able to handle far heavier loads than the log Gerome had hooked into. The cable tightened, setting the hooks. Cody heard the engine torque down as black smoke erupted from the exhaust stack. The log was not moving. It was stuck in the bottom muck. The rear of the barge was slowly pulled down and the cable stretched taut. The clutch shrieked, catching fire as the barge emitted a loud groan. Rose set the stops on the winch. For a moment, everything was frozen in place—the barge's front end tilted into the air, the cable at break point. Cody and Rose stretched toward their respective levers, staring at each other.

Bursts of air erupted from Gerome's lungs and boiled up to the surface. He heard the muffled groan and felt the barge vibrate. The Indian fanned his feet slowly to stay in place, and waited.

The barge was on the verge of breaking apart. She froze, waiting for whatever was next.

"Jump!" Cody shouted.

She dove over the edge, kicking down and under the barge. She twisted around to look for him. As the cable exploded on deck, Cody shot into the water.

A spray of bubbles chased the cable down to where it struck Gerome. He floated motionless in twenty feet of water. A bright ribbon of blood rose from his head, infused with a thousand tiny beads of air.

They followed the red stream down to Gerome. Cody swam under him and pushed him up while Rose held the air hose in his mouth. They maneuvered him to the surface and Cody climbed on deck. Rose held one of Gerome's arms above his head so Cody could pull him up. Blood cascaded from the cut across the top of the Indian's head, into his eyes, masking his face. Rose climbed on deck and helped pull him over the edge.

They stretched him out and she pressed her hand against his skull to slow the flow of blood. Cody stared at Gerome, thinking about the winch and the cable, wondering why the log had not come loose.

"He'll be okay," she said. "Bring my kit, the pillow-cases, and the bottle."

The Indian blinked, trying to clear the blood from his eyes. "I'll be okay."

The kit was a woven grass basket that held a thousand things, including several feet of fishing line and three needles.

Cody reasoned that standing, the Indian's blood would not spew out of his head as easily, so they stood him up straight. Cody helped keep him upright, and Gerome drank medicinal-smelling whiskey from a blue tonic bottle. When he was ready, Rose balanced on the ramp log and carefully stitched his head shut.

"It'll be as good as the others," she said. "Maybe better."

The whiskey burned his throat, distracting him from the pain on top. When his blood stopped seeping through his hair and down his face, he knew she was done.

She wrapped his head in a pillowcase. "Put some moss on it when you get home. Okay?"

"That wasn't bad," he said, and handed her up the bottle.

"Thanks." She took a pull off the bottle, gagged, and spewed it across the deck. "Christ Almighty, what is this?"

"That good?" said Cody. "It's Schliebe's best moon-shine." He took a drink. "I think it damaged Gerome in his brain."

"If it hasn't, it will," said Rose.

Gerome sat down on the deck and stared out at the lake. He put his hands out to support himself.

"The lake is angry," he said, and lay down on the deck in the sun and went to sleep.

His two partners sat down beside him, passed the bottle between them, taking short hits and thinking about the angry lake. Half an hour later, the sun had warmed them until small beads of sweat formed on their brows and lips. They curled up next to the big Indian and fell asleep.

---

Rose came awake to the sound of the Daimler pounding its way toward shore. Her head rested on Cody's arm. She looked around at the steam rising off the wet deck and the tangle of cable that had wrapped itself around the winch. Gerome stood in the pilot-house, guiding them home. She could see him clearly through the window—his scars and his usual savageman expression.

When they docked, Gerome said he was going to get some sleep. He walked past Gretchen, up the dirt road, and headed down the highway to home.

"I doubt he'll be back," said Cody.

"No," she said. "He thinks the lake's angry with us."

"What d'you think?"

"Why didn't that log come loose?"

"It was sunk down in a foot and a half of black muck. That's probably reason enough."

She smiled at his distrust of superstition.

"If we lifted the log from one end," she said, "and got some water started under there to break the suction, it might pull loose."

"I'm game, but the cable needs work."

"Do the cable. I'll take us out."

She slid her hand across his back and pulled him in against her. He seemed uncluttered, as smooth and simple as a stone. That quality drew her to him and made her want to touch his skin. Painting, she thought, was not about pictures.

She stood in the pilothouse and watched him sawing through the cable. She knew he was always questioning, guessing, balancing, and trying to gauge the world around him. She could feel herself surge back and forth between wanting to make love to him and the grace she felt when he was next to her, absorbed in some other world of his own making—a world of gears, machine parts, turpentine, and oil paints.

He had finished with the cable and was standing in the doorway of the pilothouse holding her kit.

"Where did you get this?"

"I made it. Why?"

"It's unusual and it's beautiful. It's very strong. I could never make anything out of grass."

"I like cloth and deerskin too. Metal and wood are not my materials."

"You built airplanes?"

"It was my job. I hated aluminum."

"I never thought about it, but I never met a woman mechanic."

She shrugged. "Men like that hard stuff."

"All along, I thought it was the women who liked the hard stuff."

"You're not so funny as you think."

He grinned, happy with his joke. "Anytime, I'll trade you some hard for some soft."

She reached down and gently squeezed him. "Good trade," she said.

"So why do men like to work with hard materials and women soft ones, when what we like about each other is just the opposite?"

She laughed. "Men need things that are easy to control."

"If that's true, why do we want women?"

"You start out wanting women. But we're too difficult. We drive you nuts, so you try iron. Iron's easy."

"How's that?"

"It keeps its shape after you've pounded on it."

He smiled and shook his head. "Did anyone ever pound on you?"

"Yes. Sister Marguerite. She used to pound the bejesus out of me."

"Why?"

"Too wild. They said I was rebellious—a bad example."

"Mother warned me about your kind: bad girls." He closed his eyes and drew a long kiss from her.

She watched him go. He walked back to the hatch and jumped down to check the progress of the pumps. Grace, she thought, was not to be taken lightly.

⚬

Once the barge was in place, Cody went down with the main cable and hooked it into the end of a log. She peered over the edge at the vague form of her lover hovering above the log, holding the cable taut on the hooks. He signaled her to take up the slack. She pulled the lever that engaged the clutch head, easing the cable over the drum. The winch felt dicey. It would slip, then jerk the cable, and slap it against the deck.

Everything tightened. The cable went taut and set the hooks. She could hear the engine lower its voice and dig in as the rear deck dipped slightly. She flipped the cog into the gear and set the winch. At the same time, she eased up on the clutch and waited.

Bubbles broke the surface from the breathing line. The log had not budged. She engaged the clutch in slight little twitches. The rear deck sank lower into the water. Now there were several tons of pressure on the cable. Her breathing tightened. Nothing moved. She could tell by the sudden bursts of air rising to the surface that this was no longer the slow, unconscious rhythm of Cody lost in thought.

She heard something pop in the hull at the same time she felt a dull thud come through the deck to her feet. There were more pops followed by a high shriek. She imagined it sounded like gunshots underwater.

She could see Cody moving slowly along the log and not much else. The air bubbles became erratic, disappeared completely, then exploded to the surface.

A black shape surged from under the log and closed

around Cody. The barge screeched and lunged forward as the massive figure grew larger and rolled toward the surface. Rose felt the roiling monster close in, sucking the air out of her lungs.

The barge stopped shaking and settled out. The log had broken free of the bottom and sent a plume of black silt to the surface. Rose set the cog and released the clutch. She leaned over the side, searching for some sign of Cody in the boiling muck. She was sure the lake had killed him. Then she saw something moving up through the darkness. Cody broke the surface smiling. Rose was limp with relief. She sat down and waited for him.

He climbed up, dried himself off, and lay on the deck to soak up the heat. He was happy to have found a simple solution to what had promised to be a major dilemma.

"I jammed the air line under the log to break the suction," he said.

"I saw a monster in the silt," she exploded. "I thought we were dying."

He finally realized she was trembling and put his arm around her.

"It scared the hell out of me, Cody. You were gone. It came up and sucked the breath out of my lungs. It was very real." She tried to shake the image. "I can still see it." They lay down in the sun and he held her.

He had misjudged the lake. He had believed the lake was simple, direct, and workable, but it was none of these.

"Did you see the silt monster because Gerome said the lake was angry?"

"Maybe," she said. He watched her shift from the world of dark magic back to the rational. "But what Gerome believes wouldn't mean anything to me if I hadn't been raised to believe it."

OGEEN STOOD NEAR THE BACK DOOR OF HIS CAFE watching the small figures of Cody and Rose lying in the sun on the deck of the distant barge. He squinted against the light, seeking signs of movement, worrying a hole in the ground with the tip of his oxblood loafer. Ogeen, the watcher, needed what he saw in the heat rising off the dark deck. Ogeen, the obsessed, had been watching for several days. The shimmering heat only fueled his fantasy. By now, he could see whatever he created in his mind's eye.

The cafe screen door opened and broke into his fantasy. He turned and found Earl, coffee cup in hand, grinning at him. Earl had been watching from the cafe.

"Whatcha fixated on there, Bill?" he asked.

Ogeen turned away and went back into the cafe with Earl trailing behind.

"I was thinking, it would be much for the better if that drifter returned to his original line of work."

"Well, you know I'm with you on that. I'll give it some thought."

"What do you mean, Earl?"

"I just thought we might find a way . . . "

"I wasn't suggesting we actually do anything."

"No. Of course not," said Earl. "Nothing actual. The power of positive thinking, that kind of thing," and he laughed.

"Yes," said Ogeen. "Always think positive." He sat down and watched the new girl refill his cup.

She heard him mumble something and leaned down, looking him in the eye. "What did you say?" she asked.

"Oh, nothing," he said. "Not you."

"Oh," she said, giggled. Her short, high-pitched squeal made Ogeen's chest tighten.

---

Cody decided a five-foot pipe attached to the end of the extra air line would make it a good deal easier to force air under the logs and break the vacuum. In the afternoon they brought the barge into Tidyman's dock and took Gretchen into town in search of a proper piece of pipe.

They drove slowly down the main street toward Bandee's hardware. A change in weather from a distant storm made the air heavy and close. They parked in front of Chevyland and walked across the street to Bandee's.

The gossip that had already defined the drifter and the Indian girl for much of the town made people forget their manners. Several stopped and stared. What had been the easy speculation of a lazy summer town was turning aggressive. People were surprised to see the simple work of their imaginations walking across the street in the hot sun.

"Is it just me," Cody asked, "or are we being stared at a little more than necessary?"

"Let's get our pipe and get out of here," said Rose. "They're giving me the willies."

When they drove back down to the dock, the sheriff was waiting with another piece of paper. It was from the court, stating to all and sundry that the new dock, recently constructed at the Springhill Dairy, would be removed. Furthermore, Cody would not be allowed to tear out the new dock. That would be done on bid. Cody would be billed accordingly. Another bid would be let for building a dock to proper specifications. He would be billed for that as well.

Cody looked into the sheriff's solemn eyes. The quiet, resigned aggression he found in the man's face made him explode. "What in the name of hell is going on?" he yelled.

"I wouldn't swear at an officer of the court," said the sheriff.

Things were beginning to unravel for Cody. The square corners and the parallel lines that held everything in check were beginning to buckle and warp.

Rose could see something strange in his eyes. He was holding back whatever violent urge was seething inside.

Cody wanted the lake's calm surface to invade his thoughts, to take over his mind, and to dispel the hatred that had jumped into his body. The lake seeped in. The glow of light off the water's surface moved through his blood, into his chest. His breathing became deeper and his face relaxed.

"You're right," he said. "It's a bad idea to swear at an officer of the court."

Rose tried to read the sheriff's response. The official crease in his pants, the high polished cowboy boots, and the hat, as well as his attitude, set him apart from her. His hat was huge. Why, she wondered, did people wear such things?

The sheriff had maintained his opaque face all during Cody's outrage and apology. Rose knew his reserve was the official's face—a solution for having power and control without bearing personal responsibility.

To Rose, the sheriff represented what passed for normal. The humor and horror of that realization turned her mouth up at the edges—an expression that was definitely not a smile.

Cody watched the play of her mouth. He had never felt so close to anyone. She turned, catching his smile, and held him with her eyes.

"We're on our own out here," he said.

Her voice was even and very direct, almost threatening. "I love you."

"Yes," he said.

With her arms at her side, she turned her hands slightly and opened her palms to him, binding them together in an invisible embrace. They were alone. Everything fell away—the barge, the dock, the sheriff, all disappeared.

For the sheriff, the landscape had shifted. He was no longer in charge. He felt as if he had been caught eavesdropping.

"Well, I have other business," he said. He walked back to the car, embarrassed and angry. The gravel spray from the sheriff's spinning tires announced his exit.

Cody watched the car lurch onto the highway, make a hard right, and shoot off toward town through the trees. The man in the hat became a series of cutouts, connected by pieces of fish line. The sheriff was going, going, gone. Sheriff was smoke.

Rose nuzzled into Cody and watched the last traces of the lawman. "Smoke," she said.

Cody laughed.

"I feel like an outlaw," she said.

"Frees you up, doesn't it?"

"We better start makin' some money, sweet cakes."

"Yes," he said. "That or leave town."

"Being on the run is not my style."

"You think they'd come after us?"

"Probably. It's what they do."

"They wouldn't catch us. We could even come back after a while and live with the Red Crows."

"Maybe," she said. "For now, let's try to make some money."

They took the barge back into the lake and anchored it out near the pilings. Cody dropped off the rear deck with both air lines and the cable. He set the tongs in a sixteen-foot log and signaled Rose. She winched the cable tight as Cody worked the air pipe under the length of the log. This time the log lifted free of the bottom without a fight.

Rose engaged the Daimler, barely moving the barge so the log would trail slightly behind the extended ramp.

As she winched up the log, it tapped one side of the ramp, aligned itself, and jumped onto the timbers. She pulled the log along the skids to the front brace, then slacked off on the winch.

Cody came up for the tongs and waved. "Okay?"

"So far, so good."

He put the air tube back in his mouth and dropped away, letting the tongs pull him toward the bottom. He found another short log and repeated the process.

"This is going to work," Rose said after they had brought up their fifth log. "We were under eight minutes on that last one."

"We'll build the shore bunker tomorrow and we'll be in business."

He was smiling and shivering, thrilled that they could raise the logs. He dried off, pulled on dry woollies, and made some honey whiskey. While Rose took the barge back to the dock, he sat on a canvas sleeping bag, wrapped in a blanket, and drank his whiskey.

He studied the windows of the houses that dotted the shoreline. The fact that he and Rose had figured out how to raise logs off the bottom of the lake would make the locals tighten up even more. There were three years' worth of logs down there. If he and Rose stayed, they would have to dig in against the town. You could get by if you were a rich bastard, or even a poor one who stayed out of the way. It was the middlin' kind they went after.

———

They tied off the barge and drove the truck back to Catherine's for dinner. When they passed the cafe,

Ogeen was coming out. He stood in the doorway and watched them go by. Ogeen had seen them decking the logs. He knew their little operation was working. Cody waved. Rose just looked away.

Half a mile past the cafe Cody turned off the highway onto the trail to the Red Crows' shacks. Gerome stood by the red Pontiac with a tire iron in one hand. Amy was standing in the driver's seat, rotating the steering wheel so the wheels were swinging from side to side.

Rose jumped out of the truck and walked up to Gerome. "Let me see your stitches," she said. She gently tilted his head down, turned his hair back, and felt the skin along either side of the stitching. "You feel okay?"

"It hurts when I bend down," he said.

"Don't bend down."

"Had to put these wheels on before Louis borrowed them again."

The wheels made a slight thump each time they reversed direction. The rhythm was persistent and even, as though the sole purpose of the red car was to turn its wheels from side to side with mechanical precision and reliability. Amy had mastered the art of steering.

"Where are you driving today?" Cody asked.

"I'm flying," Amy corrected, staring up through the windshield at the sky. "I'm flying through clouds with birds."

"You'll need wings," said Rose.

Amy was insistent. "I have wings, Rose."

Gerome pointed at the ground. "We're standing on them," he said.

The grass had been cut in the shape of wings that spread from under the car.

Cody stared up at the hawks that rose and fell in high currents above the lake. "Do you think the hawks see a large red bird with pale green wings or a car in the grass?" he asked.

Rose looked up at the hawks. "They'd see a bird, until they came down. Then the illusion would fall apart and become a car."

Cody was drawn to the idea of that brief moment between one illusion and the next. Like a trick from childhood, it was the momentary discovery of a secret place in the blink of an eye.

"What would you see in that instant in between the red bird with green wings and the car in the grass?"

Gerome looked at the hawks, then closed his eyes. "You would see God's secret." He opened his eyes. "Of course, a human being wouldn't understand it."

Rose started down the path to Catherine's. "And if you understood, you'd be a madman."

"Which comes first?" asked Cody. "God's secret or insanity?"

"Come, Amy," Rose called back, "before they drive you crazy too."

Amy had given up flying the car and was trying to follow the grown-ups' conversation. She understood that sometimes what you saw turned out to be something else. Maybe there was a gap in between where God could hide his secret. The rest made no sense.

She pushed the car door open, jumped down, and ran to catch up. She took Rose's hand and walked along in her thoughts. "Why does God's secret make people crazy?" Amy asked.

"They can't talk about it," said Rose. "That's why it's a secret."

"Why can't they talk about it?"

"There're no words for God's secret. It comes out all gibberish."

"Gibberish?"

Rose smiled. "Yeah."

"I like gibberish," said Amy.

---

Potatoes from Sally's garden and a roast from an elk that one of the young men had shot the night before made the Red Crows self-sufficient for another day. They ate and talked among themselves, ignoring Cody and Rose. The barrier between the whites and the Indians was growing thicker. Rose was no longer bringing home treats and tips. She and her boyfriend were freeloaders who had nearly killed Gerome. All this was fuel for Sally's husband, Joseph, the shaman's apprentice.

Joseph was sincere in his hatred of whites. And he knew hatred focused the turmoil of the younger men. Their need for revenge was good for the shaman trade. The pale-skinned enemy also brought the rebellious children closer to their elders. Despite the fact the whites in general had it coming, hatred had its uses.

The poisoned air in Catherine's shack drove Cody

and Rose outdoors. Gerome followed a few minutes later. The three of them walked east along the shore toward the orchards.

"Remember the hungry ghost in the orchard, Gerome?"

"The one that ate children?"

"Yes. What made that sound? It was the strangest thing I ever heard."

Gerome shrugged. "It was a ghost."

There was a reason he had followed them out of the house. "I was watching today," said Gerome. "You made it work okay. I was glad for you. Whites can do that. It is not good for Indians to work under this water."

Rose pressed his hand in hers. "It doesn't matter," she said.

"I have been thinking about the lake and what I should do," he said. "If we got the mill to leave us a logging truck, I could load off the bunker while you two were out pulling up logs."

"That would be a big help," said Cody. "We're ready to build the bunker."

---

"Roll some tobacco, Little Crows," said Catherine.

"Do you know Dee Lee who makes things fly?" Amy asked.

"No. I don't know that one," said Catherine.

"Dee Lee plays poker all day with Louie Desoto. He lives in the Louie Desoto little house. He and Gerome promised they would make the red car fly."

"Roll the tobacco, Little Crows," said Catherine. "I want a smoke before I go to sleep."

Amy dutifully got the tobacco tin and papers from the leather smoke pouch and rolled an unruly cigarette, wetting the edge of the paper with several tiny licks, and twisting the ends. She placed the damp smoke stick between Catherine's lips, took a match from the tin angel, and struck a flame. "Can you help Gerome and Dee Lee?" she asked.

Catherine inhaled. "I like tobacco," she said. The small ember on the end of her cigarette made the shack seem darker. "Of course I will help, Little Crows."

GEROME HAD DRIVEN CODY AND ROSE BACK TO THE barge so they could go down for another log before they lost the sun. The wind had picked up, roughing the water, turning it soft and gray. As Gerome watched the barge move farther and farther into the lake, its purpose seemed to change.

Rose leaned through the pilothouse doorway and ran her hand down Cody's back. "Go north," she said.

"You don't want to work?"

"I have something else in mind."

They turned the barge north and lay on the deck. The Daimler steadily pushed them on, an old mare on an ancient road beneath the evening clouds that drifted east toward the mountains.

His mouth found her mouth. They clung together, generating heat from anticipation. His fingers searched down the length of her back, like a primordial brain sliding over muscle, around the curve of her ass, and found access in the feathery folds.

She felt him spread through her in strange, illogical ways—into arms and legs, to fingers and toes. Each time she stiffened his hold tightened. His body formed around her until she was wrapped in a dense cocoon of muscle and bone.

He felt himself atomized into a million particles and drift away, intangible as mist in air.

---

It was so black a night that neither Lloyd nor Earl could find the difference between the mountains and the sky. At some point in the blackscape there were stars. There was a warm wind blowing from the west. It was the wind, a pint of Glen Geery, and several beers that gave Lloyd the idea to open all the valves on Tidyman's big tanks, spilling fuel oil and gasoline into the lake. The impulse on both their parts, like a pair of school-boys, was to see a big fire on the water.

Perhaps, because he was the more mechanical of the two, Earl's vision of the fire spread farther west into the darkness, through the pilings, out to open water. Late in the afternoon, he had seen Cody and Rose moving the barge back into the lake. It was a reasonable guess that they would anchor near the pilings. Not wanting Lloyd to change his mind, Earl said nothing about his extended vision.

Earl had a clear understanding of good and bad. He had served in Army Intelligence in France after the war ended. His good works included a black market trade in coffee, and the punishment of several Nazi sympathiz-ers, including a girl who had fallen in love with a German soldier. Earl and several others had poured gasoline in her hair and set her head on fire. War was hell, he liked to say, though he had never actually been in the war. Earl's closest friends knew the story because he told it when he was extremely drunk. They mistook his admission for guilt. But Earl had a hunger for vengeance. Like a dog in the corner pretending to sleep, he was waiting for his chance, and his chance had come.

Tidyman's father had started padlocking the tanks during the war-time rationing, when kids were stealing gas. Tidyman had kept the locks, but Earl came prepared. He fished the bolt cutter out of a toolbox in the back of his pickup. He and Lloyd started down the road in the dark. Of the two, Lloyd was quite a bit drunker. He would giggle to himself for several steps, imagining the flames spreading across the water, then he would whisper, *"Whoosh,"* and start giggling again. *"Whoosh, whoosh."* The warm wind muffled their *whooshes*, giggles, and stumbles, rolling the sounds over and over in the soft air.

They moved down the hill to the tanks, feeling along the base of the first one until they came to the valve wheel and the chain padlocked through its spokes. Lloyd held the chain away from the wheel, isolating the tank from the snap of Earl's bolt cutter.

Lloyd lunged his way from tank to tank, barely staying ahead of the spill, until they had let loose fifty-two hundred gallons of gasoline, diesel fuel, and heating oil. A few hundred gallons pooled on the ground and soaked in. The rest gushed down the bank, over the new retaining wall, and into the lake.

The two men ran back to Earl's pickup and drove east on the highway to the cafe. They parked in back by the flat rock and waited in the dark until the smell of fuel was so strong they figured the slick had made its way into the pilings. Earl got out of the truck.

"Let's try it," he whispered.

---

The restless air woke Rose in the dark. She lay still, her eyes closed as the day's images swam through her mind—strained cables, screeching clutch, Cody's shape gliding underwater. She turned on her side and reached her hand toward him, finding his shoulder. Her fingers traced his shape in the darkness, seeking her favorite curves and matching form to memory. She reached down and stroked him until he was hard and thick and filled her mouth.

The salty cream made her body ready. She came when his hand touched her shoulder. She spread her legs, mounted him, and pressed herself into his chest, sliding forward against the roughness of his neck and chin.

He sucked her into his mouth, his tongue licking out. The sensation became too intense. She tried to pull free, but he held her against him. His mouth sucked and released. She bucked and rolled away. He rolled with her.

Then he was on top, sliding forward and into her, deeper and deeper. Deeper than possible.

---

Earl tied a flour sack soaked in gasoline around a rock the size of his fist, then, poised like a discus thrower, he waited for Lloyd to get his cigarette lighter working. There were several flicks before Earl heard a low wump and saw the sack flare.

He hesitated. The wind had become erratic.

Lloyd shouted, "Throw it, throw it."

Earl spun and heaved. He watched the flaming sack arc into the night. For an instant Earl imagined he saw a flash of light in the lake and flames racing toward them, across the black water. It was an unsettling illusion.

He turned in time to see Lloyd's bright, happy face in the first moment before the blast hit. There was no *wump*—none that Lloyd or Earl could hear. The concussion blew them off their feet and knocked Earl unconscious.

The fire paused in the air above them—seething and confused, hungry for oxygen—then was sucked back toward the lake. Like bright angels, random licks of flame flew overhead. To Lloyd it seemed a miracle he was untouched by the flames. He struggled to stand up and discovered his hands were pressing against the back wall of the cafe.

He heard a deep roar as the fire rolled down the shore toward town. At the same time, the flames spread through the pilings and beyond, illuminating the barge. Lloyd had not expected the barge. It had been moored west of Tidyman's earlier in the day.

"What the hell?" he shouted.

He could not believe what was about to happen. The intense heat made the cafe wall seem cold. The cold seeped off the wall into his hands and moved up his arms to his neck. He saw the flames erupt over the barge as the cold reached his brain.

---

The sensation moved up through her belly into her chest and neck, into her head. She closed her mouth, forcing the eruption into her brain through the top of her skull. Sparks shot out across the deck and over the water.

Rose was lifted off the deck with Cody and thrown through the air, illuminated from behind by the bright, screeching air. A dark shape rose up and drew them into the water—as though death had pulled them down into the lake.

There was no pain. She was treading water, holding Cody's head free as he regained consciousness. She realized the dark shape that met them at the water was only their shadow cast from the fire. For a moment, she believed reason could explain everything.

They stayed in the water and watched the fire burn along the shore and into the pilings. Long tongues of flame rolled over the lake toward the barge, reaching out along the ramps and the edge of the front deck, until a wall of flame pressed in from three sides. The fire kept moving, licking the air, feeling its way over the surface toward them.

She pulled him toward the barge and clung to the ladder, waiting for his strength to return. The burning oil reached the back corner and turned, forcing them up onto the deck. They scrambled away from the edge and lay flat, watching the flames and listening to the roar.

Cody seemed hypnotized by the fire, until Rose touched him.

"Hi, sweet cakes," she said. "Are you here?"

His head felt thick. "What happened?"

His first thought was that diesel fuel had ignited and

leaked from the barge into the water. He sat up and saw the fire on the shore. It had ripped straight up Tidyman's retaining wall, over the bank, and ignited the standing pools of oil around the warehouse.

"We better get this thing out of here," she said. She tried to stand, but the searing heat dropped her to her knees. "Oh, Christ, Cody, this is bad."

He was too dazed to do anything. She got him face-down on the deck and crawled back to the pilothouse alone. She started the Daimler, grabbed the hatchet, and crawled out to cut the anchor line.

He saw her silhouette against the flames, bringing the hatchet down. The line snapped. He felt the barge lurch as she cut them free.

L LOYD REALIZED EARL WAS UNCONSCIOUS. IT SEEMED like a good idea—just fade away and everything would be normal tomorrow. He took Earl by the arms, dragged him to the truck, and pulled him up into the back.

Lloyd drove east, away from town. Several miles later he turned onto a dirt road that took them past fields of corn and looped through the low hills south of the lake and back toward town.

By the time they got home, Earl had partially regained consciousness in the back of the pickup. He watched the bright glow north of town. A single question occupied his awareness. Throw what? Throw what? His jellied brain stayed poised on the very edge of an answer that would never come. He did not remember setting the fire or that he had wanted to see a burning barge. He had missed his show.

The fire was burning the lakeshore between Ogeen's cafe and the city dock. Several businesses were completely gone and the air was punctuated by random explosions.

The town was abuzz with saving itself. The sirens' wail seemed to lift the flames even higher. Small squads of volunteers shot down the streets, as eager to fulfill their obligations to town and species as sperm pursuing an egg. Only here, beneath the red night sky, the collective impulse was to save the property and lives of others. For many, life's petty grievances, even the need for personal safety, seemed forgotten.

Amid the licking flames other less heroic, though equally necessary, motives were realized. New alliances were formed, promises made, and money, materials, and rezoning schemes discussed. What would be billed a tragedy in Friday's *Weekly Laker* was, for the quick few, more akin to carrion for crows.

It was early in the morning and still dark when Earl's wife found him sitting in the bathtub. She had heard him an hour before, and had lain awake waiting for him to come to bed. She wanted to know about the explosion and the fire.

His body was red from scrubbing. "I'm cleanin' up," he said. "Close the damn door."

She had seen him drunk and out of control before, but nothing as strange as this. She closed the bathroom door and went outside. She could make out clouds of smoke against the dark sky. Smoke was all that was left of Earl's fire.

———————

As soon as the fire was out around the fuel tanks, the sheriff confirmed what was on everyone's mind—it was arson. Fantastical speculations about who and why jumped around town for days. Flying saucers and Communists had already been mentioned.

By daybreak, Tidyman had talked to half the town. He wanted to know how things were going to play out. The town would have to go after someone. Of course, the county attorney would investigate the possibility of an insurance job. Tidyman did not expect that to be a problem for him. The investigation would show he would have come out better selling the business than by burning it down. His greatest concern was for Cody, whose name kept coming up throughout the night. Unless an obvious culprit appeared, Cody would become the designated villain.

---

The sun was rising when Tidyman spotted the barge far up the lake. He went out in a slender, twelve-foot, wood boat he used for fishing. Its old flat-top motor ran unusually quiet for an outboard. He zigzagged around several slicks of unburned oil that drifted north. He moved into open water, away from town and the charred remains of his livelihood.

He was nearly to the barge before Cody and Rose heard him coming. They were still horizontal, struggling into their clothes when he came alongside. He cut the engine and floated just off the end of the barge.

Rose walked to the edge and looked down at him. "You okay?" she said.

"Yeah." Tidyman laughed. "Father was big on insurance. What about you?"

"We got out. Didn't lose your barge."

Cody took his time getting up. He walked over and stood next to Rose. "Good morning. What happened back there?"

"Somebody cut the locks on the fuel tanks, spilled about five thousand gallons into the lake, and set it on fire."

"Somebody, who?" Cody asked.

"Right now they don't have anyone to pin it on. I think they'll try to make a case against you."

Rose looked at Cody and back to Tidyman. Her voice was low and calm. "That's nuts. We were nearly killed. Why would we set a fire while we were in the middle of it? How can they make a case?"

Tidyman was irritated and impatient. "They can make any goddamn case they want. You know that."

"No," she said. "I meant what kind of a case? What will they say?"

"Someone said Cody was tryin' to burn Ogeen out. The fire got his marina and damaged the cafe."

"And what about me?" Rose asked.

"They'll go after Cody. They don't care about you. This is about him."

She knew he was right. The townies had done some nasty things to the Indians over the years and always gotten away with it. In their eyes, Cody was worse than any Indian.

She watched Tidyman sitting in the little boat without his usual cigar. He looked naked somehow, almost innocent.

Cody seemed indifferent to what was being said. He

was crossing over into that secret landscape that lay beneath his paintings. He looked at Rose and smiled, knowing she would always find him.

She had her arm around Cody, holding on as much as holding him. Rose sensed the news that he was in serious trouble had no effect on him. She felt the pull of his serenity.

"They don't have a case with me," said Tidyman. "They can only spread rumors, but they'll go after Cody." He paused and looked back at the smoldering shoreline and the charred remains of what he had always considered his father's business.

"I need to talk to a couple of people," he said, "and I have to arrange a few things of my own. It'll take a while. Try the house. All right?"

"Yes," said Rose. "We'll find you."

The compact poet hunched down in the boat and twisted the throttle on the outboard. He powered away through the water, the hull nosed up, engine wound out, leaving a deep wake.

He was free and Algeria was waiting. There was nothing to keep him. Whoever torched his father's oil depot had done Tidyman a favor. He was no longer required to be the good son.

Rose watched him cut through the water. Cody had told her Tidyman had played the cello and wrote poetry. It pleased her that he could do those things and smell of fuel oil, too.

Rose started the Daimler and headed in. For the first time the relentless pounding of the engine annoyed her.

The sound that would feed them, that drew them across the lake, that kept time to their passion, that saved them from burning, was returning them to the treacherous world.

The sure gestures and tones of the legal bureaucracy were death music to the Red Crows. The courts and the police had damaged Gerome with their slow fire of words. Cody, she felt, could expect the same. He had violated too many of the town's unwritten rules. The price of being part of a community, Indian or white, was the social effort required to keep people from believing their own nasty gossip.

———————

The sheriff got out of his car, adjusted his hat, and started down the dock to meet the barge.

As they pulled in, Cody stepped onto the dock and tied off the lines. "Hello, Sheriff." His tone was direct and matter-of-fact. "Are we under arrest?"

The sheriff shook his head. "No, but I want both of you to come down for some questions."

Rose knew they were making trouble when she saw Cody smile. He made her feel gleeful and crazy.

The sheriff noticed the light flash in Rose's eyes. It disturbed him enough that he checked to be sure her hands were empty when she got in the car. She was surprised he was so keen.

Cody and Rose held hands in the backseat, gazing out at the summer day and the people along the road who watched them go by. Smoke and the acrid odor of burning creosote drifted across the highway.

Groups of kids, men and women in twos and threes,

and whole families lined out along the edge of the blacktop. They walked east, surveying the damage and talking.
The talk stopped and heads turned as the car moved past
them, leaving a wave of stunned silence, followed by a
backwash of gasps and pointing, glances and whispers—
an elongated dance of assumptions.

The sheriff's office and the jail were part of the three-
story courthouse, which had been built in the 1800s to
withstand a siege by heathens. In an act of perfect sym-
metry, the county used Indian inmates from the state
prison as laborers. The stone for the walls came from the
prison's soft-rock quarry and provided the inmates with
an obliging surface on which to record their feelings
toward the white man.

Only the hidden facets of the stones were marked by
the natives' pictographs. The exposed surfaces, cut clean
and smooth, hid evidence of the attack from within.

If you were Indian, the courthouse was the white man's
most dominant structure, the one in which you might
expect a lengthy stay, or your life to end. It came to be
known as the house of the weeping walls. Some believed
the souls of the Indian slaves lived in the stones. That the
wall in the jail seeped salty tears was evidence enough.

Rose went first. Bardenoux, the county attorney, a
tall, handsome politician, asked her to tell her version of
events of the night before. There was little to tell and
she told it.

The sheriff watched Bardenoux, rather than look at
Rose. She knew then that Tidyman was right. They
would try to railroad Cody. The county attorney was

particularly interested in establishing the fact that Rose could not prove where Cody was when the fire started.

"He was with me," was all she could say.

"Where, with you?"

"We were on the barge."

"Where was the barge?"

"We anchored by the mill pilings, below the cafe."

"What were you doing?"

"We were asleep," she lied. "It was two o'clock in the morning."

"He was sleeping next to you?"

"Yes."

"On the deck of the barge?"

"Yes."

"Are you married to this man?"

"No."

"You are not married to this man?"

"No."

"You are not married to this man, yet you were sleeping next to him on an open deck in public view?"

"It was dark."

"Do you know that people, people who are good citizens, know you are living like this?"

"Is that what this is about?"

"Did you have sex on the deck of this barge?"

"Yes. We had sex on the deck. What does sex on the deck have to do with the fire?"

"You do not have the right to ask questions."

"I can't ask questions?"

"You are unfit to ask questions."

Her leg twitched. She thought *unfit* was a strange thing for him to say. Unfit, unfit, unfit, unfit. The word became meaningless. The parts of the attorney's face seemed badly connected. She leaned forward and whispered, "You do not have the right to ask such questions. It is a matter between a man and a woman."

"I have no further questions," said Bardenoux.

The sheriff stared out the window away from Rose. He imagined her on the barge, in the flames, naked, reaching up for Cody, her lips on his lips. The fire came from their touch. Together they were the fire.

Rose stood and walked to the door. The afternoon sun threw a sharp, bright light across her white shirt, leaving her face in the shadow of the room. Her disembodied voice was controlled and sure. "We were not asleep when the fire started. We were making love. You should arrest us for arson."

———

Cody was standing on the lawn of the courthouse, watching several crows maneuver for the highest position on the branches of a tall cottonwood tree. He smiled when he saw Rose.

"They wanted to know if we had sex on the deck," she said.

"You told them?"

"Yes. I told them we started the fire."

"Now you're bragging," he said. "That's not like you." He gave her a crooked little smile and went on watching the crows.

"Are you frightened?" she asked.

"No. I feel like I'm standing outside myself, watching things happen. I should be frightened. I don't know about legal things, and I'm not a laker. What about you?"

"Whoever dumped all that fuel into the lake and put a match to it is very stupid and mean or very crazy. It's the kind of thing one of Ogeen's moron buddies would think up."

As they talked, a tall, elderly man carrying a leather satchel walked across the lawn toward them. He had a large face and reddish eyes.

"Hello, Mr. Stanley," said Rose. "Are you here to save us?"

He spoke slowly, almost in a whisper. "I gather you and your friend here need savin', Miss Rose. Mr. Tidyman asked me to speak to the county attorney on your behalf. With your permission, of course." He extended a hand to Cody. "Handel Stanley, poet, farmer, and attorney at law."

The attorney's hard hand belonged to the farmer, not the poet.

"Cody Hayes." Cody glanced down at the massive wrist and the thick fingers that grasped his hand. Evidently, his amusement showed.

"Nothing is as it seems, is it, Mr. Hayes?"

Cody smiled. "I guess that depends on what you're looking for."

"As a practical matter," said Handel, "I would like to speculate on who might have started this fire and why. Mr. Tidyman has assured me that neither of you did it. That leaves the rest of the town as suspects."

"We don't fit in this town," said Rose. "That won't make your job any easier."

"Why and who?" asked Handel.

"I'd guess it was some drunken laker's idea of a prank."

"Anyone in particular come to mind?"

"Yeah," said Rose, "about a quarter of the male population."

The sheriff came out of the house of the weeping walls and walked toward them at full stride. "This your lawyer?" he asked.

Handel acknowledged Joe's authority with a short, "Shrff."

"The county attorney wants to ask you some questions," the sheriff said to Cody. He nodded to Handel. "He's allowed in, if you want."

Cody was intrigued by how much these two men were alike, despite their physical differences, as though one had created the other. He wanted to paint them, just as they were on the lawn, under the sun, with the crows dividing the air above them.

"I'll wait out here," said Rose. She watched Cody, the sheriff, and Handel cross the lawn and disappear into the courthouse. The sense of dread that caught in her chest was what the Red Crows called bad feathers.

"Mr. Hayes," the county attorney said and nodded to Cody. "I'm Bardenoux." He gestured to some chairs and turned away toward the window.

"That half-breed woman is talkin' to those goddamned crows," he growled, then he looked around at the three men who had seated themselves near his desk. "Takes all kinds, doesn't it, Mr. Hayes?"

Cody smiled and looked up at the county attorney. "I can think of one kind I don't need any part of at all," he said.

"And who would that be, Mr. Hayes?"

Handel cleared his throat as he came forward in his chair. "That would be the crazy bastard who set that fire last night," he said.

"Him too," said Cody.

Bardenoux sat down and leaned back in his chair. "So, I hear you paint pictures."

"Yeah, some."

"Not much of a livin' in that. How do you feed your-self?"

"I'm a saw filer and I contract various jobs. I built a retaining wall for Tidyman recently."

"I heard." Bardenoux laughed. "Damn near sunk his barge." He eyed Cody. "You realize that I can charge you with arson?"

"You can do a lot of things, Mr. Bardenoux, but that wasn't my fire."

"I've heard about your fire, Mr. Hayes. Some folks are more upset about that than the fact that half the town burned down."

"Is that so?"

"It is so, Mr. Hayes. As I'm sure you will find out."

---

Ogeen had not been able to reach Earl or Lloyd. He suspected they were busy with their fears. When no one answered at Earl's, Ogeen drove through town and down the highway, past the burned-out motel to his cafe. He stood in back and studied the blackened bunchgrass and the partially burned siding.

He knew from the gossip that the fire had started as

far east as the cafe, spread west along the shoreline, and ignited Tidyman's fuel tanks. A woman on the west shore across the lake from the cafe had been awakened by the initial explosion. She saw the barge, illuminated by the fire, escape into the blackness of the open lake.

Ogeen reached down for a piece of steel lying on the ground between clumps of grass and picked up Lloyd's Zippo lighter. The top was still flipped back—an open mouth screaming, Here I am. Initials and all.

---

The next morning the sheriff discovered a bolt cutter in the hold of the barge, made some experimental cuts with it, and determined it made marks similar to the marks left on Tidyman's locks. The bolt cutter, he was willing to testify, was the same.

It was feeble evidence as far as Bardenoux was concerned. The bolt cutter was probably planted, but its presence complicated his life. The town would be hungry to get Cody. Word would have spread, raising expectations for a trial. But if he took Cody to trial, the chances of a conviction were not good once Handel got his hands on a jury. The other possibility was to leave things open, not to press charges, and to wait for someone else to turn up. Either way, it was likely to cost him the November election. His best hope was that Cody would make a run for it.

None of this had anything to do with the fact that he believed Cody was innocent of arson or that Rose was a slut. Pragmatism came before innocence or guilt.

---

Handel Stanley drove out to the cafe to see what Ogeen knew about the fire. He walked past the counter into the back room and found Ogeen at his desk.

"Hello, Billy."

"Good morning, Mr. Stanley. Let me get you a cup of coffee."

Ogeen got Handel his coffee and came back. "I hear you've taken on the drifter," he said. "You got ahold of a bad one this time. The man lives in a truck, for God's sake. He has sex with that Indian girl in plain view. Plus, he's some kind of artist. There's something wrong in the head about him."

Handel nodded. He realized what Ogeen had said was the solution to everyone's problem. "You might have something there, Billy. Thanks for the coffee."

He drove east down the highway toward the Red Crows' shacks to talk with Cody and Rose. He was concerned about finding a favorable jury in the storm of suspicion and gossip. At the same time, he had an intuitive grasp of the county attorney's dilemma. Slowing things down seemed a good idea.

Even though Cody was seen as trouble by a significant number of townspeople, he was a white man. Handel knew he could delay the trial by requesting a psychiatric evaluation at the Springhill Asylum.

Handel found Cody and Rose by the lake, watching the crows search for bugs among the stones. He eased himself down on a log, placed his large, calloused hands on his knees, and studied the crows.

"I don't like the idea of a trial anytime soon," said

Handel. "It might not even be necessary. Suppose we get the county to send you up to Springhill to undergo an evaluation for a few weeks. It might keep them from charging you with anything. I don't think the county attorney wants to try you—too much of a risk."

A small, tight knot formed in Rose's stomach. "I don't want Cody locked up anywhere. I'd rather be on the run with him. After what they did to us about the dock, I don't trust them."

Handel shook his head. "No. The deal with the dock wasn't the asylum's doing. That was the court. The asylum only filed the initial complaint. You can't blame them for that."

"Springhill might be the best thing," said Cody. "It's only an evaluation—give things a chance to die down. We can always change our minds."

"Rose, the only practical proposition is for Cody to go to the asylum," said Handel. "It's a swanky place. You can visit him when you like. Think of it as a vacation." Handel smiled at Cody. "He can paint those pictures of his."

"If you want, Cody," she said. "But I don't like it."

Handel could see he had worn his welcome thin. "Why don't you two discuss this and let me know how you want to proceed?" He shook Cody's hand, nodded to Rose, and went back to town.

———————

Two days later, Rose was sitting in the stock truck, watching Cody go through a box he had packed for the asylum.

"Linseed oil, turps, pigments, jars, rags, brushes, a dozen boards. Being on the run would be harder to take than a few weeks in the nuthouse," he said without looking up. He was going through his brush jars for the third time. "I should only take three brushes—don't need that much turps." He could feel his heart pounding. "Here's a sweater you should have." He looked at her and smiled. "Do you think they'd give me a pair of those white pants?"

She looked away, out into the blackberries and the fugitive cars. "It doesn't feel good to me, Cody. Too much can go wrong."

"If it goes wrong, we'll see it coming. This gives us time to plan something. Yes?"

His dark shape moving through the dim light aroused her. "Yes," she said. "Of course, yes. I just don't want you to leave. I don't want you to go away. Not now."

He had become a part of her. She carried him around inside—feeling his muscles and skin inside her body. She slid her arms around his waist and pressed into him until he got the idea. The sex was quick and desperate.

A slow ache moved down her thighs. Then the sound of rain began spreading through her body, growing louder and louder. The sound stopped. She heard a car door, then the sheriff's voice calling for Cody.

"Not yet," she said.

He kissed her. Then he was gone.

## LATE SUNDAY
## NIGHT

$T$he fire smoldered through the night, long after Ana
and Liz had gone to sleep. The smoke rose and billowed
above the house in the early morning darkness, drifting
toward the condos south of the orchard. The acrid odor
of magazine ink seeped through the summer screens.

Henry Red Crows pulled on his khaki shorts, slipped
his feet into sandals, and called 911 as he ran downstairs
to his van. Five minutes later, the fire siren woke the boys.
They were dressed and coming down the stairs before the
truck passed the driveway. They ran down the road,
shouting for the firemen to give them a ride to no avail.
Far off in the darkness, they saw their father in the flicker
of revolving lights wave the truck onto the narrow road
that circled around to the front of Ana Hanson's house.
He jumped on the running board as it rumbled past.

The black smoke could be seen against the early morning sky, rolling over the house and up the road toward the condos. Soon the road was lined with the sleepy curious, their children, and happy dogs, coming to see Ana Hanson's derelict house burn to the ground. Some were disappointed, others relieved, to find the firemen dousing a smoldering mound seventy feet from the house.

Ana in her robe and Liz in sweats stood in the newly spacious living room and watched the drama developing on the lawn outside. Dark shapes of men in fire hats and slickers danced their heroic deeds against the metallic light off the lake.

"It looks like a play," said Liz.

"Yes." Ana chuckled. "And I never know if it's a tragedy or a comedy. Would you like some killer coffee?"

"Sure. Could you add a little more water to mine, please?"

Ana laughed and padded off to the kitchen. Liz waited in the dark and watched the heroic gestures of the fire fighters on the lawn. The high-pitched whine of the pump truck and the flashing lights added an aura of frenzy to the many men and machines focused on the smoldering pile of old magazines. Their oversized costumes went well with their oversized effort.

"Thanks," said Liz when Ana returned with their coffee. "It's definitely slapstick out there."

"I know. We live in a time when people who try to be heroes end up looking ridiculous."

"This time's different than any other?"

"The emphasis is different," said Ana. "The old myths

were always about how to survive. That was their morality. I think there's something else now—an unstated desire to find grace as we go to our fate. We want more than just survival."

"Grace? I always thought it was about finding love."

"Yes, but love is a path to grace. Love is the last best place for our rapture."

"You don't think falling in love is a mistake?"

"You risk drowning, of course. But when I was full of youthful enthusiasm, I didn't question whether or not to fall in love. Later, there were times when I decided to avoid it."

"You actually made a choice?"

"I didn't follow through when I knew where my fantasies were leading me. Sometimes I wondered what would have happened. But I had my share of lovers."

"I want to be in love again," said Liz. "I want to feel like that again."

"There's nothing quite like it, is there?" For a moment Ana saw something in Liz's expression she recognized in herself—a longing so deep, it bordered on despair.

"But love requires you to lose yourself," said Ana. "You were always one to put things in order. It didn't surprise me that you became a statistician."

"Numbers were my default mode, Gramma. I could control them. Nothing else stood still long enough to make sense."

"Including men?"

"Yes."

Ana smiled. "You wanted a man who made sense?"

Rose stopped Gretchen on the side of the road below Tidyman's house. She was still practicing the timing to double clutch the transmission. Grinding gears the first thing in the morning seemed rude.

It had rained during the night. The sun streaming through the cool, dense air made anything seem possible. Tidyman came down the steps carrying a red briefcase in one hand and a large suitcase in the other. Rose slid over to let him drive. He put the suitcase in the back and got in.

"Good morning, Rose." He started the truck and gently shifted through the gears, picking up speed through the leaf-laced sun on the rain-black road.

"I'm getting out of the country," he said. "I'm going to a place where I can see through the everyday crap."

"Where?"

"Algiers."

"Algiers? Where's that?"

"North Africa."

"Long trip."

"Yeah."

"What will you do?"

"Write poetry. That's what I used to do."

"I heard you played the cello too."

"Yeah, that too," he said in a distracted way. It was obvious he did not want to talk. He drove into town and parked a block from the bus depot.

A life of poetry? She glanced over to see if he was serious or teasing. He was watching the bus down the street. Six passengers were in line, waiting for the driver to finish his coffee.

He tapped his fingers on the red leather case on his lap and stared straight ahead. He was a mysterious package of a man.

"Well," she said, "send me a poem."

"I'll do that. Definitely."

"Thank you for all your help," she said.

He drew an envelope from the inside pocket of his jacket and handed it to her.

"Open it later." He gave a dismissive little wave. "I want Gerome to have Gretchen. There's a title and a bill of sale, and something for you."

"How did you know Gerome would want Gretchen?"

"I saw him driving her once. He was smiling—like a kid. He never smiles." Tidyman paused. "I guess we all are."

"Are what?" she asked.

"Kids. Some of us are mean kids and some aren't so bad." He got out and closed the door. "I'll write."

He grabbed his suitcase from the back and walked toward the bus. He did not turn or wave. In his own mind he was already gone.

She watched the bus pull out. She waved to the pale windows and the reflected sky. Diesel exhaust blew into the truck, replacing the last trace of cigar smoke.

The envelope was fairly thick. The unsealed flap made his generosity seem casual and easy. Inside she found Gretchen's title for Gerome. Wrapped in a plain piece of paper was a stack of crisp new bills and another title in the name of Rose Red Crows. The money gave her a jolt. The title description made her laugh: the southwest quarter of the southwest quarter of the northeast quarter of section twenty-one and the southeast quarter of the southeast quarter of the northwest quarter of section twenty-two, township four south, range one west, including all improvements. There were no drawings. She had no idea what or where it was. Maybe it was the deed to all that twisted metal that had tied him down—Tidyman's crazy idea of a poetic joke.

She left the truck, walked the three blocks to the courthouse, and asked the keeper of records for the appropriate plans. Her property was easy to locate, because the lake and the highway were drawn in. The two sections were part of the lakefront, directly east of the Red Crows' place. The leather-bound record of deeds showed Tidyman's parents had owned the property before him.

Rose realized he had grown up next door to her. The

hungry ghost in the orchard of her childhood had been a cello.

———✦———

The asylum, by its design and landscaping, bent life as effortlessly as water bends the light. Its several buildings were constructed in 1886 by Andrew J. Bering. The labor of small, yellow-skinned men and the leverage of large engines and steel rails made Bering his great fortune, a small portion of which he spent building a mansion he called Montana Dream. Granite, cut from a Canadian quarry, was the primary material used in the construction of the three-story Main Hall. Secret, narrow stairs allowed the servants to move freely through the house without ever being seen on the grand marble stairways. Two dumbwaiters thrust massive quantities of elk, moose, goose, and native trout up through the walls to the dining room on the top floor, where dignitaries from England, Denmark, Bavaria, and Norway could enjoy the view. The French and Italians were too degenerate for Bering's taste. It was a grand time for a grand man.

He bred draft horses, sheep, and milking cows, and raised hay and corn to feed them. The hay was stacked like loaves in the field. For the corn, he built a granite-walled silo, forty feet high and twenty feet in diameter. He built a dormitory and a cluster of little houses for his workers, and a substantial guest house. A total of fifteen buildings, including the Main Hall, three stables, a dairy barn, the dormitory, the cluster houses, the guest house, a large greenhouse, and a shop and smithy, were heated by a coal-fired steam plant.

The pre-presidential Teddy Roosevelt stayed three

nights in the west wing in the fall of 1893. He killed a bear, a wolf, three moose, and forty-five Canada geese. On a photograph in the director's office, one carefully lettered caption read: BEAR, WOLF, THEODORE ROOSEVELT.

After Bering's two disturbed sons committed suicide in 1924, he turned Montana Dream into an asylum for the insane. The board of directors renamed it Springhill Asylum. They kept the cornfields, the silo, and the large black-and-white milk cows. Eventually, as a courtesy to the locals, they built an eight-foot-high chain-link fence around it, and renamed it the Springhill Dairy.

---

"Doctor Richards is away for the next four days," the receiving man said.

The sheriff looked through the ornate ironwork that separated him from the asylum official. The sheriff had no experience with the rules at Springhill. He had a delivery to make and expected some cooperation.

"Dr. Ross will be entering the patient. Please take a seat in the vestibule." *Vestibule* seemed to hang in the air.

Cody studied the high arched beams above the leaded windows and the quarter rounds of stained glass.

"I see architecture's done its job," he said. "Has a whiff of God about it, doesn't it?" Cody smiled at the sheriff, who ignored him.

The receiving man pointed down the hall. "Chairs over there."

Cody set his duffel bag by the windows. He stood, looking out at the lawn that rolled down to the sun's hot reflection off the water. Far in the distance the south shore blurred with the sky. The Red Crows shacks were invisible. Rose was invisible.

A thin man in a white coat appeared, introduced himself to the sheriff, and signed the release. After the sheriff left, the man walked over to Cody and extended his hand.

"Welcome to Springhill, Mr. Hayes, I'm Dr. Ross." The doctor had a small, angelic smile that conflicted with his official tone. "I understand you're here for an evaluation. If you will get your things and follow me, we can get started."

He led Cody up the marble stairs to an office on the third floor of the west wing, where he began the formal entry registration.

"What have you brought?" he asked, gesturing to the pasteboard box and the duffel bag.

"Just some clothes and my paints."

"A painter? Very good. Well, you will be allowed to paint," the doctor said with a charitable nod. "However, you will have to give up your boots for hospital slippers."

Then the questions began: date of birth, place of birth, parents living, parents not living, abnormalities physical, abnormalities mental? Family psychiatric profile, history of aggression, antisocial behaviors, sexual abnormalities?

The questions continued until it was time for dinner. Dr. Ross looked at the clock on the wall behind Cody, flashed his beatific smile, and bobbed his head.

"It's nearly dinnertime for you," he announced and began organizing his papers. "You will have more leeway than most patients, Mr. Hayes, as you are only here for an evaluation. However, there are house rules which everyone must obey. The ward nurse will be going over them with you."

———

Gudrin, the ward nurse, presided over the table where Cody was seated with six other inmates. She had a way of looking soft and strong, which allowed her to give comfort and maintain authority at the same time. A faint scar ran across her cheek from her nose to her ear. She dyed her hair black and cut it extremely short. "Less to grab hold of," she explained.

Gudrin was inventive. She made up a game for the inmates to play on Sunday afternoons. Each person told three stories, two real and one made up. After an inmate told his stories, the others tried to guess which was the lie.

"For some inmates it's progress if they start lying," she said. "I can always guess the lie when I play with normal people. It's harder in here. Most don't know their realities from their fantasies. But the psychopaths are great."

"What are psychopaths?" Cody asked.

"No conscience. They're great liars. The ones who can fake empathy make real good politicians. They'll be what *you* want, to get what *they* want." Gudrin laughed and flashed her eyebrows. "Real survivors."

———

After dinner she showed him to a small plain room. He stood in the middle of the room next to the white iron bed. His eyes traveled from the door, which bolted on the outside, across the barren room to the window. There were bars on the window.

Even in the dim light from the ceiling fixture, Gudrin could see the changes in his neck and shoulders, and the muscles around his eyes.

It was already dark. On the lawn below, electric lamps lit the walkway and the stone walls. In the distance, a single light reflected on the water. Far across the lake, he imagined Rose's sleeping shape suspended above the floating bed in the white church of Catherine.

Cody stayed at the window with his back to the nurse. He raised his hand to his eyes and blanked out the glow from the lawn lights. He could see the shoreline at the bottom of the hill. "Are you going to lock me in this room?" he asked, without turning around.

"Yes. We have to, until your evaluation. We can't take chances. The night staff is very small."

"How small are they?" he asked. His voice was flat.

Gudrin laughed. "Good night," she said. "See you for breakfast. Seven o'clock."

Her *o'clock* tumbled through his thoughts. It seemed like an ugly, meaningless word. The door shut and she slipped the bolt. "Good night," he said.

Somewhere outside in the maze of stone walls, a voice answered, "Good night."

———

In the morning, Cody stood at the window pretending he could see the south shore and Rose walking along the beach. Up and down the hallway the attendants were snapping door bolts back and calling out, "Breakfast." The thought of the dining hall overcame his hunger.

When it was quiet again, he picked up his paint box and a board. He walked downstairs and outside. He crossed the lawn to a stone wall, below and to the west of the main house. The wall marched from the power-house near the top of the hill down almost to the lake. It was divided by three brick walkways; halfway down the hill it intercepted another wall.

Cody chose this corner of walls for his studio. He climbed over the wall and set his board against the corner capstone. He opened his paints and began.

His hands were calloused and thick from work. At first they refused to move properly. After a while the necessary sensations came back to his fingers, and he stopped thinking about every stroke of the brush.

He painted and watched. Thoughts of Rose stayed with him through the morning. He could feel the press of her skin as the lake pressed against the sky.

At first he was left alone. He painted the sun and the lake against a black background. The lake had a bright blue surface and reflected the sun. Beneath the surface the blue became darker and darker until it was absorbed into the darkness that surrounded the sun and the lake. Where the blue turned black, Cody painted serpent's scales.

He stood on the steep lawn looking down over the other inmates and men in white pants. The angle of the hillside, the way the land dropped away below and the lake fanned out toward the horizon, made him feel like a giant. At first he was elated by the illusion of his great size, feeling its power and invincibility.

Gradually, the inmates began to converge from all directions following along the stone walls to the corner, to Cody. They maneuvered around to see what he was painting.

One man with a long, pale face sounded surprised. "That's not the lake. Nothing out there like that. Nothing."

"It's bad," said one of the men.

"It's symbolic, John."

"It's the underneath part," said another.

"Too smooth. There's no jags or lumps. Where's the caves?"

By the tone of their voices, they knew what they were talking about. Cody did not seem to exist for them. At first, they would not speak to him directly.

One of the men looked at Cody's feet, then at the painting and back to his feet. "A dream?" asked the man. This voice, unlike the others, was tentative and fragile. "Is it a dream?"

"Yes," said Cody.

They looked at him.

"I have dreams," whispered the man. "Terrible dreams."

Cody waited for the man to tell his dreams. The other inmates, as though given a signal, began to crawl over the wall and walk away, trailing along in random file toward Main Hall. The man of terrible dreams crawled over the wall and followed them. Several inmates and white pants men walked up the hill from the lakeshore.

Judging from the sun, Cody realized the defection was prompted by lunchtime. It seemed as though he had only been painting for a few minutes. He cleaned his hands, put his paints away, and climbed over the wall. As he dropped down on the other side, he looked back and saw something moving through the sagebrush just beyond the chain-link fence to the west. He thought he saw a boy jump into the ground. Cody stood for several seconds and watched the spot beyond the fence. Three more boys came running through the brush, stopped briefly, talked, pointed toward the lake, and ran off. The first boy reemerged from his hiding place and watched the others in the distance, running along the shoreline.

A loud, rasping buzz blared from Main Hall to announce feeding time. The boy turned to stare at Cody. He hesitated, looking over his shoulder to see if the other boys had spotted him, then waved to Cody and disappeared into the ground.

Cody waved, but the boy was gone.

———

Sally's husband, Joseph, did not speak to white people, so Sally was sent to tell Rose that she should be thinking about leaving the Red Crows.

"Joseph says you will bring the Red Crows bad luck if you stay here," said Sally. She did not believe this, nor did she consider herself Joseph's messenger. She felt she was warning Rose. "Joseph talks against you to the young men. He says your man lives in the house for crazy, rich, white people. When you visit him, you will bring his sickness back with you."

"Does Joseph think he'll turn into a crazy, rich, white guy?" asked Rose.

"He's bad, Rose. He'll make very big trouble for you. The young men are already angry 'cause the whites came back after the war and started hunting. They shot a lot of elk last year and before."

"Most of the whites have work now," said Rose. "They won't need to hunt."

"You believe that?"

"There won't be as many."

"I'm scared, Rose. Joseph will point the young men's anger at you." She looked at the ground and whispered, "I feel bad feathers inside me. I don't want you to leave." She turned and ran away.

Rose already knew what Sally said was true. Hearing it said filled her chest with sand. She sat down on the rocks near the water. Her breathing became deliberate. She imagined each breath, like the stroke of an oar, would draw her farther across the water.

She sat for an hour, breathing her way to the other end of the lake toward the man in the madhouse, away from Joseph, Louie Desoto, and the young Red Crows men who called her white meat.

She returned to the house and found Catherine sleeping in a haze of afternoon light. Rose sat down beside her ancient mother. She traced the angles, ridges, and valleys of bone beneath the skin that one hundred years of work and weather had worn thin as wasps' wings. Rose slid her fingers under the old woman's braids and held her mother's bony head. It seemed to lose its Catherine magic. It was just a thing. Rose was holding a skull. She felt as distant as a saint blessing stones.

The skull began to speak to her. Rose felt panicked, thinking Catherine had read her mind.

"One year when there were no salmon, a big winter storm came down on us," Catherine whispered. "It was early and caught us nappin'. We weren't ready yet. In a few days all the birds had gone, the elk and deer disappeared into the mountains, and the lake froze over. We knew it was goin' to be a hard time for us.

"When the storm passed, many people together could walk on the ice. My father made a plan. He had the tribe make sleds. We pulled them across to the north end of the lake. Then twenty of us walked over the mountain in the snow into buffalo country. The Black Dogs, who lived around there, liked to kill other human beings. So, we were careful. We couldn't make fires. We made houses in the snow to hide from the Black Dogs, and we had to whisper, because voices carry a long way in cold air.

"We drove the buffalo into deep drifts in a gully. The men would run across the snow on their snowshoes, get real close, and shoot their arrows between the buffalo's ribs. There was lots of meat. We had to bring it back over the pass in fourteen trips. Then we loaded the sleds and pushed all that buffalo meat across the ice to our camp. The lake was good to us that winter, after all."

"I never heard of a tribe called Black Dogs."

"We called them that. Sometimes, Filthy Dogs. Most of them got wiped out by their enemies and the whites. They never made a treaty. I think they're all gone."

"Did you ever see them?"

"One time. Our young men caught one of their young men who came to steal horses." Catherine's voice was becoming more animated. Her memories made her blood flow. "They tied heavy tree limbs to his feet and told him to run. The women and girls chased him and threw stones. We killed him that way."

"Did you hit him?"

"Yes. I was good at throwing."

"What did you feel like when he died?"

"We were shouting and excited. Later we were quiet, because we knew his people would want to get back at us, maybe try an' wipe us out. And it was true. Two moons later they came in the night and killed three of us. One was my grandmother and one was my best friend. I called her Fox. If we hadn't killed their young man, they wouldn't have killed my grandmother and Fox. You forget those things when you're angry."

"Why did you call her Fox?"

"She was small and fast like a fox. We wanted to know everything and go everywhere. That got us in trouble with the grown-ups.

"The day before she was killed we took a canoe and went far out into the lake. It was evening. The air was full of tiny flying things. We came to a place where fish were boiling up to the surface. We'd eaten medicine plants and could see through everything, so we looked down into the water. Little people were swimming around like bull trout. They had gills for breathing under the water. Then we saw my grandmother. She was sinking to the bottom because she didn't have gills and couldn't breathe.

"When we came home, the grown-ups were angry, because we were too young to eat those plants. We didn't say anything. The next night Grandmother and Fox were killed. In the morning, I told my grandfather I had seen Grandmother and the little people with gills in the lake. I told him Grandmother sank down because she couldn't breathe. He listened to me.

"Before they put her body in the lake, grandfather took his skinnin' knife and cut gills under her jaw and along her neck so she could breathe the water and wouldn't sink into the darkness where Loneliness could get her." She opened her eyes and looked at Rose. "Now you know what to do," she said.

"You want to be buried in the lake, like the old people did?"

"Now I am old people."

"The priest won't allow it."

"Father Pelletier will."

"The old one?"

"Yes. He'll say the Latin over me."

"A priest wouldn't do that."

"Father Pelletier was a manly priest."

Rose was ready to challenge Catherine's assertion that a priest would tolerate a lake burial when she grasped what her grandmother meant by manly priest.

"Good god, you were lovers?" asked Rose.

"It was long ago."

"There's a surprise." Rose imagined her old mother and the priest wrapped in his black robe, their toes protruding—his white and hers brown. She remembered the priest's beautiful accent, his graceful hands, and a silver cross.

"No one suspected," said Rose. She smiled and amazement spread through her voice. "You were so proper around him. You fooled us all."

"I was being proper to fool the white man's god. When you were a girl, we were already old. Proper was what was left of us."

"You were always trying to trick the gods," Rose teased. "And you did very well—you lived to be very old. Now you have to behave."

Catherine whispered, "That's what a Red Crows would say." Rose felt a tremor of laughter resonate through the old woman.

They were quiet. Rose watched the light change inside the little house and thought about tricking the gods. Her observation made her a Red Crows in her mother's eyes. She wanted to be her mother's daughter, but she no longer wanted to be a Red Crows.

Outside the magpies raised a ruckus with a bluejay. Catherine listened carefully, finding words in their racket. "Bad birds say bad things," she whispered. Shouting and cawing, the birds flew away. With the confidence and certainty of a small child, Catherine said, "Gerome will make me gills."

Catherine actually expected them to cut gills in her

throat after she died. Rose was not so sure. She could not take a knife to her mother's throat. Could Gerome? she wondered. She spread her white fingers along the dark skin of Catherine's neck and squinted her eyes. The idea of gills did not particularly bother her. The physical act of pushing a knife into her dead mother's flesh was another matter. Rose guessed that Gerome could not take a knife to Catherine, either. It would be a test, she realized, not of Gerome, but of how well she knew him.

---

The inmates began to suggest ideas for paintings to Cody. Often they simply told him their dreams. Since their dreams interested the doctors, they should interest the painter of pictures as well. Painting other men's dreams became a way to pass time.

One man thought the natural color of blood should be yellow. His own blood had been yellow before he was attacked by magnetic ray thinking. Another inmate believed worms were crawling through his brain, interrupting his thoughts and making concentration impossible. Worse even, he could feel the worms moving around inside his head.

Several days later, Cody gave the man with worms in his brain a painting of the worms emerging from a human head. The following morning the man came to thank Cody for curing him of worms. He explained that the worms understood they were supposed to leave his brain. When he woke, they were gone. The man was fascinated to discover that they were not bad worms. They meant him no harm. They just did not know any better.

For the patient who mourned the loss of his yellow blood, Cody painted a naked man with outstretched arms and legs. Yellow veins sprouted through his body like tree roots, cobalt blue angels danced on his bald head, and he was smiling through a lemon yellow beard. The sprouting yellow and the dancing blue overwhelmed the young man. "Oh, thank you, oh, thank you," he said. He repeated his mantra of *thank-yous* across the lawn and up the hill to Main Hall, where he deposited his treasure with Gudrin for safekeeping. On some days, he went to the nurses' station and asked to see the painting several times.

"All right," said Gudrin. "It's a real pain in the ass, but if it makes you happy . . . " His gaze met hers. She smiled, reaching down into a secret place under the counter, and set his painting against the glass for him to see.

He would stare at the sprouting yellow veins and the dancing blue angels, letting them spill into his mind and splatter around until he was bathed in color. "Yes. Thank you, thank you. Yes," he would say, and smile, and walk away.

A heavyset man, who knew his guns, told Cody his dream. "In my dream, I am a bigger man, bigger than you see now. On my head is a big hat that blocks out the sun. The hat is like those that cowboys wear. Bad men point their guns at me. I have my gun in one hand and my bullets in the other. I have to put the bullets in the gun before I can shoot, but when I look down, the bullets turn into minnows and swim through my fingers. All the time, even when I'm not dreaming, I can feel the minnows wiggling through my fingers." He held out his hands and spread his fingers for Cody to examine.

———◆———

One day Cody watched a thick man with thick, black eyebrows standing off to the side, talking in incoherent strands of words. The man began waving his arms up and down. He reminded Cody of Tidyman conducting fish.

"Do the fish sing for you?" Cody asked.

The man turned and stared. His pale skin went crimson. His agitation quickly escalated to a shaking rage. "What the hell is that supposed to mean?" the man yelled, attracting the attention of several other inmates.

Cody kept painting. He spoke calmly, almost to himself:

I knew a man who spent months in a submarine under the Pacific Ocean. He said they had a machine for listening to ships. The machine made a pinging sound that traveled through the water and bounced off a ship. The time it took for the ping to return told the distance to the ship. One day a sound came back, distorted and strange, surrounded by a lonely, high-pitched song. The entire crew of thirty men stood absolutely still, hardly breathing, and listened. The singing came closer and closer until it was on the other side. The men pressed their hands against the steel and felt an unbearable loneliness pass through their bodies. Some of the men cried. The singing stopped and the ocean was silent.

Cody looked up from his painting. "Some believed it was a sea monster, others said it was a large school of tiny fish."

The angry man turned back to the lake, fists still clenched, and his body rigid. The maddening noise inside his brain gradually surrendered to the thousand imaginary voices beneath the water. His hands relaxed, his arms rose above his head, and he began conducting his singing fish.

One of the inmates ignored the singing fish. He was staring past Cody into the distance. Cody turned to see what the man was so fixed on. The boy who had disappeared into the ground several days before was standing against the fence, fingers laced in its links, watching the conductor of fish. Cody waved and the boy waved back.

"Hello," Cody called out to him.

"Hi," the boy replied. He seemed sad. Cody wondered if he was lonely or if he felt sorry for the conductor of fish.

The inmates watched the boy gradually descend from sight. After he had vanished, the men stood watching the spot on the horizon where he had been.

"Who's the boy?" Cody asked.

"The director's son," said a small, nervous inmate. "He has trouble with some of the other boys."

Dr. Neal Richards, the director—a psychiatrist, father of the disappearing boy, and Cody's doctor—was a tall man. He knew he was extraordinarily handsome. His mouth turned up at the corners in the slightest of perpetual smiles. He had grown the beard common to his profession—a somber, authoritative mask of precisely pruned hair, because smiling was inappropriate. Smiling confused people.

After his return at the end of August, Dr. Richards found time to work Cody into his schedule.

The room used for the interview was empty except for a simple, straight-backed chair in the center, facing a row of six high windows that looked out over the lake. The afternoon sun reached across the polished elm floor, halfway to the chair. A redheaded attendant in the usual white pants stood by the chair.

Cody nodded. "Hello," he said. The attendant was silent. Cody wondered if the man could talk.

As Cody moved around the periphery of the room, looking at charts and displays, the shock of red hair kept turning, always facing the potentially violent inmate— on the alert for sudden moves.

The sun reflected off the floor, illuminating a glass case against the west wall of the office. The case held seven gray lumps the size of baseballs suspended in separate sealed jars. Their Latin labels were written in artful flourishes of purple ink. Cody guessed the lumps were the brains of animals.

On the wall next to the case, a framed diagram of the human brain hung from the heavy molding board that circumscribed the room. Narrow lines emanated from brain parts to small flags that identified various areas.

Cody read aloud: "Infundibulum, cerebellum, uncus, chiasma? Who makes up these names?" he asked.

The attendant was not about to be distracted. He was a little frightened—Cody was a drifter and an artist who had busted up the dock with a barge and set the lake on fire, a classic P&D, as the staff referred to the psychotic and dangerous. Once a staffer had his nose bitten off by a P&D. There was also a rumor that Cody was a Communist. The attendant had no intention of losing his nose to a psychotic-Commie-artist.

As Cody studied the lumps in the case, he realized they could be human brains—small, deformed, diseased, or mutilated brains. He could see the small ghost of the attendant's reflection in the glass, waiting to pounce. The man's vigilance unnerved him. Thinking of the brains as human sickened him. As he moved away from the case, the window light erased the attendant's reflection. Cody turned to keep his eye on the redheaded man, wondering what the attendant's brain looked like—its size and shape. It struck him that the attendant saw him as not quite human either—as something strange and deformed that should be sealed in a glass jar in a glass case.

Being seen as subhuman himself made Cody angry. He thought of Joseph Red Crows' rage, bailing water in a fury on the sinking barge.

He smiled at the attendant. "Have you ever heard of white man's dogs?" he asked.

The attendant jumped back. He pulled a black leather, lead-filled sap out of his pocket and hunched forward, feet apart—braced for an attack. He looked ridiculous. Cody laughed.

The psychiatrist, Dr. Richards, observed this scene from the doorway. He stood, holding a file folder and a notebook, waiting to see what would develop. When Cody and the attendant noticed him, he stepped in and closed the door. His impulse, given Cody's laughter and the attendant's sap, was that the inmate was dangerous. He looked at the attendant. "Do we need restraints, Jerry?"

"I don't think so, Doctor. This pea brain was just talkin' a little crazy. I was ready for him." They stared at the man by the brain case, waiting to see what he would do next.

Cody knew he was trapped in their opinions. He did not even dare explain why he had been laughing. The psychiatrist's presence filled the room, pressing the light from the air.

Although Cody knew he should appear to be normal, that was almost impossible. The asylum was a zoo of multiple meanings—nothing stood still, nothing was simple and straightforward. Everything he did would be seen as insane or as an attempt to fool the doctors. His thoughts darted around, glancing from surface to surface. He imagined his brain, sealed in glass, shrunk to the size of a baseball.

When Dr. Richards smiled, Cody smiled back automatically. That was normal enough, he thought. There was no other reason to smile. They had total control. Would it make any difference, at this point, how he behaved? What the hell, nothing he did mattered. The air seemed to decompress slightly.

Cody walked toward the psychiatrist and extended his hand. "Hello," he said. "I'm Cody Hayes."

The psychiatrist hesitated for a moment. Jerry tightened up, ready to lunge, until the doctor extended his hand to Cody.

"I'm Dr. Richards," he said, then gestured toward the chair in the middle of the room. "Why don't you sit down, Cody, and we will begin."

The attendant positioned himself behind the chair. Dr. Richards walked back and forth, along the windows, studying the file in his hands. He stopped and looked over at Cody, then turned his back to his subject, and continued to read.

Cody could only see the hunched and headless silhouette of the psychiatrist against the light, and wonder, what is he thinking, what is so damned important?

Still facing away, Dr. Richards spoke in a calm, almost gentle, voice. "You have an interesting file, Cody. As you know, you are here for a pretrial psychiatric evaluation. Part of our examination is based on your response to the charges being brought against you and your response to other claims and observations that are included in your file. With that in mind, let us review your case."

Dr. Richards turned toward Cody and gave a solemn nod.

"It states here that you are an itinerant worker who lives in the back of a cattle truck, that you do odd jobs and paint pictures, that you were engaged in a highly risky logging project, that you had sex with an Indian woman in public view, that you destroyed the asylum's dock with a barge, and that you are suspected of setting a major fire that threatened human life and caused tens of thousands of dollars in damage."

Cody smiled. "I didn't set the fire."

Dr. Richards did not respond. He walked to the glass case and back, rereading parts of the file.

"The preliminary staff report indicates there is a possibility that you may be seriously disturbed, Cody. This is nothing to be ashamed of. Many mental illnesses can be improved with therapy. And, let me emphasize, this is only a preliminary report. Our ongoing evaluation will divulge any inaccuracies or inconsistencies."

The doctor placed the file on the windowsill. The room was quiet. In the distance, beyond the fence, Cody could hear the magpies.

"Do you have any questions, Cody?"

Cody shook his head. "No, Doctor. No questions."

"Then, perhaps you could start by telling me why you would want to start a fire."

"I didn't start the fire, Doctor."

"The county attorney's report claims that you did. Are you saying this is not true?"

"Dr. Richards, I haven't been charged because they don't have a case. I don't mean to be rude, but what difference would it make what I said? Your mind's set like a post."

The psychiatrist fiddled with his face, touching his nose and patting his beard. Being scrutinized himself,

Cody became sensitized to the doctor's peculiarities—
his thin fingers patting the mask of graying bristles or
touching his nose, his habit of looking down at his legs.
These gestures left the impression of a purely abstract
mind floating through the room, trying to locate a body.

Cody had never known people who were discon-
nected from their bodies. You could not work with your
hands, he realized, unless you were part of them. If you
lived in your mind all the time, sooner or later, your
body would forget about you.

"No. Not like a post, Cody. All I have to go on at
this juncture is the material in your file. If it is inaccu-
rate, you are the only one who can remedy the situation.
It is in your best interest to answer my questions."

Cody looked at his bare feet. He liked the feel of the
wood.

"Depending on our findings, we may want to see
how you respond to therapy."

Cody looked up. "What therapy?" he asked.

Dr. Richards pulled out a pocket watch and held it at
arm's length. "No more time today, Cody. We'll schedule another session soon," he said, nodding good-bye.
Then he was out the door.

ROSE GOT UP EARLY TO MAKE A FIRE IN THE PIT BEHIND Gerome's shack. She stuffed a chicken with sourdough crusts and the last of the dried cherries, then pinned the cavity with splinters and stuck the bird on a spit. She kept adding kindling to keep the flame high and hot. When the bird caught fire she flicked water on it. The faster it cooked, the sooner she would see Cody.

Four Red Crows children came out of the shack and stopped, surprised to see her. They whispered, "Good, hello, oh hi, morning, Rose, Rose," all in a jumble and smiled.

"Hi," said Rose and held up a mason jar. "Would you like to pick me some berries?" They took the jar without a word and ran to the berry patch. After they returned the jar nearly full, they disappeared into the bushes again. Rose guessed they went to hide in the abandoned cars to wait for bears. It was time for the bears with their gangly cubs to come down from the mountains to work the lowland blackberry bushes for breakfast.

Spying on bears was forbidden because, it was said and said often, bears were spirits and dangerous. Girls especially were not to look at a bear or say its name. Rose remembered bears were trouble. She hid in the bushes in the old Model T to spy on them. Catherine caught her and sent her to Father Pelletier, who made her say five Our Fathers and scrub steps.

Rose packed her chicken, the berries, and a quart bottle of Indian beer in a cherry crate, and set it on the passenger's side of the stock truck. Beside the red Pontiac, she could see down on the tops of three cars in the patch. The Model T had rusted into the ground and been turned into blackberries.

"You kids be careful," she said to the car tops, and started the truck. The smell of old cars still reminded her of bears.

She headed north in a set of ruts known as the east side road. The ruts kept changing size and shape, slapping the front tires, jerking the steering wheel from side to side. The Slocomb Creek bridge was closed for repair, which required a ten-mile detour to the temporary ford.

Rose was oblivious to the pain of the drive. The wobbly wheels and herky-jerky steering, the detour, and the endless dust went unnoticed. She was not driving, she was sailing to see Cody.

Just before the asylum, the road curved away from the lake, through some low hills and sandstone outcroppings behind the complex of buildings, until it came to a gate on the west side of Main Hall. She parked the truck, stated her visitor status at the gate, and was allowed to enter on foot.

Cody was at his usual place on the hill where the walls came together, working on a painting of his interview with Dr. Richards. The interviewing room had been opened up like a box and flattened out. Everything inside was flat: brains, glass jars, the case, diagrams, the psychiatrist's headless silhouette, the chair, even the red-headed attendant, Jerry.

Cody had been working on flat Jerry when he heard a truck approach. It took him a few minutes to realize it was his truck and Rose. He could see the truck pulling up to the main gate. His arms shot up with his shout. He flew up over the stone wall and landed running.

Running alarmed the attendants. It meant trouble. Running set them off, like dogs after cats. Several shouted and pointed. Some chased up the hill after Cody. Others, nearer the gate, ran to head him off.

As Rose stepped through the gate, she recognized Cody running toward her. Her legs quivered. He was fly-ing over the lawn to her, his eyes seeing into her eyes, aware only of Rose.

The frenzy of running feet hitting the ground inten-sified their elation. In the instant before it happened, Rose saw them all coming together: surprise, shock, and convergence—Cody with Rose, with attendants, with chicken, berries, and beer.

The two attendants who were still standing tripped over those on the ground. They were all trying to reach Cody, who was on the ground trying to shield Rose.

"Just stop," Rose said, her voice calm. "Everybody stop. It's all right. He was coming to see me."

All the white pants stood up.

"No running," warned one of the men. "You shouldn't have been running."

Another watched the beer spilling on the ground.

"Liquor's not allowed," he said. They all turned and walked off.

One man looked back. "No necking, either. No type of foolin' around, period. And clean up your mess."

Neither Cody nor Rose moved. She waited. The attendants were farther down the hill, looking the other way. When he touched the palm of her hand, she seemed to explode, covering his face with frantic kisses—ears, eyelids, mouth, chin. She ate him up, then she started laughing.

"What's funny?" he asked.

"Not good to make men in white pants feel bad," she said.

They reclaimed the chicken, a handful of blackberries, and what little beer was left in the bottle.

"They have lots of rules here," he said as they walked down the hill toward the dock. "You heard—we're not even supposed to touch."

"I *want* you. There's got to be someplace."

"Nowhere I know."

She brushed against his shoulder. "Nowhere?" She pointed back toward the powerhouse smoke stack. "What's that?"

"It's the steam plant."

"Not a monument to psychiatry?"

"That too." He laughed. "And the maintenance shop—people fixing stuff. This isn't the first time I've thought about a place. It's like a prison here."

"I was teasing," she said. "Let's forget where we are and have a picnic. Can we eat on our dock?"

"It is ours, isn't it?"

"Yeah," she said. "We own it."

"I think we're still paying for it. It's on layaway."

"Today," she said and raised her eyebrows, "the place is ours."

He reached for her, then pulled back. "Oh, no touching."

She laughed and threw her arms around him.

"That's my studio," he said, pointing to the intersection of stone.

"Show me."

They detoured from the path and walked across the lawn. Cody vaulted the wall and retrieved his painting of the flat room. In his earlier ecstasy, he had knocked the board off the wall, facedown into the grass. They stood with their heads together picking debris out of the paint.

"It got smeared," he said.

"You can fix it."

"Yeah." He sounded doubtful.

"It's flat."

"It's the room where the psychiatrist interviews people. That's him."

"The dark thing?"

"Ummm. He's bent over reading my file."

She studied the details in the painting. "What are those?" she asked.

"I think they're brains. They're in glass jars."

"Brains? He has people's brains in jars? Really?"

"I think so. Small ones. Something was wrong with them."

"Cody, that's horrible. It's wrong to keep a person's brain in a jar."

"It's pretty strange, all right."

"Does he think something's wrong with your brain?"

"Probably. But he's not going to put it in a jar."

Rose laughed. "You don't understand. It's a white guy disease," she said. "If they have jars to put brains in, they have to find brains to put in the jars. That's how they work."

"I'm a white guy," he protested. "I don't do that."

"Oh? Put a chain saw in your hands, and you have an irresistible urge to cut down trees, don't you?"

"All right. Yes. Trees will fall. It's true."

"So if you want to keep your brain in your head, we should start thinking about where we're gonna go."

"Let's not be hasty. Maybe they'll find who set the fire. We don't want to live on the run, unless there's no other way."

They walked down the dock and set out their feast of stuffed chicken and blackberries. They ate their fill and had a few sips of warm beer.

"Catherine hardly eats at all. I think she'll die soon—she's ready to die. The Red Crows want me gone. So, even if the sheriff finds who started the fire, we won't want to stay around," she said. "We'll want to go away— for a while, anyway."

"We could come back after a few years and live on the lake."

"We'd have a place. Tidyman gave me his parents' old house. It's the white one, east of Catherine's shacks, with the orchard."

"Why did he do that? Is something wrong?"

"No. He was well insured and he was very generous. He gave us some cash and Gerome got Gretchen. He escaped to be a poet."

"Where?"

"Algiers."

"Tidyman escaped? That's good."

"Where would you go?"

"I don't know. Have you heard of Camloops?"

"In British Columbia? Lots of salmon."

"There's a mill there."

"So practical, but crazy," she said.

"That's the trick of this place. You want a normal life here, but *wanting* a normal life makes you crazy."

"What about New York or Los Angeles?"

"What could I do in a city?"

"You're a painter?"

"Yes, but I couldn't do that there." Then he remembered his reaction to Tidyman's need to go back to Algiers to write poetry.

"You can do anything you want, Cody."

"What do you want?"

"I want to go to a real school."

He laughed. "They might have one of those in New York City."

"You'd want to go there?"

"Sooner or later."

"Okay, New York City."

"Why not?"

"Good."

"Well that's settled." She leaned to kiss him.

"No touching," he said.

"We'll see about that." She lifted her skirt and straddled him.

From his third-floor office, Dr. Richards studied the pair on the dock through his oversize, World War I field artillery binoculars. The image frustrated him. It was impossible to focus clearly through the office window, which was closed to prevent the inmates from knowing they were being observed.

He could see the woman on the dock, her back to him, with her large black skirt spread out around her. She partially blocked the view of Cody, who was leaning back on his elbows, looking up at her. They seemed to be talking and laughing.

The psychiatrist played with the focusing knob. Cody and the woman were in high spirits. Visits were a rarity at Springhill, and interactions between patients and visitors were nearly always stilted and morose. Cody seemed, in the doctor's mind, to be enjoying himself much too much. Perhaps he was in a manic phase.

The dinner buzzer blared across the lawn. Rose stiffened and twisted around, looking for the sound. Then she bent her head to his chest and laughed. Cody lay on his back, smiling at her.

"It's closing time," he said. "They turn me back into a frog in ten minutes."

They gathered the remains of their picnic and started up the hill. Rose was laughing and hugging him. He stopped and, holding her head with his hands, kissed her.

"No touching," he said.

"I think we're invisible."

The gatekeeper let Rose out. "You two can talk through the gate if you want," he said. "It's not allowed, but I'm off duty, now."

"What about touching?" asked Rose.

"That's not allowed either." The gate snapped shut and the attendant went off to supper, smiling to himself.

"Ah, a white pants in human form," said Rose. "I'll have to change my tune."

Cody reached through the bars and pulled her close. "Never trust a gatekeeper with a sense of humor."

"Trust one who breaks the rules," she whispered.

A voice from the front of the hall called, "All in for count." They squeezed hard against the wrought iron and kissed good-night through the gatekeeper's grill work. She closed her eyes as they separated so she would not have to watch him walk away.

---

In the morning, Rose cleaned, and scrubbed, and washed clothes. Catherine slept most of the day. Rose was hanging clothes on the line in back when she realized nobody had come around. The children were not out in the berries or playing in the lake. She wondered if the Red Crows had abandoned the place. Some days they would visit the mountain Red Crows on Belfast Creek.

Rose had finished hanging clothes and was walking toward the front door of Catherine's shack when she saw Stephen Red Crows, a very tall boy, about sixteen years old, running along the shore from the west, which meant he was coming from town. Young Indians did not go to town alone.

She went inside and stood back out of the light. The boy turned up from the shore and ran to the other shack. Rose was waiting in front when he came out a few minutes later, carrying a leather pouch and a duffel bag.

"Stephen, what's going on?"

The boy looked away and ran between the two shacks, then turned east toward the mountains. He had not come from town. He had seen her in back, hanging clothes, and made a wide circle around the shacks to avoid her.

Sally had warned her things had gone bad, but it was much worse than Rose had imagined. When the boy ran toward the mountains, she felt a slow spasm in her stomach and sat down in the grass. The air buzzed with the sound of insects. They want me to die, she thought. The shacks started to spin and she closed her eyes.

When she stood up, there was a crow on Catherine's roof.

Rose shouted, "Go away, crow-face—useless bird." She felt foolish shouting at a crow—nothing could stop the old woman's dying, nor the Red Crows' listening to shaman bastards. When she went inside, the crow flew away.

Rose made soup from yesterday's bones and brought it to Catherine.

"What's that smell?" Catherine asked.

"Good, you can smell. It's soup. Have some."

"I am not hungry."

"When will you eat?"

Catherine waved the soup away. "They've all gone, haven't they?"

"They're in the mountains."

"They think they'll catch your man's sickness from you. Silly fools."

Rose was silent.

"How are the crows?"

"They don't count for much anymore," Rose answered. It made her feel guilty to dismiss the crows.

"It doesn't matter," said Catherine. "Crows are just a way to think about your life."

The admission surprised Rose. "You don't believe the crows can talk?"

"Age makes you crazy or it makes you practical."

Rose did not think of the old woman as practical. She wondered how Catherine could place her peculiar and final request in the regions of sanity. "What is practical about being buried in the lake with gill slits in your throat, Mother Red Crows?"

"You never know where you might be going, so bein' buried in the lake with gills and Father Pelletier's Latin is practical." Catherine looked at Rose and cackled. "When I was a child, they said old women played stick games with the devil."

———⊙———

Rose lay in bed that night with her mother, listening to her breathe and the crickets drone. In the distance, she heard a truck downshift, then the sound of Gretchen coming through the grass. It was quiet again. She waited, watching the open doorway.

"Rose?" Gerome hesitated. "Are you awake? Come have a talk."

She got up and went out. They walked back to the truck to sit in the cab. Gerome liked being inside the truck, surrounded by metal.

"Joseph believes the lake is angry. He says we have lost our luck and you will make us crazy."

She tried to see his expression. "Do you believe him?" she asked.

To her surprise, Gerome was laughing. "It has already happened," he said. "Everybody is acting crazy."

They sat for a while without saying anything. She leaned her head out and looked up at the sky.

"I guess I should move out," she said. "I can always live in the stock truck."

"Well, I'll check on Catherine. Where will you go?"

She laughed. "Not far. I'll want to come back at night and see her."

"Yeah. She's gonna die soon."

"I know. She won't eat."

"She lived a long time. She's tired."

Rose told Gerome that the Father and Catherine had been lovers. He had no memory of them together. She told him about Catherine seeing her mother sinking into the dark lake, but she did not mention what was expected of Gerome. They told stories and laughed and held hands in the dark until their tears dried.

The temperature began to fall while they sat in the truck, and the lake became choppy. Gerome drove back to the mountains before the rain came.

———※———

In the morning, Rose awoke to a steady, cold drizzle. The sky was covered by a gray cloud that came down and hid the lake. She packed her things and put them in the stock truck. She returned to the shack to say good-bye to the sleeping Catherine, kissed her eyes, and left.

She drove the truck up through the wet, green grass to the highway and headed toward the mountains. Not quite a half mile later, she turned off toward the lake onto an overgrown road along the east boundary of the property Tidyman had given her. She thought about introducing herself to what were now her renters, but she was in no mood to talk to anyone. Near the lake, she turned the truck around and backed down into a cluster of cotton-woods. It was a secluded place, out of sight, away from the Red Crows.

Rose went in back and stretched out on the bed, face-down. She tried to imagine what it was like to wake up and be Cody. With her eyes closed, she rolled over and lay on her back. The sounds of the lake and the crows' caws were muted by the wooden walls. Turpentine and linseed oil mixed with the faint odors of gasoline and grease. She opened her eyes enough to see the row of curved oak slats that supported the roof, and beyond that, the doorway and the gray sky. For a moment he seemed to be every-where—surrounding, almost touching her. The sweet anticipation of his presence faded and left her alone.

At night she walked along the shore to Catherine's. Gerome's truck was parked in back. She crawled into bed with her old mother, cradling the shriveled woman against her stomach. After hours of holding Catherine and listening to the rasping in her lungs, Rose fell asleep. An hour later she woke, startled and anxious that the Red Crows had discovered her. She listened in the dark, but the only sound was Catherine's breathing.

When dawn came, she left the shack and walked back to the stock truck in the cottonwoods. It was colder than the day before and had rained most of the night. As she approached the truck through the trees, she could see something had happened. The hood was open, as if shouting at the rain.

She walked closer, a step at a time, listening for the intruder, but the pounding in her head drove out all other sound. The truck windows were shattered. Every tire slashed. The back door had been kicked off its hinges. Inside, tools and clothing were scattered and covered with paint. Several of Cody's paintings had been thrown into the brush. Rocks were used to smash the carburetor and spark plugs. The hole punched through the cast iron block guaranteed the engine would never run again. She leaned over the fender, reached far in, and ran her fingers over the bright iron exposed by the engine's fatal puncture.

Rose walked around the truck, stunned by the fury that had driven the destruction. She continued to circle the vehicle, stopping many times to examine details of the vandalism, until there was nothing new to discover. All dents, scrapes, broken edges, and tears were touched and studied until they lost their power to surprise and terrorize. They became, in her mind, artifacts—evidence of ritual rage and the exorcism of fear.

Had there been more than one attacker, she wondered, or had several come in the night? From along the shore or from the highway? Did they speak? Was there a plan or did it begin with a single, angry blow? She imagined they would have stopped and listened in the dark. Then there would be another blow, and another, and another, until they were in full frenzy. And when they had finished, she wondered, were they elated in their camaraderie, or filled with fear, or even remorse?

She collected the shards of window glass and set them in patterns on the running boards. The rest of the day she spent cleaning inside the truck.

In the late afternoon, she found several undamaged cigar boxes filled with Cody's treasures—extraordinary stones, marbles, seed pods, and feathers. There were metal parts to mysterious machines, seashells, pieces of ruby glass, and notebooks filled with pressed flowers. She sat on the floor of the little house until dusk, examining one thing, then another, and putting them back in their boxes. Her head was filled with images of the vandalized truck and her lover's secret treasures. That night she was the archaeologist of rage and a curator of passion.

***

Cody had been working on a painting of the white church of Catherine since early morning. Painting involved millions of minuscule decisions. He constantly examined the possibilities of light and color, contrast and shape. After a few hours of focusing on a particular image, his mind would relax. The defensive barriers would fall away, leaving him unusually open and, in a way, naive. It was the state of mind he liked best. It made him easy and it let him see with an innocent eye.

"Interesting," said Dr. Richards, who had come up behind Cody and was standing a few feet back and to the side. It was possible he had been there for several minutes.

"Oh, hi," said Cody. He kept painting.

"I don't believe I've seen that technique used before."

Cody pulled back for a moment, then leaned into the painting again. "I like dots and lines of pure color. It's more intense. You get to see each color at the same time your eye mixes them together. If I do it right, they shimmer."

"Oh, yes, I see," said the doctor. "Very clever. Have you been at this long."

"Since this morning."

"I meant, how long have you been a painter."

Cody laughed. "Oh, not long. About three years."

"After the war?"

"Yeah. Right around then."

He had added lace around the edge of the bed, letting it flow slightly out and up. Catherine was lying in the center. He had painted her dress dark blue and her skin dark reddish brown. She was surrounded by the white of the quilt. The bed floated above the floor the way Cody remembered from the first time he had seen her. The perspective was slightly skewed, making the bed look as if it were coming off the picture.

The painting seemed amateurish and crude to the doctor, a lot of effort for little reward. "What do you like so much about painting?" he asked.

Cody carefully dabbed tiny white dots onto the picture, turning zinc oxide into floating lace. "I like how it feels."

"And how's that?"

"When it's working, I feel like everything is right on the verge of . . ."

"The verge of what?"

"Well, of something hidden, I guess."

"Go on."

Cody stopped painting and looked at the doctor. "It's like being in a doorway between my life and some-thing else."

"I see. Could you describe this something else?"

"Why?" Cody asked.

"Well," said the doctor, "I can understand your reluc-tance, it's a sensitive and complex subject. It's something we should discuss later, anyway." He started to leave, then stopped and looked at Cody's hand. "I don't believe painters usually put their fingers in the paint like that," said the doctor.

Cody looked down at his colorful hand and smiled. "I don't know," he said, surprised he had never thought about it before.

A thin man in his sixties, who wore a black wool over-coat, had been watching Cody and the doctor. He was dignified and exceptionally fine featured. He avoided contact with other inmates, though he was curious about the man who painted. When Dr. Richards returned to Main Hall, the inmate ventured forth. He walked up to the stone wall and reached over to shake Cody's hand.

"Hello, I am Elemente Duval. Would you be kind enough to answer a question for me?"

"Hi, I'm Cody Hayes. What's your question?"

"Do you think it possible," Elemente asked, "that a particular image might kill whoever chanced to see it?"

Cody was used to bizarre behavior and strange questions. He looked at Elemente's perfect features and thought about his question. "Wouldn't it be more likely that certain images would kill certain people?"

"I would like you to speculate about a single, deadly image."

"Well, I don't think it could happen."

"And why?"

"Because none of us sees the same thing the same way. Our memories affect what we see, and our memories are all different."

Elemente's eyes tightened. "Suppose a man has lost his memory. His memory is gone. He has no family or friends, no past. What does he see?"

"Perhaps he would only have ideas floating around in his head."

"Yes, just vague ideas, unattached to real experience."

"You've lost your memory?"

"Yes."

"Is that why you're here?"

"I do not know why, or for how long. I do not

know, even, who I am. I believe their machine stole my memories."

Cody went back to painting his white dots. "You know your name."

"Yes. Just my name, Elemente Duval, and the past seven days. Nothing more."

"How do you know that's your name?"

"It's what the attendants call me."

"What kind of machine steals memories?"

"The electrocution machine," he said and put his fingers to his temples. He made a sizzling sound with his tongue. His head shook. "Your muscles try to tear themselves away from your bones. It's terrible."

Cody looked at Elemente, wondering what had happened to the man's mind. "Why did you ask about an image that could kill?" he asked.

"Sometimes I have a thought that just comes. Then I have to worry about it. But you have eased my mind. Thank you."

"Sure. Anytime."

"I want to show you something." Elemente scrambled over the wall and started toward the fence. "Come, come," he insisted.

Cody followed him across the grass to the fence near where the boy had disappeared into the ground.

"There," said Elemente, pointing into the sagebrush on the other side.

Cody peered at what seemed to be a dozen or so round stones scattered among the sagebrush. Then he noticed they were moving.

"See them?" said Elemente. "Many small, gray bunnies."

They stood for several minutes with their fingers hooked through the fence, absorbed by bunny antics, until another shape caught Cody's attention. Someone, hidden in the sagebrush, had been watching them. All Cody could see was a face in the shadows close to the ground. He assumed it was the boy he had seen before—the vanished boy. Cody waved.

The boy scrambled from his hiding place and came to the fence. The bunnies hopped out of his way.

"Hi," said the boy. "Are you going to paint a picture of my rabbits?"

"I was thinking about it. What's your name?"

"Teddy. Theodore. They call me Teddy. My father is the head of everything here."

"I'm Cody and this is Elemente."

"Hello, young man," said Elemente.

"Are these really your rabbits?" asked Cody.

"I don't know. They're just here, I guess. I come through the tunnel to watch them. They'll come up and take things from my hand and let me pat them. They like me."

"You came up through a tunnel? What kind of a tunnel?"

"It's for the steam pipes from the boiler room." He turned and pointed toward the tall brick chimney. "They heat all the buildings with the steam."

"Why would the tunnel come out over here?"

"There was a building here, long ago. It burned down

before my folks came. The tunnel was all boarded up on this end, but I kicked the boards out with my foot." He kicked against the fence to show his strength. The fence shook and the bunnies scooted into the brush. "Nobody knows I go through the tunnels. It's my secret. My father would be really mad. You won't tell, okay?"

"Okay," said Cody.

"Your secret is secure," said Elemente.

"You can go to places through the tunnel that aren't above ground," said Teddy.

"What kind of places?" asked Cody.

"I found a house where an old woman lived. She wasn't home, but I saw all her stuff. I think she's a witch."

"Why do you think she's a witch?"

"Her house disappeared. I can't find it anymore. There are some places you can only go to once."

Cody smiled. "I can understand that."

The bunnies had returned. One came up to Teddy and nibbled at his shoelace. Cody wanted to show the bunnies to Rose. He had gotten used to seeing things with her.

## EARLY MONDAY MORNING

Ana had gone back to bed after the fire trucks left, leaving Liz to contemplate the risks of passion and desire. When the sun came up, Ana reappeared as though she had been beckoned for duty. She smiled at her granddaughter and sat next to her on the couch.

"Have you been here all night, Elizabeth?"

"Yes. I've got a lot on my mind."

"You're going to have to pack soon."

"Last night, you asked if I wanted a man who made sense." She laughed and began swinging her leg back and forth, watching the shadow dart across the boards. "Actually, there is a man, and he doesn't make any sense at all."

"Not the chirper from Tokyo?"

"Tom? No. This man's a painter. His name is Andrew. He lives in a storage building on a dock on the Charles

River. He's been traveling for the last ten years. He's from Senegal, very black."

"You're in love with this man?"

"Let's just say I know where it's going."

"Well, I'm impressed."

"Why?

"Painters are better than musicians."

"You're teasing me again."

"No. That's just my experience."

"Really?" Liz's attempt to subdue her delight made her sound as though she had swallowed a gasp. Laughter took them over, fracturing all reserve, and left them weepy with relief.

"I would never be the one," Ana said, catching her breath, "to tell you not to take risks."

"Were the risks you took worth it?" Liz asked, wiping her tears away.

"I thought so. But don't forget all those homeless people on the streets of Boston. . . . "

"Yes?"

Ana held up her palms in a gesture of futility. "Victims of romance."

Liz rolled her eyes. "Deranged by love?"

"Of one sort or another."

Liz took Ana's hand and studied her slender fingers. "You have beautiful hands, Gramma." She was having a hard time looking Ana in the eye and continued talking to her hands. "I didn't think you would understand any of this."

"I'm not sure I do, but that's not the point, is it?"

"You understand the important part."

"You haven't known him very long, have you?"

"How did you know?"

"Tom still thinks you might marry him."

"I've only seen Andy four times and once was when we met."

"How did you meet?"

"One evening there was a fire in a warehouse across the river. I went down to watch the fireboats. There was a man ahead of me walking toward the end of the dock. I loved the way he moved. He was easy and elegant. I wanted the dock to go on and on so I could watch him walk."

"But he stopped—and what happened?"

"He was watching the fire and he said something, but I couldn't hear him over the sirens. After a while, I got up the nerve to ask him to repeat it. He said, 'Serpent's breath.' Then he pointed to a face in the water made by the reflection of the burning building. We talked. He told me he was a painter. Before we went our ways, he drew a map to his place on a scrap of paper.

"I taped the map on my computer at the office and thought about this man all week. When I woke up on Sunday, I had a picture of the map in my head. I got up and went out to find him.

"That was two weeks ago. I've seen him three times since then. His clothes always smell of turpentine and oil paint." She paused, remembering the painterly scent. "I know it sounds silly, but I saved one of his paint rags. I put it in a plastic bag and brought it with me."

There was nothing Ana could say. Her memories came in waves. The pungent scent of turps and oil paint seemed to fill the room. She walked to the window and stood quietly facing the lake.

"Gramma? Are you all right?" Liz asked. She went over and put her hands on her grandmother's shoulders.

"Don't worry, Elizabeth. I'm fine."

Liz held her, leaning forward to kiss the back of her head. They stood, watching the lake.

"There is something you could do for me before you go," Ana said.

"Of course. What is it?"

"Would you mind leaving me your paint rag?"

"You want the paint rag?"

"Yes, I do."

"Well, sure. I'll get it out of my bag."

"You could just leave it on the dining room table."

"Sure. Gramma? You're laughing. Why are you laughing?"

ROSE LAY ON THE BED IN THE DARK IN THE VANDALIZED stock truck. There were nuns in her thoughts. She remembered them coming down the hall that night—swishing skirts and rattling beads—and into the room to take her baby.

She left the truck and walked back along the shore toward Catherine's shack. The old woman was awake, waiting for her.

"I stayed awake," Catherine whispered, "because I need to tell you how to run your life." Her laughter rattled in her chest and she started to cough. Several minutes later she got her breath back and reached up to touch Rose's face. "Listen to me. Get your man out of the crazy house and go away with him. Okay?"

"Okay."

"Soon, before it's too late. Go soon."

---

Rose woke when the sky was flat, before light reached the earth. It was quiet in the white room. Catherine's arms and legs reminded Rose of dark, twisted roots. She curled around her mother's fragile body, pressing her warm belly against the old woman's cold, bony back, as though one lover were absorbing another.

Rose slid her hand over Catherine's leathery breast and waited for the beat of her heart, unwilling to start the morning without her mother's touch. There was no breath, no beating heart, and no touch. Rose listened to a distant crow call to another—as if the old crow woman had hopped out of bed in the night and flown away.

Rose went outside, picked up a rock, and threw it at the roof of Gerome's shack. "Catherine is dead," she called to the Red Crows.

Gerome came out half asleep in an undershirt and pajama bottoms. "Catherine died?" he said. He was quiet for a long time, listening to the words in his head, not believing them. Rose took his hand and led him into Catherine's shack.

Gerome stood over the bed, looking down on the woman who had raised him. He began stroking her hair. He drew his breath in short, deep bursts.

"She wants to be buried in the lake, Gerome. She wants the Father to say Latin over her, and she wants you to cut gills in her neck so she can breathe like a fish."

"Yes, she told me."

"We should bury her after dark, when the whites are sleeping." She smiled, but Gerome was slow and serious.

His breathing had returned to normal as he began to think about the burial. He was already absorbed in the rituals of magic and tribal politics that embrace human death.

"It will take a while for everyone to get here," said Gerome. "We will have to wait until tomorrow night. Will you ask the Father?"

———◆———

Rose waited on the steps behind the church until Father Tallie appeared in the doorway of the rectory and gestured for her to come with him. The rectory walls—square-hewn, whitewashed logs—muted the outside world. The thick wooden floor absorbed the sound of their feet and confirmed the sense of isolation. She followed Father Tallie through the library to the Father's room.

The young priest tapped on the door frame, then stepped into the room and announced, "Your visitor, Father."

She had not seen him since she went away to Indian school. He sat upright, supported by a large horsehair pillow, his hands folded carefully on a dove-gray blanket. His hair was longer now and white. The eyes she remembered, because they were a pale, transparent blue. He stared at her in silence, trying to place her in the congregation, or in the baptismal lineage.

"Please come closer, so I may see you," he requested.

She walked to the bed and stood next to him. He reached up for her and lifted his head slightly, as though he expected a kiss. She leaned forward, apprehensive at her lack of proper priest etiquette.

He inhaled sharply. She drew back, more startled than had he kissed her.

Father Pelletier looked wistful. "The abandoned girl?" he asked. "Your name was Rose, wasn't it?"

"Yes, Father. It still is." She laughed. "How did you know? Do I smell abandoned?"

He smiled at her lack of propriety. "No," he said. "The odor of smoked deerskin clings to you, and Catherine Red Crows raised a white girl with flying eyebrows."

Rose watched his face change. He understood Catherine had died. "Early this morning," she said.

He nodded, then patted the bed for her to sit down. The old priest took her hand.

She thought about how pale he was in his white room and how dark Catherine had been in hers. "She wanted to be buried in the lake and for you to say the Latin. It will be tomorrow night."

"It would be impossible, Rose. I can barely walk. But there is someone else I believe would understand." The priest paused and smiled, realizing how much he was about to reveal. "Be sure to cover her throat." He saw the flicker of surprise. "Catherine and I had no secrets," he said.

Rose took this to mean that he assumed she knew they had been lovers. Perhaps he was testing her. She waited.

"Your mother was the only woman I ever knew."

There was a fragile tone in his beautiful voice, as

though he were trying to confess something. Rose felt awkward. She got up to go, but Father Pelletier held her hand. He looked noble, she thought, even pure.

"I felt no guilt for failing God," he said. "I only felt remorse for failing Catherine."

Rose glanced toward the door, concerned that someone had overheard. The old priest released her hand. She was still unsure of her place or if he expected a response. "I don't believe you failed Catherine," she said. "Perhaps you disappointed yourself, Father."

He smiled and opened his elegant hands in a small gesture of acceptance. Still, she had second thoughts about having spoken so directly to a priest.

---

In the late evening, canoes and boats from all around the lake began to converge in the bay in front of Catherine's shack. The people came ashore, made fires, and set up camp for the night. There was some drinking and two fistfights broke out. The old people shamed the combatants into making up and returning to their families. Fights always confused the old ones and made them feel sad, but the young men and women, even those who hated violence, were drawn in by rage.

After dark, several groups came together and sang and drummed until late into the night. Rose listened from inside Cody's truck until she could no longer resist. She jumped down and walked along the shore until she came to the first fire. A log that had washed up on the beach became her hideout. She crouched in the dark and watched the people singing and drumming.

She wanted Cody next to her. Physically she missed him, she wanted to see and touch him. What she missed most, what made her lonely, was that he was not there to see this with her. What they discovered together was more interesting and vital than what they found separately.

When she grew tired of watching, she returned to the truck and lay down on his bed. She found herself making plans for where and how they could live on the run. Getting out of the country altogether seemed a better idea than New York. She was thinking about Cody in Mexico when she heard a tap on the side of the truck.

Gerome called to her, "Sister, the priest has arrived. It is time to bury our mother. I have a boat for you."

---

The Indians pushed out into the dark lake and rowed north for nearly an hour, following Gerome's boat, which held Catherine's body on a small, crosswise raft. Rose watched Catherine's still form gliding over the black water toward her. She imagined her mother's hands, open and reaching out for her.

Gerome stopped rowing and everyone clustered around. A dozen lanterns and several burlap torches were lit and held aloft. Their collective light appeared to glow from the white wool blanket that covered Catherine at the center of the many boats.

The boat carrying the priest came up and scraped to a stop alongside Gerome's. A boy held up an electric lantern wired to a set of dry-cell batteries in the bottom of the boat. The priest tried to stand, but the boat was too unsteady. The boy set the lantern down to help the priest, illuminating his face. In that brief moment, Father Pelletier made passion timeless.

Rose felt a quiver through her body. Catherine's ancient lover had come to bury her after all.

The Father resigned himself to his seat. A murmur of relief passed through the floating assemblage. He waited until it was quiet and began his blessing. "This woman, whose beauty and wisdom were God's own invention, this mother of many mothers, who made life here on this earth possible, we are about to return to the lake of her dreams." As she had requested, he said the blessing:

*Domine, Jesu Christe, Rex gloriae,*
*libera animas omnium fidelium defunctorum*
*de poenis inferni, et de profundo lacu.*
*libera eas de ore leonis,*
*ne absorbeat eas tartarus, ne cadant in obscurum.*

He raised his hand and with stately grace made the sign of the cross. "*In nomine Patris, et Filii, et Spiritus Sancti. Amen.*"

When he had finished his official duties, he reached forward, tilting the boat to its limit, and pulled back Catherine's white shroud. He looked into her face for a moment. He raised his crucifix to his lips, then touched it to hers. He nodded to Gerome, who slid Catherine's raft into the water. The blanket floated free, exposing her throat and a necklace of delicate, ivory gills.

Rose looked at Gerome. He glanced at her and smiled. Gerome had given grace to Catherine's final wish.

Catherine was tied to the raft, which was weighted with stones. She held her father's favorite knife in one hand. Her unbraided hair floated out in all directions, then she sank from sight.

In the late afternoon, an attendant came for Cody and escorted him to the room with brains in jars. He waited alone for the doctor for a half hour. There was no Jerry this time, only the brains and the window shapes on the floor, compressed into sharp angles of light. He was standing by the glass case studying the folds in the brains when Dr. Richards came in.

"Do you find my brains fascinating?"

Cody laughed. "Yes," he said. "Even before I knew they were yours."

Dr. Richards looked at Cody for a moment, analyzing the implications of his remark. "Yes," he said, flatly. "That was funny, Cody."

The doctor was wary of humor. He understood its destructive power. Not only was humor often an expression of hostility, it was destabilizing. Smiling and temper tantrums posed similar quandaries—the boundaries on behavior could shift all too rapidly. Laughter was a hysterical condition even in normal, healthy minds.

"Do you have an opinion as to what kind of brains these might be?" Dr. Richards asked.

"Since they're similar to the diagram, I assumed they were from children or retards."

"They are underdeveloped human brains, though the subjects had full motor responses."

"Why do you have them in jars?" Cody asked.

"They were part of an experiment that determined the upper limits of electroconvulsive shock. After the subjects had died of natural causes, their brains were removed and examined. The experimenter's widow gave them to me when I was a graduate student."

Cody felt slightly nauseated. Another normal response, he thought.

Dr. Richards cleared his throat and walked to the windows. "Please have a seat so we can begin."

Cody sat down. He was conscious of his bare feet. It would have been better to have worn his slippers. He put his feet under the chair and focused his attention on the doctor.

"I have been thinking quite a lot about your paintings, Cody. There's been some interesting work recently in the field of psychiatry, comparing the art of several institutionalized psychotics with art from primitive African tribes. I thought you might be interested, given your fascination with the local natives." He handed Cody some black-and-white reproductions of several drawings.

"There is a similarity, not only between the imagery of the psychotic and the primitive native, but also between their thinking. They have in common delusional, magical, and highly paranoid thinking. The paranoid believes certain people are out to get him, that they attack his mind with secret rays, or broadcast thoughts to him, or that people in the government are arranging the events in his life. The primitive, on the other hand, believes powerful animal spirits control his life and that he must perform all manner of rituals and prayers to ward off destructive forces. The primary difference between the two is that the psychotic is alone—isolated from all of humanity—whereas the primitive's paranoia is determined and sanctioned by his culture.

"This morning the staff confiscated several of your paintings that were in the possession of inmates. I felt your images—those exhibiting psychotic properties— were potentially damaging to other inmates."

Cody gradually began pushing his feet out in front of him, toward the bright wedge of light.

Dr. Richards went on, "Your paintings appear to have been the result of a paranoid-schizophrenic dementia."

"They are the dreams of other inmates, Doctor."

The doctor patted his beard. "If that is true, you may be reinforcing their pathologies. Perhaps you are disturbing yourself as well as the other inmates. Have you considered that possibility?"

Cody smiled at his toes so close to the wedge of sun. He did not want to hear the doctor's voice or to answer any more questions. The room was silent for several minutes.

The doctor cleared his throat and waited. Finally he asked, "Are you refusing to cooperate with the evaluation process?" Cody simply stared at him. "In case you do not understand your situation, let me explain," said

Dr. Richards. "This is a pretrial evaluation. The county is obligated to pay the expense of keeping you here until the evaluation is complete."

The doctor began speaking rapidly, tapping his fingers lightly against his beard under his earlobe.

"The county attorney has requested a thorough report based on a long-term evaluation. Your behavior during the evaluation will certainly affect the nature of my report. That behavior includes your willingness to cooperate or not. Cooperation is important in the psychiatric process."

"What does *long-term* mean? Several weeks?"

"I expect you to be with us for several months, Cody. I'm interested in how you respond to some therapies."

Cody repeated *some therapies* for his own amusement. How far, he wondered, were they going to take this? The zapper was used to threaten and to subdue. It destroyed your memory. Were they going to shock him because he knew talking was pointless?

The sun crept across the floor, reaching for his toes. His skin was damp, as though he wanted to evaporate. He thrust his bare foot into the luminous wedge and began to laugh as the sun swallowed his toes.

"Would you care to explain what you find amusing?"

"Just looking for a way out, Doctor. I'm ready to leave, anytime. I don't need my brain zapped."

Doctor Richards stroked his face, paused, and began flicking the tip of his nose with his forefinger. "Let's have another session in a few days. You may see things differently after you've had time to think. Thank you for coming, Cody."

I N THE EARLY MORNING, A FEW HOURS AFTER CATHERINE'S funeral, Rose lay in the truck thinking about the bottomless lake. The serpent of Loneliness had coiled itself around her heart.

Something was moving around outside the truck. She peered through a broken window and found Gerome studying the damage.

He shook his head.

"It's not your fault, Gerome," she said through the window.

"This should not have happened. They are not bad boys. How could they do this?"

She jumped down from the truck and went around to where he was standing.

"There's so much of you to be sad, when you're sad." She put her arms around him. "It's all right. I'll fix it up."

He opened the hood and looked at the battered engine. "Lots of money, Rose."

"I have some money."

"You're going to need your money." He stared at the engine while he tried to make a plan that would fix everything. After he thought it through, he said, "I'd like those kids to fix Cody's truck. I'll find glass for the windows and put the door back, right away. The rest will take a lot more time and some money, but I could have that red car running real soon. In a couple of days, maybe. Then you'd have something to drive."

"Thank you, Gerome. Do you think Amy will give up the red car?"

He made a feeble attempt to smile. "I came to tell you that the fellow from the cafe was looking for you yesterday."

"Ogeen?"

"Yeah. I told him I'd tell you."

"Could I use your truck? I want to drive up and visit Cody. And I need to see Handel about getting Cody out of that place. I guess I should find out what Ogeen wants."

———

Rose walked straight through the cafe into the back, looking for Ogeen. An accident with a sack of flour had him flustered and covered with powdery white smudges.

He looked up and saw her. "Oh, hi," he said.

"Hi. Nice effect. You look ghostly."

"I've been better." He laughed. "I came by to see how you were doing, that's all."

"I'd be doing all right if I could get Cody out of the funny farm. I thought I'd talk to Handel today—see if there's anything new on the fire."

"New? What do you mean?"

"Well, we both know Cody didn't start that fire. That leaves the whole town to consider, doesn't it?"

Ogeen found a towel and was trying to brush the flour off his clothes. "I suppose so," he said.

"You've got a pretty good idea who started it, don't you?"

"I wouldn't say that."

"How is Earl doing?"

"Oh, fine. I guess. You think it was Earl?"

"Maybe it was you."

"No, Rose. You know better than that."

"Maybe. Well, I'm going in to town to see Handel. Thanks for checking on me. I'll be fine." Rose started to leave.

"Handel's not around. He's in court till two and he'll be tied up till three."

She stopped and turned to Ogeen. "How do you know so much about Handel?"

"He's, ah, doing some work for me."

"He's your lawyer?"

"Well, yeah."

"Really? For how long?"

"He was my dad's lawyer. So, quite a while."

"You know all about our case, don't you?"

"I know some, sure."

"Sure?" Her voice began to rise. "You're right in the middle of all this, aren't you?" She was close to shouting. "Handel, Earl, the county attorney?" She glared at Ogeen. "Did you set us up? You phony bastard."

"I swear I didn't have anything to do with the fire. If it *was* Earl, I didn't put him up to it."

"And if it was Earl, you didn't want anybody looking

in his direction, did you, Billy? You were the one who helped push this whole thing on Cody."

"They didn't need any help from me. And other than Tidyman, your drifter didn't make himself any friends around here. It was his fault as much as anybody's."

She left the cafe, got in the truck, and headed up the road toward the asylum.

Her fists clenched the steering wheel the entire trip north. She charged along, fighting ruts and slamming through potholes for thirty miles. She focused on the problem of how to get Cody out of the asylum and make a run for it. By the time she reached the Springhill gate, she was perfectly calm.

———

"Lean forward," he said. "A little more."

"I can't," she said. "I'll lose my balance."

She held her arms slightly away from her body like wings at rest, the palms open, toward him, cushioned by the air as though she were landing. Behind her a dark, rolling storm moved down the lake toward them.

Her white dress lifted around her thighs. She was ready. He lay down on the dock, flat on his stomach, looking up at the flying woman against the violent sky, and began to paint. He painted fast, faster than usual because of the storm. The sun angled down, illuminating the woman, holding her in the slant light against the dark sky and the churning lake.

———

From his office in Main Hall, the psychiatrist watched Cody stretched out on the dock, passionately attacking his work with pure color. The intensity of the painter and the woman, charged with the electrified air of the coming storm, disrupted the doctor's mental detachment. He was aroused and angry. He set the binoculars down, walked to his desk, and leafed through Cody's file. He dispelled his own sexual desire and rage by referring to his clinical interpretation of the painting. As the certainty of his science allowed him to regain his composure, his fingers found the shiny Bakelite knobs of his mentor's ancient shock machine. Rationality was his godsend and savior—his version of luck.

———◆———

Faces were the hardest part—getting the expression right. Cody had the details down—the eyes and eyebrows, the perfect line of her nose, then her lips. The smallest stroke seemed to change everything.

Lightning cracked in the distance and thunder rumbled across the lake toward the painter and the woman on the dock.

"Move your arms out a little, and back," he said.

"Like this?"

"That's perfect."

"Paint fast," she said. "The rain is coming and the light is leaving."

Cody began sketching the flow of her dress, her arms, and her hands, with quick brush strokes. He stopped for a moment and looked at her. "I have to get out of here, Rose," he said. "The doctor wants to roast my brain."

She stared at Main Hall, trying to find the psychiatrist's lurking shape in the window reflections. The asylum's dignified opacity only deepened her rage.

"There's no way to get you out legally," she said. "Handel is Ogeen's lawyer. I'm sure they're protecting one of his friends, probably Earl. I think Ogeen's afraid the whole thing could find its way back to him and he'd be blamed for the fire. They don't want you getting out of here any time soon."

Cody knew Handel had been his last hope with the legitimate world. He dipped the tips of his fingers into the jars and examined the colors in the angled light, then he began to paint again.

"There're tunnels for the steam pipes," he said. "They connect the buildings. One comes out on the other side of the west fence. If I can get into the tunnels, I can escape without much trouble." He looked at her and smiled. "It'll have to be at night—as soon as possible."

She could see the psychiatrist coming down the hill toward them. It began to rain. "Closing time," she said.

"Yeah, we better get inside."

"Your doctor's coming," she said. "We have to talk fast."

Cody stood up. "Can you come back tonight?"

"There's a place a mile down the road on the west side where I can pull off into the trees and park near the lake. You can see it from here. I'll flash the lights. I'll wait for two hours. If you don't show up, I'll keep coming back until you do. I'm driving Gretchen because your truck was vandalized by some of the kids. Gerome's going to fix his Pontiac so we'll have something to drive until he gets the truck back together."

"We should have gotten out when you were here before."

"I wish we had. I love you." She pressed against him and kissed him. "Here he comes."

Cody could feel the footsteps on the dock. He wiped his hand and put the paint jars back in their box. Then, holding the box with the new painting balanced on top, he stood and watched Dr. Richards come down the dock. Two attendants in their white pants waited at the lawn's edge. There was a strange aggressiveness in his slightly jaunty stride, his jutting beard, and angry eyes. He stopped several feet away.

The ancient parts of Cody's brain bristled. Every hateful thing came into focus. He knew the doctor could destroy him. He deliberately dropped the box, splattering blue paint on the deck.

Dr. Richards panicked at Cody's loss of control. He waved to the attendants, who ran toward them.

"Don't do anything you'll regret, Mr. Hayes."

Cody did not move.

Rose's hand touched his arm. "We'll get away," she whispered, frightened he would explode.

The tone in her voice froze his heart. Whatever happened, he dreaded the thought of her being diminished by fear.

Dr. Richards waved the attendants back. They stopped short and waited.

Cody looked at the blue paint on his bare feet. "Sorry about your deck." His voice was flat, almost automatic—without a hint of apology or irony. He wanted to kill the doctor. Rose's fear was all that kept him from trying.

Dr. Richards nodded to Cody, accepting the non-apology. "I would like to talk to Rose alone, Cody. Would you mind waiting for me in 311?"

Cody turned to Rose and drew her against him. He kissed her as though it were the end of them.

"Excuse me," said the doctor. "I can't allow this. You must leave now, Mr. Hayes."

"We'll be all right, Cody."

Cody picked up his box of paints and the unfinished painting of the flying Rose. He walked up the hill to Main Hall without looking back, oblivious of the thick blue paint that dripped down his pants.

Rose could not take her eyes off him. When Cody finally disappeared into the hall, the doctor demanded her attention.

"You need to know that Cody is an alienated, aggressive, and manic personality. He is potentially a danger to you and to himself. I'm afraid he will need extensive treatment."

"There was nothing wrong with him before he came here. Why is he suddenly so dangerous?"

"He may have been psychotic before and kept it hidden. Possibly it was something triggered by the blast. Perhaps it's war related."

"If he is insane, Doctor, this place is what did it to him."

The doctor ignored her. "You need to consider your own part in his illness. The intensity of his interest in you seems much greater than what would be considered normal."

"I'm sure you are a big authority on what's normal, Doctor. But you don't know what you're talking about. You use your words. You have your rules. And underneath all that, you're a bully and a cheap quack."

"I have studied the two of you together, and today I have seen his painting of you flying. This intensity is a manifestation of projected delusions. I have researched the field of romantic delusions rather thoroughly. His obsession is unwarranted and unnatural. His paintings are rife with these sorts of things."

"He paints for himself. What he really sees. How is that unnatural?"

"You have just described for me the behavior of a schizophrenic."

"You're the madman. You're the one who should be locked up."

From a window in 311, Cody watched Rose and Dr. Richards on the dock. Things seemed to become animated, at least on Rose's part. The doctor turned and said something to the remaining man in white pants.

The attendant grabbed Rose by the arm and marched her down the dock. At the foot of the hill, she tried to pull free, but the man twisted her arm behind her and grabbed her hair. She was forced up the hill toward the gate. The doctor walked away from the scene as quickly as possible.

Cody tried to open the window, but it was painted shut. He began yelling and pounding against the glass. He wanted to run downstairs, but two attendants were already in the doorway and more were coming.

He slammed his fist through the window and bellowed, "Let her go!" Glass shattered on the steps below. His fist was covered with blood.

The attendants charged across the room at the bloody madman. Cody leapt toward the glass cabinet and pulled it down between them. The brain jars exploded, cutting into an attendant's leg. The man screamed. Cody bolted but got caught in a melee of bloodied white pants, glass, brains, and leather straps. Dr. Richards came in while they were kicking Cody's inert body.

"That will do," he said.

———◈———

As Rose stuggled with the attendant, she heard the glass shatter in the third-floor window and Cody's yell. He sounded like a lunatic.

The gate slammed behind her. She stood in the middle of the road, listening for his voice amid the splatter of raindrops on Gretchen's hood. The coming storm and the electric air made her feel dead in contrast. She got in the truck and drove to her hiding spot in the trees.

She waited until the sun went down, then began flashing the lights every half hour or so. Between flashes, she sat in the dark with the windows down and listened. The lights were bound to alert the asylum staff that something was going on. Rose was sure they would send somebody to investigate. No one came. There was no sign of Cody.

She spent the next day collecting berries and roots. In the afternoon, another storm came up. She stayed in the truck listening to the rain pelt the cab until she fell asleep.

Late in the evening, she was awakened by a heavy thump. The long tongue of a grizzly bear trailed across the driver's side window, testing the glass for edibility. Glass was new to the bear. Rose hoped he could not see her lying there. He would run off if he did, and she wanted the company.

The bear's tongue found the gap at the top of the window and slipped right in. It wagged around for a moment until his nose detected something strange. The tongue withdrew and the bear peered in, its paws on either side of its head, as though to block the reflection. Its beady eyes searched the inside of the cab for the source of the unusual odor. He discovered the light of Rose's watching eye, snorted loudly, and departed rapidly.

She was delighted by the way he held his paws by his face to see in. She looked out the window. The bear had vanished into the trees.

How did he know to do that? she wondered. How does a bear who's never seen glass know to block the light with his paws? Maybe he knew about glass, knew to lick the rain off the window to see inside.

Darkness closed in from the trees and the sky, allowing the asylum lights to emerge from the distant mist. The rain continued through the night. Every half hour she flashed the truck lights, and waited and listened.

"This time it will work," she whispered. "This time he'll come. This time. When I count to one hundred he'll come. I know he'll come."

When it was daylight, she drove south to what she still thought of as home. She had no plan other than to wait for a few days and go back to the asylum.

———

Cody regained consciousness in a small, white room to the strong smell of disinfectant soap. A kindly looking, pale man with sparse, blond eyebrows was leaning over him. The man was manipulating Cody's throbbing nose.

"This is going to hurt," said the man. Cody groaned as his nose was yanked back into place. He tried to move his arms but discovered they were bound to his body by a restraining jacket.

The man patted Cody's shoulder. "I'm Dr. Shales, Mr. Hayes. Your nose is broken and you have a deep cut in your right hand. Other than that you have some soft tissue damage to your back and neck. Can you feel your toes?"

Cody tried to respond, but his jaw would not cooperate. He managed to nod his head. Dr. Shales's faraway voice seemed to come in and out.

". . . before I go back to town . . . if there's organ damage."

———

When he woke he wondered why he was lying on the floor by the open window. Cold air spilled over the sill, flowing over his body. The air felt like water. He could see the underside of his bed where the mattress pressed through the spring frame. His paint box and the boards were gone. A white, gauzy lump lay on the floor near his head. After a moment he realized the lump was his bandaged hand. His brain refused to work. He had the vague feeling his brain was in a jar.

Footsteps in the hallway stopped outside his door. He heard the key turn and the door open. He faced the wrong direction to see who it was. The expectation of having to move or of being moved made him wince. The door closed and the feet went away. As bad as he felt, he suspected it would be worse.

Another set of steps, this time a woman's, returned with a larger set of keys. The door opened. The keeper of the keys hesitated, then stepped into the room. The door closed.

She came toward him, stepped over his gauzed hand, and closed the window. His eye traveled from the white shoes, up the white hose to a garter belt. It was a sexless experience. There was no secret thrill nor even a sense of invasion.

She knelt down and looked in his eye. "Cody? Can you hear me?"

He recognized Gudrin, the nurse who had shown him to his room that first day. "Yes," he said.

Gudrin helped him sit up. "You've got to control yourself around here or they'll do it for you." She unwrapped a stack of soda crackers from a napkin and set them on the floor next to a bowl of oily, yellow broth. She squatted down with her white knees pointed toward him and offered a spoonful of the broth. He opened his mouth. It was hot, salty, greasy chicken soup, the best he had ever had. He tried to smile. Gudrin was serious.

"Cody, when the swelling in your face goes down, they're going to start you on a series of shock treatments. Whatever you do, don't fight them and don't show fear. They'll hurt you if you fight. They'll think you're psychotic if you show fear, and they'll give you more shock."

He chewed the soda cracker slowly. His jaw hurt. "Elemente?" he asked.

"Most patients don't have measurable long-term effects from the shock."

"What about Elemente?" he said, and took the bowl and spoon from her.

"They don't know about Elemente yet. It may take him months to get his memory back."

"Maybe years? Maybe never?"

"He's not typical, Cody."

"He said he feels like a ghost."

She looked at his battered head and heavily taped nose. She touched his arm to reassure him.

"Is Rose all right?" he asked.

"The woman?"

"Yes."

"They didn't hurt her. She drove away in that old truck."

"I want to get out of here."

"I can't help you," she said. She took the empty bowl from his hand.

"Thanks for the soup," he said.

"Sure." She helped him into bed and turned out the light. When she reached the door, she turned, "Don't try anything until you're better, okay?"

For a moment, she was illuminated in a wedge of light from the hallway. Then it was dark, and the clutch of keys rattled in the door. He listened for her to walk away, but there were no footsteps. He imagined her standing in the hall light waiting for him to escape.

---

The white tiled walls of the shock room reverberated and amplified all sounds. To overcome the boom of voices, everyone talked louder. Normal speech was impossible. Cody lay on his back staring up at a row of small-paned windows near the ceiling.

"Have you ever tried this on yourself, Doctor?"

"Please allow the nurse to proceed with the injection."

"What is it?"

"Curare. It's a muscle relaxant. We will also place a rubber mouthpiece between your teeth. These measures will prevent your muscles from tearing away from the bones and your teeth from shattering."

Elemente had not made up anything. Cody understood they could easily kill him. It was dangerous to fight them.

Cody watched the nurse work a needle into his vein and inject the curare. He caught a glimpse of someone unfolding a straight razor. It flashed past his eye. They were shaving his temples.

He could feel the curare relax the muscles in his back and neck. Then he had to work at breathing, as though someone was sitting on his chest. He was gasping for air when the nurse inserted the rubber mouthpiece between his teeth.

Several attendants had come in. They surrounded him. Their hands held his arms and legs to the table. The cold electrodes were slipped over his head and pressed against his temples.

His body tensed at Dr. Richards's authoritative little barks.

"Set voltage?"

"One ten," said the attendant.

"Set duration?"

"One five."

"Set variation?"

"Fifteen."

"Set series?"

"Five. And initiate."

T HE LIGHT PULLED HIS EYELID BACK. THE BLAZING white made the sand fleas inside his brain explode. He tried to close his eye, but it was held open.

"How are we feeling?" an attendant asked and released the grip on his eyelid.

The sand fleas stopped popping in his brain. His tongue, like the air, tasted acidic and burnt. He could not open his mouth. His jaws ached from biting the rubber mouthpiece. Little spasms torqued his body from his neck to his toes. His chest hurt from trying to breathe.

Ogeen was walking to his car when she pulled up in front of the cafe. He came over.

"Hello, Rose. You look like you've been rode hard and put away wet. What's up?"

"I have a favor to ask."

"What kind of favor?"

"Find out what they've done to Cody and if he's okay. Will you do that?"

"Well, I'll ask around. I don't know—"

"Please. You owe us that."

"I'll do what I can. It may take awhile."

"Thank you." She started to leave, then smiled. "I need a lemon pie."

"A whole pie?"

"Indians invented lemon meringue, Billy. It's an old Indian food."

"Are you kidding?"

"Where do you think Meringay, Montana, comes from?"

She drove up the highway to the orchard and eased Gretchen down the narrow road through the cherry trees to the stock truck. Gerome was there, cutting cardboard patterns to make new windows. The red car was parked next to the truck.

"I thought you might be here," she said. "I have a lemon meringue pie for you."

"Thank you. Meringay is my favorite."

"There's your car," he said. "Dee LeClair and Amy helped. They want to do some more to it."

"What's some more?"

"Overbore the block and mill the heads. Dual carbs and a three-quarter cam. They think you should have a getaway car."

"Sounds like something I could get away in. Has Amy talked him into making it fly?"

Gerome laughed. "Of course. She has complete faith in him."

"Faith's required," said Rose.

———◦———

Cody felt befuddled and weary. Small gusts of wind laced rain across the water. There was something he was supposed to be looking for, something about Rose. It was at the edge of his mind, just out of sight.

He heard someone coming down the dock and turned to find a trim little man he vaguely remembered.

"Follow the rules," the man said. "Follow the rules—you will be all right. Everything according to plan."

"Follow the rules," Cody replied. It was the first thing he had said in several days. They stood together and watched the rain on the water. The chill of the rain closed around him. Something had happened to Rose, something terrible, and he had forgotten.

Without looking at Cody, the trim man said, "Do you remember my name?"

Cody felt empty and blank. "I'm sorry, I don't . . ." The name jumped up at him. "Elemente?"

"Yes, Elemente Duval." He looked at the purple bruise that spread from Cody's nose to his eyes and at his gauze-wrapped hand. "You've been in a fight."

Cody had forgotten the fight. He looked down at his bandaged hand. "Yes," he said, "there was a fight."

He remembered Rose being hauled away. They had no reason to hurt her. She was probably all right, he decided.

He reached up with his good hand and carefully touched the bridge of his nose. "I lost."

"How was the zapper?"

Cody laughed. "Real hell. I couldn't even remember my own name for a while." The rain picked up. He was starting to get cold. "I need to get inside," he said.

"Do you remember the woman who came to visit?" asked Elemente.

"Nothing they could do would make me forget her."

They had started back toward Main Hall when Cody remembered Rose was to signal him with the truck lights. He turned and looked back along the shoreline.

"Elemente, have you seen lights near the lake? Flashing lights?"

"Yes, car lights. They flashed every half hour for two nights. All night. I sleep very little."

"When?"

"Three weeks ago."

"Three weeks? No. Damn it. Three weeks?"

Was Elemente teasing him? What had happened for the last three weeks? Had he missed her?

"Were there other lights?" he asked.

"If there were, I did not see them." Elemente twitched. He felt awkward, as though he had failed his duty. "I am sorry. I will watch for lights every night."

"You won't tell anyone about this?"

"Of course not," said the trim man. "We are getting wet. Should we go inside now?"

"Yes. Let's go back."

---

Winter had started to move down from the Arctic. All day snow sifted out of the flat, white sky. Even though his breath hung in the air, he was unaware he was coatless. He wondered what month it was. That acidic, metallic taste was in his mouth again. His jaw hurt and the spasms in his back twisted his shoulders. He stood on the dock and watched the snow disappear into the dark water. An attendant was coming down the dock for him.

"Dinnertime for you," said the man with white pants.

"I'm fine," said Cody. "I'm waiting for someone."

As the attendant reached for Cody's arm, he slid across the slick planks. For an instant, he flailed for balance. His arms froze above his head in an awkward dance, braced against the inevitable. The white pants sailed over the edge and into the water.

The frigid water charged the attendant's anger. He shot up screaming, thrashing the water and ready to kill.

Cody did not offer his helping hand.

"You need to cool off," he said. He turned away and walked back up the hill to Main Hall.

The attendant walked out on the shore. His clothes weighted him down and he was out of breath by the time he caught up to Cody near the front door. He struck Cody in the back with a fist, slipped, and went down on the steps. Cody's reactions were unusually slow and ponderous, as though he were swimming in pudding. The attendant came off the steps in a rage and lunged at Cody. After a struggle, Cody pulled the man down and sat on his chest. He laughed at his own lack of aggression. Several attendants charged through the door and pulled him off their wet colleague.

***

It had been cold for several weeks. A covering of snow had fallen before a massive cold front moved down from Canada and gave the lake a skin of ice. Rose parked the red car far off the road, among the stark trees, and walked back along the shore toward the asylum.

She stood out of sight in the trees, wrapped in Gerome's heavy wool coat, watching the hillside and Main Hall—willing Cody to be the next one to open the door. The reflection on the glass would shake, the door would open. It was never Cody. The crunch and squeak of patients' shoes in the cold snow carried down into the trees. The blown snow whipped at her legs. She pulled the coat tight and walked back to the car along a path through the trees made by the deer. There were no tracks from her bear with the long tongue.

She started the engine and ran the heater to get warm. When it got darker, she drove nearer the shore where she could see the asylum and began another long night of flashing lights. Futility was beginning to shade the pain of her longing, as though she were waiting for him to come home from a war that had ended years ago.

Her letters had been returned. When she had tried to visit, she was denied entry by a bland, lispy man who knew nothing of his predecessor, the bender of rules.

Ogeen had told her they were still running electric current through his brain. He was getting along fine, Ogeen had reported, thinking she would be pleased. Under the circumstances, getting along fine with the pocket Nazis meant you were a collaborator or brain dead.

Through the library she had managed to get two scientific papers on electroconvulsive shock. The first was a gruesome history of the treatment and a statement about the need for more research. The other was jargon and another plea for more research. She had gleaned that nothing was known about how convulsive shock actually worked, that it was used primarily to control inmates and to keep them docile, and that it could damage their memories. She tried to ignore the thought that Cody might be made to forget her.

When the early storms came, she had insulated the stock truck. The walls, the ceiling, and the floor were thick with layers and layers of corrugated cardboard. Each day she went longer without eating. She would lie in bed watching the fire in the woodstove through the isinglass, trying to recapture the summer with Cody.

The ache in her chest drew her inward and her memories began to drift away like vapors, preferring the empty frigid air to the weight of her loneliness.

She sat in the car, curling and stretching her toes to keep warm, one foot and then the other. It was not impossible, she thought, that he could tap on the window at any moment.

When she was a child, Catherine would tap on her head when she was upset. "Makes the worry leave," said the old woman.

———

He looked out the window of his room. The landscape was not recognizable. It was white. The sky was overcast. Men in brown and gray coats were walking along the pathways or standing on the hillside. Far below, spreading to the horizon, was a desolate white expanse. It must have been a lake because there was a dock. The dock and the stone walls were familiar.

He did not know if it was before Christmas or after. One day was like the next. He sat on his bed or looked out the window. His body seemed thick. He was always tired and taking naps. Gudrin came to take him to the dining hall three times a day. The food tasted strange. Adding salt made no difference. He unscrewed the cap from the shaker and poured salt on his potatoes. An attendant made a note of his behavior and took his food away. He did not mind. He wanted to sleep, anyway.

One afternoon he was standing in his room, looking out the window, when he noticed someone outside the fence in the trees near the lake. He was sure it was a woman. She stood there, half hidden and motionless, waiting for someone. He watched her for almost an hour. Finally, when it was getting dark, she turned and disappeared into the trees. He did not want her to go.

That night he woke up thinking about Rose. He must have been dreaming about her. No, that was the night before. He thought about the woman in the woods. That could have been Rose. She was waiting for him. He could have gone down and talked to her through the fence. Of course, it wasn't her at all. She wouldn't just show up, on a cold day in the snow, and wait in the woods.

Why had she not come for him? She became his mystery. Did she live only in his mind, an illusionary composition of many women, both real and imagined? If she were real, who was she? Was she in love with him?

He had no proof of her existence, only the vaguest of memories, all jumbled, confused, not adding up or making sense. He was confined in an asylum. That was all he was certain of. Did that mean he was insane?

He watched the crows flying over the frozen lake, and opened his window to listen. They cawed to each other, complaining, he guessed, about the cold and the deficiency of mice and other edibles. He remembered crows complaining about how clumsy and rude people were—how they mashed the stones. But how did he know what they'd said?

He heard the key and the door open. It was Gudrin to take him to dinner. He turned back and looked at the white lake.

"Did I ever tell you about the lake?" he asked.

"What about it?"

"I don't remember. I was hoping I'd said something about it before. I only remember that it was a story I'd heard, maybe when I was little, about the lake and Loneliness. Loneliness was at the bottom of everything. I never told you?"

"Sorry, no. Nothing about the lake."

"Did I say anything about a woman named Rose? Do you know anything about her?"

"She was the one who came to see you. You painted her picture on the dock the last day she was here."

"I painted her picture?"

"Yes. Do you remember painting?"

"No. I didn't know I could."

"They put your paints in storage. I'll see if I can get them back for you."

———◦———

Several days later, Gudrin set a large box with his paints and paintings on the bed. After she left, he began going through the box, taking each painting and examining it in the window light. One painting showed a boy surrounded by bunnies, standing near a small cave. The boy was smiling and pointing to a bunny at his foot.

He took up the painting of Rose flying against the storm sky and stared at it for a good part of the morning. With a dry brush he began to trace the lines he had painted months before. His body felt large and thick. His hands were stiff.

He studied every detail of her face until he could remember his hand making those fine strokes. He touched the brush to the corner of her eye, traced along the lower lid to the nose, down the perfect line to the flare of her nostril, to her lips. He felt as though she were speaking to him. He set the painting against his nightstand and stared at it until he went to sleep.

When he woke, in the afternoon, he opened his paint jars and stuck the tips of his fingers into the colors. He was afraid if he actually tried to paint he would ruin what had already been done. Instead, he pretended to paint. He held the white finger close to the painting and moved the brush back and forth without touching the paint. He pretended he was shading the folds in her dress—hundreds of zinc white flecks mixed with black for the vibrant gray. Specks of white, yellow, and red gave shape and color to her arms and the open palms of her welcoming hands.

After he had re-created every stroke in his imagination, he actually touched the brush to the red finger and in the upper right-hand corner began to paint a small creature. Its form was vague because he did not know what he was painting. The red blur sprouted wings.

Rose would return and help him escape. How she intended to do this eluded him. He believed the key to his former life and to his freedom could be found in the painting. It became his fixation. For hours every day he stared at the painting. He would daub the brush with one color and then another, holding the tip next to the board, waiting for an image, but none came to him. Nothing was revealed.

He left his room and walked down to the dock to see if anything in the landscape might arouse his memory. The air felt dense and still. Behind him, to the north, it had begun to snow. He was looking out over the ice, trying to remember the lake in summer, when a small, trim man walked down the dock toward him.

"I have good news," said the man. "Last night there were lights on the lake." He looked into Cody's eyes and knew his friend remembered nothing. "I am Elemente Duval."

Cody's blank expression distressed Elemente. He became animated, gesturing, and speaking louder to overcome the quiet of his companion.

"Several weeks ago we stood there on the dock," he

said, pointing a few feet ahead. "It was raining. You asked me about the flashing lights. I had seen the lights. The lights were very important to you. A signal of your woman's love, I assumed. You were very upset because you had missed her lights. I said I would watch for them again and I did see them, but I could not find you to tell you."

"I don't remember the flashing lights," said Cody.

"No, of course. You never saw them, but you knew they would be there. She had come to signal her love for you." Elemente pointed down the shoreline to where he had seen the lights. "They were there, near the lake, at night, all night and the next and several times since." As Elemente watched Cody's face, his heart sank. "All night, the lights called to you."

Cody knew the lights must be from Rose, but it was the painting of the bunnies that came to mind—small, gray bunnies huddled around a young boy standing by a cave. Cody could only guess that the painting, fixed so vividly in mind, had something to do with Rose.

"Small, gray bunnies?" he asked Elemente, as though he were repeating a menu item.

"Bunnies. Yes," Elemente cried.

He grabbed hold of Cody's coat sleeve and pulled him along. "The bunnies are the secret," he shouted. Then they were running through the snow toward the fence, with Cody only half aware of what was happening.

"Remember the boy in the steam tunnel?" Elemente was shouting and pointing toward the fence. "The tunnel will take you outside to the lights at night, to your woman." He was laughing. "You had planned to escape."

His effervescent laughter mystified Cody. The intense little man seemed out of place in the white landscape, rattling the chain fence. Maybe Elemente was simply insane.

Elemente pointed to a shallow gully on the other side of the fence. "Everything depends upon many small, gray bunnies," he said with a grin. "The lights always happen two nights in a row." He was breathless. "They happened last night," he gasped. "She will be there again, tonight."

Cody could see a slight depression where a heated tunnel might have melted the snow, or it could have been a deer trail. The depression led to the shallow gully. He realized he had put the tunnel entrance in his painting with the bunnies even though he could not have seen it. He must have believed the boy about the tunnel, or he may have painted a story Elemente told him. Perhaps the whole thing was in Elemente's mind. But Cody had to risk the possibility that the strange, little man was sane.

"Find the tunnel and be ready," instructed Elemente.

Cody studied the buildings, imagining the connecting tunnels and where he might hide. He knew he would have to find a place where there were windows that looked out on the lakeshore. The most obvious building would be the greenhouse, though he could not remember if he had been inside. How strong was the tunnel door? Would the night watchman be checking?

"Where is the door to the basement in Main Hall?" he asked.

"I do not know," said Elemente. "But there are other ways to get into basements. This was once a mansion. Such places had narrow, hidden staircases for the serving staff. Many had small elevators called dumbwaiters. These ran from the basement to the banquet rooms. There's a room on the third floor that would have been used for balls and banquets."

"How do you know these thing, Elemente? Were you a servant or a man who had servants?"

"I cannot remember anything of my own life. However," Elemente laughed, "I recall a grand stairway from the underside of the banister."

Cody smiled. "To the manor born?" he asked.

Elemente looked up at Cody, delighted to be so highly regarded. "I remember the details of living, but I do not remember living. I am like a book of instructions that sits on a shelf, unread."

"Yeah. I have the same problem. I seem to know a lot about logging," said Cody, "but don't remember being a logger. That part's a blank." He turned and stared up at the third floor of Main Hall. "Where is the room that might have one of those little elevators?" he asked.

"It's the center one on this side. It has a glass case full of jars with mushrooms floating in them. Do you know the one?"

Cody remembered the sound of breaking glass and the smell of formaldehyde. "They were mushrooms?"

"I thought so. You don't think so?"

"I don't," he said.

"I was sure they were mushrooms. What else could they be?"

"Could they have been human brains?" Cody felt bewildered.

"Of course," shouted Elemente, suddenly agitated. "They have put our memories in jars. Is it any wonder, then, that we cannot remember our lives?"

---

Cody stood in the doorway, looking into the old banquet room on the third floor. The room was familiar. He remembered seeing someone's bare foot in a shaft of sunlight. Now it was overcast. There was no sun on the floor. The light was soft and diffused. The room seemed peaceful. As he walked to the window, he could see that one of the old panes of wavy glass had been replaced with a clear one. There was no case with brains in sealed jars. Instead there was a brass pull recessed in the cherry wood panel where the case had been.

He slid the panel back and found Elemente's little elevator. It had not been used for years. The elevator made Elemente seem slightly more trustworthy, as though the dusty box and its frayed rope were the last vestiges of the little man's sanity. Cody could not really believe Elemente had stayed up all night for several nights watching for the lights, much less that he had seen them. There was something too fantastic and strange about the man. Elemente seemed to vibrate.

Cody tested the pull ropes, letting the elevator down and drawing it back up. Then he grabbed the rope and gingerly eased into the box. He barely fit. He waited for a moment, listening for something to give way. Everything held. He slid the door shut and slowly lowered himself to the basement.

He found the main steam pipe and followed it to where it disappeared into an arched brick tunnel, four feet high and two wide, with a concrete floor. The crawl space was shared by the pipes and tubes carrying water, electricity, steam, and condensation. These were held to the ceiling with corroded iron brackets.

Cody crawled into the dim hole and pulled the door closed. The air was hot, even though the ten-inch steam pipe was insulated with thick layers of corrugated asbestos. Moisture condensed on the bricks and seeped down onto the concrete floor. He felt his way into the tunnel, one hand pressing against the wall, the other sliding along the belly of the steam pipe. He crabbed his way through the darkness for 150 feet until he came to a junction with a tunnel on his right. More pipes from the steam plant joined the main tunnel, forcing him closer to the floor.

He had expected to find a tunnel on the left that would follow the hill down to where he had seen the boy. It was not there. He began crawling on his hands and knees through the dense hot air toward the greenhouse. Broken mortar and pieces of rusted iron littered the concrete floor, cutting into his knees.

His hand slid along the damp wall, feeling from brick to brick, searching for the passage that could lead him back to the old world of his memories, his freedom, and Rose.

He wanted to will the other tunnel into existence—

to slide his hand over the next brick into a void of dank
air. He would look into the endless black and see the
faint flash of headlights and she would be waiting. But as
each brick slid by beneath his hand, it was replaced by
another slippery brick and another—an endless, mes-
merizing train, until it seemed as though hours had
passed. Perspiration seeped into his eyes. The heat began
to cook his brain as the bricks and pipes streamed by in
the dark.

Then his hand was reaching into air. The stream of
bricks had stopped. He felt woozy and fell sideways into
the void in the bricks. The thin edge of light in front of
him became a crack in a door. Cody pushed. It felt weak
at the hinges. He put his shoulder against the door,
braced his feet, and threw his weight into it. He flew forward, into the light, with a splash.

He was lying in a shallow pool of cool water, staring
up at the evening sky. Large snowflakes fell from the light
onto the greenhouse roof. Each flake melted as it
touched, collecting into larger and larger drops that broke
and ran in long, thin streamers down the slanted glass.

How fortunate, he thought, to be faceup and not
facedown. He lay in the water, anxious that he had not
found the tunnel to the outside. Had he passed it and
not known? He was soaked, his knees were bleeding, and
he was surrounded by water lilies.

The greenhouse was built into the hillside and connected to the main tunnel. Cody had broken the door
off its hinges and lunged forward over a walkway into
the shallow pond. He stood up, dripping water, and

peered back into the access tunnel. He guessed that the main tunnel continued west to the staff compound, Dr. Richards' house, and, he prayed, to the secret tunnel. If there was no other way out, he would have to hide in his psychiatrist's basement—the mental patient's last refuge.

It was growing darker. They would be looking for him. In squishy slippers, he negotiated his way through rows of exotic succulents, cacti, and tropical flowers. As he approached the windows, the thin, erratic coating of ice distorted the winter landscape. Far to the south, soft streams of reflected colors seemed to melt the frozen lake, pulling it up into the evening sky.

He scratched a small patch in the thin layer of ice and peered out at the shoreline west of the asylum where Elemente had claimed to see lights. He began to shiver. He pulled off his wet clothes, wrung them out, and hung them on a large cactus. His slippers had fallen apart.

He went back to the window. The wind had picked up, gusting snow down toward the lake. From time to time he had to scratch away the ice that formed from his breath. An hour later he was shaking. He crouched down by the frozen glass and waited.

Was it irrational to expect her to come for him? He could not guess how long it had been since he had seen her. He tried to remember the change of seasons. Had he been there in the spring? Was this the second winter? He may have been there for years. It seemed like years.

Through the swirling snow, he saw a set of lights moving, as though they had drifted off the horizon toward the lake. After several minutes the lights seemed larger. They appeared to be car lights, but they had to be on the ice, which seemed impossible. The ice could not be thick enough to hold a car. And if the lights were all in his imagination, why didn't they make more sense? If they were his lights they would be on a road, not in the middle of a lake. The lights kept coming. They were less than a mile away. He stumbled through the dark to the light switch by the door and flipped it twice. Two bright flashes illuminated the entire greenhouse.

The car lights were still out there, moving across the ice toward the asylum. The driver, if there was a driver, ignored the flashes from the glass house. The lights were coming in fast.

Outside the greenhouse, attendants began shouting— they had just seen their escapee's naked silhouette against the illuminated glass. A man cupped his hands against the glass and peered in. Another was trying to open the door. A third man was running toward the greenhouse, shouting he had the key.

Cody flipped the switch again, illuminating the glass house. The lights on the ice flickered twice, like a bad connection, then went dark. It could have been a signal or just a loose wire. Perhaps Elemente's story was making him see things, but the plan was all he had.

Cody stared into the darkness, waiting for another signal. People and dogs had gathered on the other side of the glass. An attendant kept his flashlight trained on Cody while the watchman had a little fit with the keys.

"Get that goddamn light down here, you idiot," he snarled. "Let me see the hole."

Cody had no choice. He had to believe Rose was out on the ice waiting for him. As he ran toward the tunnel, he heard glass shatter, then the door open.

"Hold it right there," someone shouted.

Their lights found him and the dogs went crazy. Their yapping exploded inside the glass house. Cody ran to the tunnel and wedged the broken door behind him. He backed his way into the main tunnel, then started crawling west.

After thirty feet the air seemed to cool. Then he felt a slight breeze coming from the left. The pipe to the left was capped off, which meant the tunnel had been abandoned. There was nowhere for the tunnel to go except under the fence where he had seen the boy disappear.

The tunnel followed the slope of the hill down to the secret door. After several yards the floor became icy. He started to slip, skidding and picking up speed. He shot along through the darkness, ricocheting off the bricks. For a moment he felt himself falling forward, swimming through the darkness. He slammed against a door.

The booming yap of the dogs brought him back to the fact that he was trapped. He pulled his legs under his body, lay on his back, and kicked the door open. The blast of cold air clenched around his body, reminding him he was naked. The strange, warm sensation in his right foot made him reach down to touch it. There was a deep cut in the arch. A bright flash of light from the lake illuminated the blood against the snow. He looked up, but too late to locate the precise direction of the light. Behind him he could hear dogs and men. He began running. A sharp, cold wind pushed him forward. The wind blew snow off the hillside and across the ice.

He could not believe the lake was frozen hard enough to support a car, but that was where the lights came from. He ran onto the lake, leaving a trail of dark footprints on the ice.

He heard the motor first, then saw the tapered, torpedo-back outline. The dome light came on—she was reaching over, holding the door open for him. He caught the handle as the car picked up speed.

Hot air blasted from the heater hitting his ice blue legs. The warmth of the car made him laugh. He remembered his legs. The watchman's huge dog was trying to get in the car. Somewhere in the blowing snow men were shouting. The dog was howling with delight. Cody pushed him away.

"Close the door," she said, "before you freeze."

Several levers sprouted from the floorboards, something he had never seen in a car before. Gerome's Pontiac had undergone a major transformation.

The lights from the dashboard illuminated her face. She reached out her hand for him.

The windshield wipers slowed as she gunned the car forward, spinning across the ice. She reached down and moved a lever forward. He could hear the screech of something sliding out from under the car. Another lever engaged the propeller. The engine picked up its pitch until it was wound tight, screaming under the strain. He felt the car lift off. If they stayed even with the storm, he thought they might make it out.

Below, the dogs and men seemed to cling to the ice, then blur beneath them.

The car climbed higher, into the blowing snow. She turned and tacked along the front edge of the storm, east, toward the morning light.

She looked at him. Her eyes were shining. She was smiling. He slid across the seat to her and ran his hand through her crow black hair. He could not believe she was real. The engine drowned out all other sounds. He watched her mouth to see if she was talking. He realized she was laughing.

## MONDAY
## MORNING

*L*iz studied the painting of the flying Rose, wondering how she could pack it to take back with her. As she lifted it off the wall, she saw something in the figure that surprised her. She took the painting into the living room, where Ana was investigating the contents of a small wooden box.

"Gramma, the woman in this painting wasn't an Indian, was she?"

"No, Elizabeth. She wasn't."

"So Rose wasn't Indian?"

"No, she wasn't."

"The legend had it wrong, then?"

"Yes."

Each surmised what the other knew. The blast of a car horn from the back gate signaled the arrival of the Red Crows' airport service.

"You have to go," said Ana.

Liz laid the painting on the dining room table and went to her room for her bags. She returned, set the bags down, and put her arms around her grandmother. While they held each other, Liz studied the painting on the table. All these years, she thought, it had lain hidden in the basement and its secret with it.

"Are you ready for me to hang your picture in the living room?" Liz asked.

"Thank you, Elizabeth, but I would like to spend some time thinking about where I want it to go, and besides, your ride is waiting."

Ana reached into her robe pocket and held out her closed hand to her granddaughter.

"Here," she said, and dropped something smooth and hard into Liz's hand. "Have a stone."